# A BURNING HUNGER

## BY DERRICK KNIGHT

*Let my stomach burn with hunger, but
let me never leave my country.*

Interview with a Sahel farmer in
*At The Desert's Edge,* Panos 1992.

© Christian Aid 1994

Published by Panos Publications Ltd
9 White Lion Street
London N1 9PD, UK

First Published 1994

British Library Cataloguing in Publication Data
A catalogue record for this book is available from the British Library

Christian Aid supports health, education, agriculture and other projects in more than 70 countries worldwide. It also campaigns in the UK to overturn the injustices which disable the poor from helping themselves.

Panos Books is the wholly owned trading subsidiary of the UK charity Panos London. Any judgement expressed in this book should not be taken to represent the views of Panos or any of its funding agencies. Panos Books publishes authoritative, challenging, accessible books offering new and seldom heard perspectives on sustainable development.

Editor: John Montagu
Managing editor: Olivia Bennett
Production and text design : Sally O'Leary
Cover design: The Graphic Partnership
Cover photo: Derrick Knight
Maps: Philip Davies
Printed in Great Britain by Bell and Bain, Glasgow

# CONTENTS

# FOREWORD

The story of 'development' in Africa is now nearly 40 years old. In Africa, that is about one generation. In the annals of international affairs it could be said that Africa's unique contribution was to put 'development' on the agenda — in other words, to internationalise the development enterprise for the first time in modern history.

By the Eighties, by universal consensus, conventional development had failed — miserably. The scene of greatest catastrophe was none other than Africa. But what followed? Instead of repudiating it, the UN launched yet another version which I would call 'The Africa Development Summitry Enterprise Inc.'. The year is 1986 and, ever since, no continent has been the object of such relentless summitry of agencies, each with an apparent life of its own, with every organisation trying to outdo the next. This is where we are today. The centre of gravity of African development is still outside Africa.

But the story of development has also been told in different ways. What Derrick Knight has offered us is among the best that I have read from the grass roots. Only a handful of multi-disciplinary story-tellers have an eye both for the critical relationships in development and for the key actors or animateurs. The 'World of Hacchim' in Chapter Eight is the linchpin — a story woven over 30 years which is invaluable for development education here in the UK and Ireland.

I venture to suggest three reasons why *A Burning Hunger* should appeal to the general public, especially to the supporters of development agencies, and why Christian Aid should hold it up as a model during its campaign on 'Who Runs the World?'

First, this is a story from Senegal, one of the leading francophone African countries and one of only six with which Christian Aid has a special partnership. It represents a major cultural contribution, too, when indigenous culture is one of the casualties of the shameless balkanisation of Africa. Against a background of Anglo-Saxon cultural hegemony and French colonialism, the book is the product of a true partnership.

Secondly, my faith in the role of research at the grass roots was greatly boosted by the challenge within the story of Hacchim. For me, it brought back the memory of Amilcar Cabral, that most original of African thinkers. He affirmed that without discovering who the people were, what their basic conditions were, and their actual and felt needs, there would have been no basis for waging a struggle for liberation in Guinea Bissau.

Finally, a word about vision. If we listen to the Hacchims and Thiernos of this world we will find that they have a vision of a better future. It is what has sustained them. They are able to see ahead because they belong to the ranks of people who are creators of history. We in the development agencies are working alongside them and, for our own inspiration, we need to explore our relationship with them. It is the quality of this partnership which provides our own vision.

**James Oporia-Ekwaro**
**Head of Africa at Christian Aid**

# ACKNOWLEDGEMENTS

Among the many people in Senegal who gave me their friendship and guidance I would like to thank particularly:

Ousmane Ndoubo Ba
Thierno Ba
Cire Boccum
Aboubakary Deme
Ousmane Diakhate
Madame Ndeye Sokhna Faye
Ousmane Faye
Madame Djienaba Ouman Ndiath
Waly Niane
Hacchim Ndiaye
Raoul Ndiaye
Samba Ndiaye
Oumar Sy.

I also thank the members of women's associations, cooperatives, village development groups in the Senegal River valley; in Diomandou, Guede Village and Guede Chantier, Kas-Kas, Madina Niathbe, Mafre, Mery, Nenette, Ndioum, Nguidjilone, Ouressugui.

I owe a debt of gratitude to Elajh Dia, the President of the Association for the Development of Ouressugui in France, and a respected campaigner in the cause of migrant workers everywhere.

I am also grateful for the support and encouragement of the staff of ENDA Tiers Monde, in particular Jacques Bugnicourt who has always been generous with his time whenever I have passed through Dakar, to explain development issues and to offer a critique or a shrewd *tour d'horizon* of current work and thinking; also Emmanuel Ndione and the team of ENDA GRAF in Grand Yoff, and the staff of the old Centre de Bopp and of the Centre Ahmadou Malick Gaye (CAMG), its new incarnation.

I would like to thank the members of the ceramics workshop at CAMG who opened my eyes to the obstacles facing would-be small entrepreneurs in an economy such as that of Senegal.

I owe a special debt to Oumar Sy, the Secretary General of USE, the non-governmental organisation in Dakar which manages CAMG and the Integrated Project of Podor (PIP), and to his colleagues who smoothed my path, opened doors and made invaluable suggestions about content.

In France the close and cordial links with CIMADE, Christian Aid's sister agency, provided the first germ of the book when it sent me to the Centre de Bopp in 1968, and its team have always been supportive especially in their concern and contacts among migrant workers and exiles, contacts which I have more than once plundered.

None of these friends and contacts have any responsibility for the opinions and errors which are in the final text, nor have my employers at Christian Aid who allowed me the time to develop the project and complete it.

# INTRODUCTION

David MacDonald

**Wally Niane**

Waly Niane, a calm and thoughtful young man in T-shirt and cotton trousers, is sitting on a thin mattress on the floor of a shack made of packing cases, beaten tin and matting papered with newsprint pictures from cheap magazines. Prominent are coloured pages from *Soviet Weekly* — not because Waly is politically interested but because it is given away down town in large quantities and is therefore the cheapest wallpaper to be found in Dakar. The room is barely two metres each way. There is room for two double mattresses on the beaten earth floor, a tiny table and chair, an oil lamp. Any clothes are hung on a wire. The men who use this cabin have very few personal possessions, not even a change of clothes.

Waly has been out of work for two years. He resigned from the army after refusing an 'invitation' to join the ruling political party or say goodbye to the hope of promotion. He isn't bitter but he is very tired. He's been walking around town for a very long time looking for work and not finding any.

**VOICE FROM BEHIND THE CAMERA:** This is your place, is it?

**WALY:**    Yes. There are six of us living in the one room. There are problems, but we manage — three in one bed — three in the other. When it's cold we sleep well. When it's hot, it's difficult to sleep three to a bed. It's pretty much the same everywhere in this district. We get by somehow. We put up with each other. Living in the same place keeps us together as a group.

This is a short extract from a series of documentary films I produced for the UN in Senegal in 1969. I make no excuse for starting with it. If I had never been asked to make those films I might never have gone to Senegal. If I hadn't gone to Senegal I might never have understood some of the more insidious ways in which poverty undermines the self-respect of ordinary people in the South, nor might I later have gone to work for the British aid agency Christian Aid which had projects and programmes in West Africa, enabling me to return there a number of times as a staff journalist, most recently in 1992. If I had never made those visits across the years it would have been difficult to gain the perspective of change or lack of change which they gave me and the germ of this book would not have taken root.

In 1969 I wanted to know how the people of a developing country like Senegal felt about the progress of its government and the international aid agencies in steering them towards a better future and what their expectations were for themselves and their children. I kept up the same line of questioning in the years that followed, adding the question, how were they themselves involved in their own development?

The same sort of question might be put again today but in the light of the known facts it would have to be put differently: how is it that, 30 years on, your country has still been unable to raise its people's standard of living, and what are you doing about it? Do you feel let down by the conditional loans and financial expertise offered by the international aid community, especially that of the

IMF and the World Bank whose package of financial aid and structural adjustment has been imposed since 1979? It was this package, according to most observers, that had worsened the poverty of the majority of the population.

Even a superficial look at available statistics showed me in 1992 that in general the Senegalese were eating less, earning less, growing less than they were even a few decades ago. In the countryside the market price of cereals had not kept up with the rise of the cost of living and it had become impossible for the peasant farmer to grow enough on which to subsist and pay other necessities. As a result, in a country theoretically self-sufficient in essential foods, food production per capita had fallen some 40% since 1965. In 1986 daily calorie supply per head fell below the World Health Organisation (WHO) daily requirement for good health and remains below it at the present time.

Adult illiteracy remains between 70% and 80% while only 10% of the school age population is able to attend secondary school.

A country's consumption of energy is seen as a good indicator of a nation's economic good health but in Senegal consumption per head had fallen in 1990 to less than half what it was in 1965.

Figures in the UNICEF report of 1990 on the situation of women and children in Senegal showed that the nutrition of these groups was falling both in quantity and quality, and that pauperisation of families as a result of economic measures taken under structural adjustment programmes had led to increased prostitution as a way of keeping a family home going.

Even World Bank figures showed that the proportion of the national budget devoted to public health had shrunk from 9.2% in 1970 to 4.8% in 1989 — well below the level of 9% considered as an acceptable minimum by the WHO.

Reported malnutrition among under fives has risen by some 8.2% since 1965, which indicates both a greater degree of poverty and a lowering of standards in primary health care.

The figures also showed that in the complicated fields of international trade and finance things had gone badly wrong and the country still teetered on the brink of bankruptcy even after many years of expert advice from the country's international donors and bankers.

It is not as if there have been no attempts at putting things right. There have been five-year plans and plans for agriculture, plans for self-sufficiency in food production, special plans for industrial investment. Senegal has basked in the approval of the western developed nations for its principled stand on human rights and democratic procedures, for its statesmanship in world affairs and until recently for its internal peace and stability.

It has benefited from preferential amounts of overseas aid and as a favoured partner and client of France, its former colonial master. As a former colony it has enjoyed a special status with the European Community for its exports. Yet the economy of the country is in tatters.

Ten years ago, as the extent of the country's economic disaster became a full-blown crisis, private and public finance was increasingly difficult to negotiate and the government was forced to accept the terms of a rescue package devised by the IMF and World Bank in the form of a so-called structural adjustment programme of tough economic reforms. The SAP, as it was called, was a 'magic' formula which the economists of the international banks believed could be used anywhere in the world to boost the economic prospects of poor developing countries.

The process was intended to produce a lean and more efficient government and to liberalise the economy by abolishing all state agencies and enterprises, removing subsidies to farmers, opening up the economy to private enterprise and investment. All of these measures, if carried through effectively, were expected to be painful but necessary steps if recovery and growth were to be grasped. Such plans accorded with the economic theories in fashion throughout the industrialised world at that time but failed to take into account the very different problems faced by poor developing countries.

The harmful effects were quickly observed and documented by aid organisations directly involved in the development, health and education of the poorest members of the community. UNICEF demanded 'Adjustment with a human face', a programme which gave priority to the alleviation of poverty caused by IMF and World Bank measures. The UNDP brought out its Human Development Report which echoed the concern of UNICEF by showing that many of the previously accepted statistical indicators produced by the World Bank and other UN bodies did not reflect the true negative impact of change on the poor.

During the Eighties, a period during which Senegal was forced to submit to some 11 separate structural adjustment packages, long-term official debt had increased from 1 billion US dollars to over 3 billion.

A large number of expert economic observers believe that the structural adjustment programmes have failed. They blame either the banks for imposing an inappropriate treatment which they should have known was unlikely to work, or the Senegalese government for taking the money and avoiding its essential conditions.

There are already in print a number of learned analyses of the economy of Senegal and of other developing countries with similar problems. Sub-Saharan Africa has attracted special attention because it is seen as the graveyard of so many 'good' development ideas and plans. This is not another of those texts. Instead I have tried to listen to those who live at the margins of society; voices unheard by the media who have no space for the more humdrum battles of survival and well-being. These are often people with a limited view of the world. They may often not understand what a white person from a far off land is doing in their patch of the country asking questions. On top of that the local languages mean all dialogue has to be fed through an interpreter, who may choose to alter the words to suit himself. But often the answers throw light on the big questions in unexpected ways. They give substance to an otherwise abstract kind of debate. And there are lessons perhaps in the lack of such material among the mass of development writing of recent years. Where is the evidence there of dialogue with the population who are 'being developed'?

My earlier attempt to do something similar on film in the Sixties when I talked to villagers, newcomers to the city and university students about future development, led me to think it might be possible and useful to tread similar ground in the Nineties. Maybe find some of the same people, remind them what they said in the past. Ask what has changed. In so doing I hoped to discover some answers but also to convey something of the warmth, the thoughtfulness and the courage of a people all but forgotten, their voices lost in the drama of events in other war-torn and violent areas of the world.

The populations of the countries of Sub-Saharan Africa are among the poorest in the world. The Senegalese are such a population but the people of Mauritania, Mali, Gambia, Burkina Faso, Niger, Chad, Guinea Bissau, Guinea, Sierra Leone and Ghana face similar problems. They have been working and waiting for a breakthrough in their living conditions for a long time. As one old man said nostalgically: 'When is this independence thing going to end? We are tired of it.'

The first time I visited Senegal was in 1968. I was an emissary for the United Nations and had been commissioned to do a job of work for a consortium of agencies — UNDP, World Bank, FAO, UNESCO, CESI — working in the developing countries. Though an outsider, I had the coveted blue UN laissez-passer which reduced airport officials to a state of spaniel-like devotion. I was ushered into a world of chauffeur-driven cars, air-conditioned offices, expense account hospitality, and million dollar aid programmes. I was there to see the progress made by a developing country in the first UN Development Decade and try and picture its climb over the next ten. Everything was big. The words global, overall, ceiling, macro, national development strategies, urban renewal, industrialisation, infrastructure, implementation, peppered the discussion. I struggled to bring it down to earth, to work out what it meant to villagers and shanty town dwellers.

The second time was in March 1981 as a staff journalist for Christian Aid, an agency which channelled small sums of money donated by the British public to alleviate poverty and to encourage development work. I found my own way around in rattle-trap taxis or over-crowded buses. The talk here was of peasant farmers, harvests, the cost of firewood, where exercise books might come from, gardens, seeds, hand pumps, families, mud bricks.

The contrast could not have been greater. Two wholly different languages of aid, two different patterns of development. The large-scale, officially backed aid programmes on the one hand — the miniature, village or family ones on the other. Macro and micro, perhaps Ying and Yang. Or maybe fundamentally opposed and at odds!

As years went by it became clear that 'top down' and 'bottom up' development ideas were often in conflict, although in principle devoted to the same ideals. When the large-scale, top down efforts failed they often caused widespread social damage, even loss of life. When the small-scale actions failed they may have affected a few, but being close to the people, the cause of failure could be more readily seen and remedied. The small-scale or grass-roots approach of the voluntary agencies has often led to the support of new ideas with small groups, accompanying them rather than directing them, making the most of small resources and solidarity. The UN and the national aid budgets had to go through the host government. Their programmes necessarily became high profile, high budget, top down, hierarchically organised, broad brush actions.

Nor was it simply a matter of scale. Until the end of the cold war there was a political agenda in almost all aid programmes. There were friends and enemies, deserving and undeserving; morality took a back seat, giving rise to the famous quip by a US President about a vicious South American dictator the US were supporting — 'he may be a son of a bitch but he's our son of a bitch'. Development, whether official or voluntary, has seldom been free of hidden agendas. There have been few clear and agreed guidelines. It is uncertain whether we are any nearer to an answer.

There was a further question, which all who have compared countries that have made great strides in the growth of their economies with those which have scarcely moved at all, ask themselves from time to time. Is there something about a country or about its people which makes it eager and able to develop — whatever one means by the word — and something about another which disables it? Why is it that some of the formerly poorest countries in the developing world have been able to climb into a league of newly-industrialised countries which aspire to be among the richest countries in the world, while others stagnate in conditions only marginally better than they had 30 years ago? Are some people — by tradition, hardship or philosophy — immunised against development strategies?

The question has often been answered in terms of 'Oh a country remains poor because it has no natural resources to exploit', 'had no appeal to either of the super-powers when they were building up allies in the developing world and spending their cash freely' or 'suffers from environmental handicaps'. By visiting one of the most traditional and deep-rooted societies in the rural hinterland, the Toucouleurs and the Soninke peoples along the middle valley of the river Senegal, I hoped some kind of answer might emerge. These people, who had been knocked out by the 1973 drought which had virtually destroyed their livelihood and their environment, were now facing a revolutionary change in their agriculture and their living conditions brought about by the completion of a major dam-building and irrigation scheme in the middle of their communities. If it were true that change was held back because of stubborn traditional thinking, then what chances had they of avoiding a bleak, poverty-ridden future? In particular how were they coming to terms with the agricultural revolution on their doorsteps as a result of the construction of huge dams on the very river which provided their livelihood and *raison d'être?*

My employers, Christian Aid, had been supporting a major training and awareness-raising effort by a Senegalese NGO — the Union de Solidarité et Entraide (USE), through a project known as PIP — the Integrated Programme of Podor, which worked closely with villagers in the middle valley. I had both filmed and toured in this heartland at various times since 1969 and it seemed a good place to go to listen to what people had to say. While the cities filled up with new citizens, could the village communities survive? How did they see their future?

# PART ONE

# CITIES AND CITIZENS

# CHAPTER ONE

# THE POWDER KEG:
# Dakar at crisis point

*Every time you feel the heat of the street...look into the eyes of the people who have possibilities, and ask them, "Why is it like this...?"*

**President Aristide of Haiti in exile**

On my first day in Dakar in 1992, I hailed a taxi-driver from the pavement of Avenue Ponty for a journey across town. Four taxis tried to beat each other to my side regardless of other traffic or pedestrians. Shouts and horns of protest were met with gross gestures. The streets might be crowded but there were few fares in the present recession. Survival was the name of the game.

'Too many taxis,' muttered my driver. 'The authorities have issued far too many cab licences. A few bank notes added to the forms and *voilà*. You can't really blame them, they're as desperate to make ends meet as anyone.'

Unlike many cab drivers who prefer to turn up their radios rather than talk, Mamadou was quite ready to launch into discussion. He needed only a few words of encouragement. We crawled down a side street which should have been a short cut but was full of stalled traffic surrounded by young men offering a bizarre variety of unlikely goods — coat stands, cuckoo clocks, gilt-framed mirrors, pink rabbits, feather dusters, back numbers of *Newsweek*.

'Just look at this,' remarked Mamadou. 'It's become a plague. Dakar is bursting. It can't cope. All these young people without

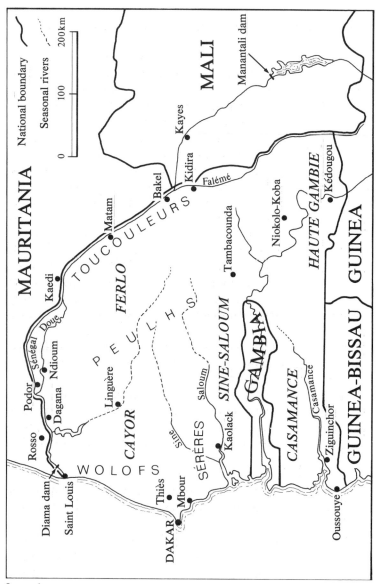

Senegal

work. You can see the fear in their eyes. They're lost, angry, betrayed.'

Hands pummelled the windows, the windscreen was blotted out with pink and green tinsel and false fur. Mamadou revved the motor to frighten those in front. There was a yell of protest. We got away.

'Ah *monsieur,* we are in a real mess and I see no end to it.'

A day or so later a bus driver was beaten almost to death by an angry crowd after he knocked down an old man who stepped in front of the bus. For 24 hours angry citizens all over the city not only boycotted the company buses, but stopped and emptied the passengers off any they found still working. The poor were so frustrated a small spark was enough to set them alight.

We escaped into an avenue running along the dockyard walls. Inside the wharves were empty. The once booming port through which flowed all the trade and supplies for a huge French colonial territory, a coaling station for merchant ships routed around West Africa, now welcomed one or two container ships a month and a battered coastal trader or two up from Casamance with fish and fresh fruit. In the tourist season a rare visit from a cruise liner for a few hours shopping gave the mass of street traders, beggars and charlatans a brief feeding frenzy. The loading and unloading which kept hundreds of unskilled workers and their families alive was a thing of the past.

'I wasn't a chauffeur for a bank without something rubbing off, even if it was only the smell of money,' Mamadou continued, following his train of thought.

'You see what's happened. The government has had to shift the burden of its debt out of its hands into the private sector. But it has not tackled the spending of those gentlemen in high places who still live on the fat of the land. In my view all they have done is replace one time bomb with another possibly much more dangerous one.'

Taxi-drivers were not, in my past experience, as ready to speak openly about their government's failings as Mamadou. This was something new.

'I get all over town. And what is going on? I'll tell you. Unemployment? There's never been anything like it. People chucked out of steady jobs. Out of 4 million workers, 3 million are out of work which the rest have to support. I'm one of them.

'Poverty? We were poor before but it's become an intolerable burden. Intolerable! Even we Senegalese who think ourselves so smart in eking out money resources are losing the struggle to make ends meet. So people are quarrelling in the street. The gaiety, the spontaneity, the good feeling for life has gone. The police are jumpy and taking it out on people. There's much more crime. Robbery has become common.'

Mamadou was middle-aged, sober-looking, not a man I thought given to tall stories. He had worked for the same bank for 20 years. Then he was *deflaté* as they call it here, in the widespread job-shedding which followed the tightening screw of the structural adjustment programmes of the Eighties forced on the government by the IMF and the World Bank. At least he kept his car as part of his redundancy and was able to get a taxi licence.

'You say you've been here before. How do you find things?' Mamadou asked. I said that I thought the place looked much more run down, people looked tired, the street traders who used to pursue one enthusiastically but with good humour had become shifty and vaguely threatening. There were so many more young people sitting around sullenly waiting, sleeping rough. The character of the place had soured.

'*Voilà,*' said Mamadou. 'There's no sign either of things getting better, despite what is said in *Le Soleil,* the official daily newspaper. We're in an economic catastrophe and our leaders don't seem to see it. I don't see any sign of a plan which might lead to a solution. We are sinking under the weight of daily problems.'

We swung round the Independence Monument with its tall concrete needle flanked by the national symbol, the Senegalese lion. The real lions had either been hunted to extinction or moved south as the desert encroached and their preferred habitat was stripped bare.

'...And the leadership is keeping up a standard of living and a profligate style of government which is quite immoral in contrast with what we ordinary Senegalese have to bear. Tens of thousands don't have enough to eat while they and their cronies are making off with the loot or living in luxurious houses, driving only the newest of foreign cars which cost tens of millions, all at the cost of the ordinary citizen. I know, because I used to work for some of them and even now I get to run errands for people in the villas — heh! you could say *châteaux* — on the luxury estates. There is no belt tightening out there, that's for sure. No will to change things. No talk of social justice.

'I tell you, you may still think us a quiet, settled, stable country with an obedient population, but we are sitting on a powder keg. It is a situation that cannot continue for ever.'

Ten years ago people were still prepared to give a new government time to fulfil its promises. In February 1981 I had to travel by collective taxi to northern Senegal. It was a Friday and business was quiet in the bus station. The best deal was the last seat in an old Peugeot which already had five male passengers about to leave for Louga, a town a third of the way to where I wanted to go. From there I might get a ride to St Louis.

We set off. Most conversations in the beat-up cross-country taxis are in a vernacular tongue and exclude the European passenger. On this journey a bumptious but charismatic young man insisted on speaking to his fellow passengers in French. They were forced by rules of politeness to respond in kind. His subject was politics. President Senghor had recently stepped down from power to allow the nomination of an experienced and, at the time, highly esteemed younger politician Abdou Diouf. It was a politically significant event which sent signals all over the continent. Senghor was the first African leader since the early independence days who had voluntarily retired from office without being pushed or otherwise deposed.

'He's a hard worker and a moral man,' said my neighbour.

'I'm looking forward to great changes and there's going to be a fresh start,' said another.

'People will have to buckle to, it will be a time of great austerity but it will be exciting,' said a third.

'Ah,' said the young man, 'the thing about African regimes is that the leaders think that the people are there to be told what to do, which is the old African way. Things will have to change.'

Yes, I thought, but how?

'It's a question of getting ministers who are technically effective and able to lead their own bureaucracies. The lower echelons also need to be competent. It is not the case at the present time.'

Today that same government, though tired and without respect, hangs on to power while lacking any policies the population is prepared to trust.

When I arrived in Dakar in 1992 I needed a pair of cheap plastic sandals so I went to Sandaga. It's a cliche but a true one, that if one wants to feel the pulse of a great city one goes to its biggest popular market and looks and listens to what is going on.

Sandaga has been the city of Dakar's principal market for generations. Every day it bursts down the Avenue Emile Badiane from the once fine colonial citadel, now the commercial and government hub of the country, towards the Medina. A giant bubbling larva flow attracting thousands of traders of all kinds, ready to burn the naive or the unwary. Here you can buy a 'Cartier' watch for 2000 francs (£5) or a bottle of 'Chanel' for a third of that. You can have a luxurious gold-embroidered wedding costume run up in a couple of hours or 5 tonnes of rice loaded on a lorry in less time than Nigel Mansell needs for a pit stop.

In the *souk*, a labyrinth of dark inner stalls spilling over with cloth, leather, hats, jewellry, plastic goods, I ended up dissecting the world with a couple of elders and a nephew who sold those gold lamé mules decorated with sequined bows and butterflies much favoured by the elegant and flirtatious ladies of Dakar. He didn't sell plastic sandals but he knew a man who did. Would I sit down and wait? It was an open invitation for a chat.

One of the old men wore his campaign medals on his *boubou*. 'Yes, I did the war. I fought the Germans to help you Europeans out,' he said chuckling. 'Now look how you show your gratitude. Where is the generous hand of true comradeship? I get an ever so little pension in memory of that time. It's not enough.'

The nephew David cut in. 'The country is having serious problems at the present time and it is all to do with the politics of the IMF.' It came out just like that. I had said nothing about my interest. I was just a visitor. 'The economy is in a drift,' David continued. 'There are hordes of unemployed. Everybody is trying to scratch a living by fair means or foul. Thousands of policemen have been laid off. They were given three years' wages which wasn't adequate. They were given no advice on what to do with it and they had never seen so much cash at one time. It all disappeared in the first three months. Family demands, difficult to refuse without losing face. Now there's a lot of unhappiness. Factories have closed, workers laid off without any prospects. Any fool could have seen what was likely to happen. It's no good taking tough measures if you cripple the very people you need to get things moving, is it? I tell you, the economy is like a train which can only run on its rails. If one removes the rails how can it go forward?'

There was a lot more chat like that but conversations of this kind tend to go round in circles and there were plenty of distractions, jokes to share, people to greet. And yes, a pair of sandals appeared as if by magic. They fitted and the price was right. On this occasion nobody tried to exploit the stranger. Perhaps the pleasure of the conversation had something to do with it. 'Come back and buy something nice for your wives,' said the old man.

Back in the cool dark depths of the hotel foyer, to which I had retreated to escape from the overpowering heat, I fell into conversation with a young man. He looked bookish and gentle. He was rubbing his hands anxiously. They were fine long-fingered hands. I took him to be a university student. One of the junior receptionists came over and told him to wait. The cook, she said condescendingly, would see him shortly.

'Are you looking for a job?' I asked.

'I am hoping to get a job in the kitchen. I gather there is one. I want to talk to the chef but he's busy so I'm waiting.'

'Are you a cook?'

'No I'm a musician. I have done part of my degree course but I can't afford to continue to study. I play several instruments. I want to compose. I have already made a tape.'

The previous night, in the bar next door to the cafe where I was eating, a small band had opened its set with a yearning rendition of 'Over the Rainbow' which seemed in the circumstances an apt theme tune both for the country and its people.

It had also been a nostalgic visit. The cafe was staffed by the same dignified and now elderly Toucouleur men who had temporarily migrated to Dakar in the Sixties from far upstream on the River Senegal to top up a poor season's income. I had met them in 1968 and again in 1981. They dreamt of going home but they were still here and sending money home to their families.

'So what are you hoping for here?'

The young man was clearly humiliated by the prospect.

'There's a job at night, washing up and helping out. I know what you're going to say but there is nothing for me elsewhere. This is my last chance. I have to eat. I have to stay in the city or I will never have a chance.'

'I hope you succeed.'

But he didn't. The cook, a Serere from the Sine Saloum region south of Dakar, had preferred one of his own people.

Many young men and women with more experience or useful skills to offer than the young musician had been flung aside as the economic crisis got worse in the Eighties.

Ousmane Diakhate was one of them.

'I've been unemployed since the end of 1987. There's no dole like there is in Europe. Yet one has to get by somehow. I haven't any other source of income. I look for work all the time. My parents live in Rufisque, on the coast just south of Dakar but I stay in Dakar, dossing down where I can because that's where I shall find work if there is any to be had. I have just got a temporary job for a few days filling in for a friend who can't do it.'

Ousmane was driving a group of European aid agency people around the north of the country to visit programmes they supported. He was not only a good driver but took great care of the vehicle with which he was temporarily entrusted. He was in his late twenties, congenial, neat, educated, self-disciplined, fit, efficient. I asked him what he had done before.

'I have been a mechanic. I wasn't trained but I have picked it up in a variety of jobs. I have done lots of things. I have acquired quite a few skills. I haven't got diplomas or anything but I can do things. I was in a deep sea trawler for a while and was promoted by the company who owned the ship to a supervising job in their fish processing factory. Then the firm went under in the economic crisis of the Eighties and I found myself on the street. Unfortunately I was one of thousands in the same boat.'

'What now?' I asked.

'The problem for me is that when you say you are a jack of all trades it doesn't mean you are a specialist in anything. You go to an interview and answer truthfully that you can do such and such a job, yet you have no papers to show for it. Those

Christian Aid/Derrick Knight

**Ousmane Diakhate**

who come along with proper training stand a better chance. I have just got to go on trying.'

Back in 1968 the numbers out of work were much smaller but exactly the same problem existed. This is how I portrayed the problems of unemployment in a scene from my UN documentary film in 1969. The situation seemed bad at the time but is now a hundred times worse.

> **VOICE:** Waly, what is your routine?
>
> **WALY:** Every day we go looking for work. Every day it's the same story. My mates Arfang and Mass who are labourers go round the docks to see if there is any unloading work to be had. I take the long walk up to the plateau where most of the business offices are. They are still mainly in the hands of foreigners. It's footslog all the way and I have regular stops. I have friends who keep their ears open so you call on them wherever they are — a garage, a warehouse, a merchant — and you hope they'll introduce you to their bosses. Most of them don't or can't.
>
> **VOICE:** So how does one get a place?
>
> **WALY:** It's really tough. In fact most jobs have to be paid for. A present is needed for the person giving out work — it's sort of expected. Now it's difficult to buck the system. Well, we can't find that sort of money, so what we do from time to time is to pool what we can put together for one man who then bribes his way into a job and tries to get the others in later.

Waly, like thousands of others, was a village boy pushed towards the city by the poor living conditions and lack of work in the countryside. In 1968 the population of greater Dakar was about half a million. In 1992 it was over two million and it is now growing at the rate of 4% per year: that is 80,000 new citizens to house, provide social services for and find work for. New attempts at town planning and providing new suburbs with modern sanitation, water and electricity are overwhelmed by numbers. The combination of the recession and the conditions imposed by the World Bank for the country's eventual economic recovery has decimated jobs and closed many of the government services which might have provided some support to the poorest sectors of the population. Most of the new arrivals are young and impatient. Tens of thousands have improvised jobs or found ways of earning money in the informal sectors — street trading, food stalls, portering, making things, begging. But there are an increasing number who have been forced to resort to crime, mugging and pickpocketing.

Traditional family custom obliges families already on the border of survival to shoulder the burden of so-called dependants. The economic difficulties are so great that fundamental values and beliefs have been weakened. Family obligations, up to now sacred, are one vulnerable area. Colleagues in ENDA GRAF, a local independent voluntary organisation offering training and practical help to balance household budgets in a poor suburb, took me to meet a housewife who was struggling with a typically heavy burden. She was typical of thousands of women keeping a home together but she was unusual in the degree to which she succeeded in managing what can only be described as a negative budget. Here in miniature was an allegory of the state of the nation and a clue to why society had not blown up in the face of government failure to provide the social structure necessary for its people's prosperity.

'My name is Ndeye Sokhna Faye. I am 34 years old. I have a very large family. My husband is 68. We live in the house he bought years ago when he had a little money. He is now retired. I have seven children  and some other dependants, not counting the sons of my husband by his first wife. They are unemployed and have to be cared for.'

She was what Jane Austen would have called 'a comfortable and obliging person', with the face of an angel, remarkably open and direct, and with sparkling intelligent eyes full of good humour. She bore no outward sign of the weight of responsibility which she began to expound, a weight which I heard everywhere has to be borne by thousands of women.

'I have also been asked to look after the teenage daughter of a cousin. She could go out to work but has not found any so far. She stays at home with me. So in all there are 15 people at home at the present time.'

Knowing that women have less chance of education than men I

asked whether she had been able to go to school. She giggled without bitterness.

Ndeye Sokhna Faye

'Not much to speak of. I was at school for only four years and then I got married.' She paused and then burst out. 'I do want to continue my education now. I really do. I have strangers in the house who don't speak Wolof. I want to be able to talk to them. It's a real nuisance. I would go back to school right now if I had the chance. I would also like to be able to speak better French but with all the demands on my time and the need to keep a very careful budget, it is too difficult.

'It tires me out trying to make ends meet. My husband no longer works. He gets a company pension of 4,000 francs (about £9) per month but it cannot be relied on. It can come months late or not at all. I used to have four rooms to let but with a bigger family I now only have two. My lodgers do not pay on time and find all sorts of excuses to avoid having to pay. I don't see much of that because my husband collects it and has his own problems.

'I have many relations who help me financially from time to time or with whom I can do some trade or other. I expect you know our Senegalese system. You do a favour here and receive a favour there. We take part in little local savings clubs — *tontines* — in the township. They can help if you are in trouble. My women friends and acquaintances all have some little schemes going to help us survive, favours, exchanges, loans, savings schemes, buying and selling. This is what helps a family keep going for months even when the bread-earners are not bringing in enough to keep the large number who have to be fed and cared for.

'I stay at home except when I get a holiday job. I take the place of a friend who has a regular cleaning job when she goes on holiday. Just a few weeks a year. At home I make and sell ice, ice creams, custards and other sweets. I sell these either at the door or to women I know in the district to earn a few francs in hand for the daily housekeeping expenses. It goes on food.

'My step-sons who are in their early twenties don't wait for breakfast. They go off early to look for work. One is a mechanic, the other a plumber. They occasionally pick up some work by the day or the week. The rest of the time I have to feed them. They invite their pals as well. They are mostly unemployed. There is such a lot of it. It is very hard. The boys are very unhappy.'

As she spoke, Sokhna kept a lively smile on her face as if all these problems were trivial matters. Even now the Senegalese laugh about their desperate problems. 'How come?' I ask.

'That's how it is,' replied Sokhna. 'I have all kinds of difficulties but I laugh all the same. I can't help it.'

To give a human face to structural adjustment and compensate for the social damage which resulted from its agenda of job-shedding, the big UN agencies, notably the ILO and the UNDP, were given funds to finance some essential training and temporary job schemes known as 'Insertion' and 'Re-insertion' programmes — in other words, new jobs for new workers and new jobs for the long-term unemployed. The purpose was to help people like the younger members of Sokhna's family and thousands like them needing work. In reality they work no better than similar government-sponsored schemes in Europe. Many Senegalese I spoke to regard them as a farce, a bit of play acting or as they prefer to say 'prestidigitation' — a conjuring trick to massage the statistics and hide the fresh cracks in the economy caused by the tensions of the SAP rules.

Some of these schemes, proudly publicised with giant hoardings, seem to be little more than creating new areas of street pavement or curb-stoning roadsides in remote villages.

'Teaching young men to do this kind of thing or hiring people for a few months to put curb-stone along a road when the country is in the middle of a deep economic crisis is going to solve nothing,' said a Senegalese colleague as we drove past one such scheme up country.

A few blocks away and still in the district of Grand Yoff, four young men, all in their twenties, were at work putting the finishing touches to a newly renovated single-storey building, all fresh paint and oiled woodwork. It was a new pre-school centre for underprivileged children of the district. These four were part of a group that had not been prepared to wait until the economy picked up. They were launching their own lifeboat to help themselves and others too.

'We were pretty desperate, but we arrived at the conclusion that we had to do something like this,' said Alassane.

'I remember that it was about the time of the new law about the withdrawal of the state from many of its traditional activities, services and state-run business enterprises. There was a lot of talk about organising the informal sector of the economy because it was said that most of the money ordinary people had to spend came from it. Nobody had thought very hard about it before, but it began to look like a lifeline. Young people have always dreamed of a good office job. All of us with a bit of education had the same ambition. I myself did my studies in accountancy. That was the sort of office work I wanted to do. But then came the squeeze. The government dismantled many offices, state agencies, companies, made thousands redundant, cut its budgets in all directions. It was mayhem. The company I worked for went bust. We were told that it was bankrupt. The bosses vanished overnight. We discovered that for five whole years they had not paid our social security dues. Work was not to be had. So what could we do? We had to do something, that was clear.'

'That's right,' continued Diop. 'We were not prepared for the sudden withdrawal of the government from so many services and for the wave of redundancies that followed. We were unable to find alternative work. So we talked long and hard and decided to try and raise funds for a scheme which would improve our chances and meet a real need in the community. We spoke with various local NGOs, to local elders and to members of the town council of Dakar. Many of them were prepared to help. You see there is a very real need to try and improve the educational chances of the very young. The majority have never been in school. They are illiterate. Often the children who start school have to leave very early because their parents cannot afford the expense. We didn't have to be experts to see how the education of children is suffering as schools go on double shifts and teachers are laid off. Really education is in a mess, so we thought we might be able to make a contribution both to education and to the country's development.'

I was curious to know what these obviously alert and able young men thought of the state of the economy now.

'The economy is getting weaker, that's for sure,' said Diop. 'The only people who manage to get jobs now do it through personal contacts, or *la petite porte* as we call it — a backhander — a traditional fiddle.'

'You have no such contacts in high places of your own, then?' I asked. The question was met with exclamations and gestures which could only be translated as 'What a hope!'

Indeed what they said was true, if the available statistics were to be trusted. Despite some 30 years of independence, there is scarcely any major industry in Senegal. Almost every manufactured item still has to be imported and adds to the international debt, which amounted to 3.74 billion US dollars and still rising in 1990, and syphons away any revenue which might be used to re-launch the economy. During the years of the structural adjustment programmes, production in industry, manufacturing and the service sector, already minuscule, have all declined. The old BATA factory, once the pride of the Dakar industrial zone, has long been a derelict wreck, all broken glass and shrubs climbing through the roof. The prices of the few exports Senegal has to offer — groundnuts, phosphates, textiles, preserved fish — have fallen steadily and continue to do so while the cost of imported goods from the industrialised north continues to rise. A slimmed down civil service can only keep going with regular drafts from USAID.

The decimated customs service is unable to prevent widespread smuggling over the long land frontiers. So where are the jobs to come from which will provide a meaningful income for all the hundreds of thousands of young people like Ousmane, Alassane and Diop arriving on the free market place with high expectations? That is the question on everybody's lips. Neither the government nor its financial advisers in Washington nor in Paris have the answers.

# CHAPTER TWO

# SAMBA AND FRIENDS

In the grey dawn light filtering into the dusty courtyard of a family compound in Anglemousse, one of Dakar's crowded shanty towns, a shirtless young man begins to stretch sleepily while an old woman prepares a charcoal fire to boil a kettle. Other young men, just as sleepy, follow him. One goes to a water gourd, a five gallon jar kept off the ground on a tripod of sticks, and spills a ration into a small enamel bowl. An old man emerges from a shack at the back of the yard. The old woman gives him a jug of water with which he begins his ablutions before the morning prayer. Outside in the alley, as the light increases, many people can be heard on the move — mostly outwards, walking.

The first young man crouches by the fire and chews a chunk of dry bread. This is Samba. The old man is his father, Mamadou Ndiaye. The others are all either close relations or members of a village group struggling to live and work in the city. These are migrants, most of them without education and skills, still with one foot in the village but attracted by the strong magnetic pull of the town where there is movement, excitement and a freedom from traditional obligations.

This is a scene in one of the films I made for the UN in 1969. They were real people. Samba was then in his early twenties. He was one of the few with a regular job. What he earned he shared with others less fortunate.

In 1992 Samba lives in Guediawaye, one of the satellite

**Dakar and its hinterland**

townships of Dakar. He is now middle-aged, burdened with family responsibilities, and when I strolled into his compound without warning after an interval of many years, he was still shirtless, slim, beaded in sweat, up a ladder and supervising the extension of a couple of rooms in brick and slate to his overcrowded house. We fell about like a couple of schoolboys and when we had exchanged greetings in a proper Senegalese way I explained that I hadn't known whether I was going to be in Dakar. I only had his old work address and didn't know until I was able to use the phone whether he was still there and whether I would find him.

I had seen him once since 1969. In 1982 I had arrived in Dakar on the way to visit various farming programmes up country. I had a yearning for contact with a real Senegalese family. I thought of visiting Samba but had lost touch completely. The shanty town where he had lived was now a model housing estate. There was nobody left who lived there 20 years ago. In Senegal, however, there are nearly always ways of finding people through village, family and caste groups. Samba was a Serere, one of the main ethnic and language groups in the country and distantly related to the Toucouleurs in the North. In the city they stuck together.

The desk clerk at the hotel had a friend who was a night-porter in another who knew a Serere who had lived in the shanty town where Samba's father had lived before a great fire had destroyed it. The town council had shipped everyone out beyond the city outskirts to the sand dunes of Guediawaye. There was a chance that Samba had gone there too. I took the greetings of the first to the second man who couldn't answer my question but had a brother who might. Would I come back tomorrow? Yes, he had learnt that the Serere people had been in a block managed by Ousmane Fall. The Sereres are one of the main ethnic and language groups in Senegal. My new contact thought they had all moved together with their block leader. He suggested that if I found the block leader, a well-known former soldier, I would surely discover the whereabouts of Samba. In due course I found myself seated most formally in the reception room of Monsieur Fall in Guediawaye, patiently swopping experiences from our past. He was not about to let me go until he had a story or two for his own old boys' network. In the meantime a 'child' — in this case a man in his fifties — could run across the block and make sure Samba was at home. As it turned out, almost the whole family from the old place were at home.

Samba's parents, already elderly in 1968, were still alive in 1982 but old Mamadou was lying in bed and coughing badly — probably, I noted, chronic bronchitis. Not too sick, though, to remember the farcical turn of events when we had dragged him off to the sheep market in 1969 to film him haggling with wily

Peulh traders for a *mouton* to sacrifice on the Tabeski feast day. He was a serious and dignified believer and had been reluctant to play act. We were offering him the cost of the sheep but in exchange we wanted a convincing display of bargaining. Some of the traders backed away, refusing to be exposed to an evil eye. It was all very well having the old man cannily feeling the meat below the wool but useless without a price being debated. We had given Mamadou a limit of 6,000 CFAs, a generous sum at that time but seeing us taking pictures, the traders tried to take advantage. Worse and most offensive to the old man, they thought he was our stooge. The verbal exchanges became quite salty. In the end price and pride and the cameraman were satisfied.

Back in 1992, Maamadou was dead but Samba remained in the same house which had grown to shelter an extended family. He still worked for the same company, the Senegalese Power Generating Company SENELEC, and had advanced up the ladder of promotion from labourer to control room supervisor. He was coping pretty well in the midst of the country's long economic crisis. I was anxious to know what he remembered of those early days.

Samba thought for a moment. 'Well, there were no houses in Anglemousse,' he said. 'No solid buildings of any kind. There were only shacks — corrugated iron and wood. My father ran the compound where we lived. It was he who taught me about household budgets. My father was a poor man. He had retired. There was only my mother and I at home. My big brother was away. Yet we consumed 120 kilos of rice a month because all the young Sereres lived with us. If you came home at ten o'clock at night or later there was no bed space left indoors. Prosper, the dancer who worked in the theatre, was always last. Every day he would cry out: "And where am I supposed to sleep?" Someone would always answer, "I've left your bed outside." He slept out of doors all the time because he didn't finish in the theatre until very late at night.' Samba chuckled. 'I used to make sure to come home early to get a good spot.'

'It seemed that everybody was hustling, looking desperately for work,' I commented.

'I was lucky. I was already working. I began to work for the SENELEC in June 1968. I was 24. Only three of those living with us had jobs, the rest were out of work.'

David MacDonald

**Samba Ndiaye: aged 24, 1969**

How I had met Samba for the very first time in 1968 seems now to be important in showing the way that 'development' was then being promoted.

I was in Dakar looking for a way of visualising the dilemma of rural migrants in an African city who had neither education nor skills to find work easily. It was another episode in the series of films I was making for the United Nations. I had learnt of the existence of self-help groups and popular savings schemes within all the shanty towns and popular housing zones of Dakar. Some were linked to a political patron, some to a holy man, some to a village, some to an ethnic group. In all of them one was likely to find a mixture of employed and unemployed young men and women sharing a common cause, and committed to mutual support. I had a feeling that the answer might lie in such a group. I might then explore the ways in which they managed. But how was I going to find and select such a group in the seething shanty towns of Dakar?

It was soon clear that my UN contacts did not have links with the poor at the grass-roots level. Their people worked from air-conditioned offices with local counterparts in other air-conditioned offices. You would rarely find them with their feet in the mud. Friendly government officials and politicians did have such contacts but their groups were the creatures of patronage and party favours. The groups they sent me to see, though fascinating in terms of the way local politics could be manipulated, were no real help.

I had also taken to West Africa some alternative introductions from Christian Aid for whom I had recently made a film about pastoralists in Kenya. There were only two contacts in Senegal. One was the Protestant Church, which I discovered catered mainly for the families of European diplomats and expatriate workers.

The pastor was a city gent with a gold watch chain and a three-piece suit. The other address was the Centre de Bopp.

The Centre de Bopp was originally founded by the local Protestant Church (which had by 1968 distanced itself) and CIMADE, the French Protestant aid agency. CIMADE created the Service Oecumenique d'Entraide (SOE) to manage it. It acquired a piece of land in the Dakar suburb of Bopp close to one of the poorest and most crowded *bidonvilles* called Anglemousse. The word *bidonville* is very descriptive. A *bidon* is a large tin can or an oil drum. It is beaten flat to provide a roofing tile or bit of wall. Anglemousse was built out of the drums and packing cases thrown aside in the docks and the port.

On the edge of Anglemousse, an all-purpose community centre was built with a view to providing activities and training for the impoverished youth of the district. There were then, and still are, too few opportunities for the young to acquire real skills. The centre was complemented by a small health clinic and an eye unit in whose operating theatre specialists restored sight, removed cataracts and corrected other problems, as a charitable service funded by the churches and aid agencies linked with the World Council of Churches.

In 1968 the social and cultural activities of Bopp were managed by a large jovial Dutch missionary known as Monsieur Bob. The work of the medical centre and clinic was maintained by a quiet and efficient British nurse called Irene Bosnanski and a staff of local assistants.

Monsieur Bob was open-minded and friends with everyone. He went about the poorest quarters on missions of mercy at all hours of the day or night. The Centre was crowded and something was going on from morning till late at night. The guiding principle was to serve the poor and to avoid all possible religious favouritism or political patronage. It didn't mean that religion and politics were taboo matters for discussion. On the contrary — but they were debated on neutral ground. Monsieur Bob listened, counselled, negotiated, made suggestions and tried to solve problems firmly but gently. He was respected and admired by Muslim, Christian and Animist alike.

The inhabitants of Anglemousse were mainly the very young who were still villagers at heart: 45% of the total population of Dakar in 1969 was under 15. Bopp catered, within its modest budget, for the local youth — unemployed, illiterate, unskilled, unmotivated, alienated, searching. Development experts have always seen them as one of the great hidden and wasted assets of developing countries and yet have continually failed to find resources to mobilise them.

Early in our acquaintance Bob told me:

'If a boy working on the land planting millet can only earn 20,000 CFAs a year (then £30) and if he can at least earn 100 CFAs a day or 36,000 a year by polishing shoes in Dakar, however precarious this seems, why should he work on the land? The producer is not valued enough — the middleman takes too much.'

Bopp had few expensive facilities but it was an oasis in a parched urban desert. Its main attraction was a hard asphalt basketball pitch with evening floodlighting and a surrounding fringe of shade trees. Basketball and Bopp were then and are still inseparable in the sports calendar of Dakar. Dozens of teams have been nurtured and coached for local championships which they have often dominated. There are not only teams of young men and young women but teams of children whose stars hope to be noticed and recruited by their elders. Inside the gates, Bopp is free of the customary shackles and religious dogmas which often imprison the minds of the young in Senegal. Vocational training schemes were started for boys and girls. The small compound was packed with workshops, classrooms, meeting rooms, a small library.

On that very first visit I quickly discovered that if one wanted to know what was going on in Dakar, indeed in the whole of Senegal, Bopp was the place. It had the collective ears and eyes of its thousands of users. They came from every corner of the country. It was a place of hope. It was free. It was packed. In the evening basketball players and their fans surrounded the court. In the main block students came to study, others to discuss current issues, often with an eminent visitor. In another room women were learning how to sew and do embroidery with which to earn a little cash. Some, more modest, wanted to learn to read and write. Musicians and dancers rehearsed and sometimes performed.

Monsieur Bob listened to my request. He took me on a tour of Anglemousse, a human beehive. In the labyrinth of alleyways some were so narrow that you had to edge your way along sideways. Extraordinary overcrowding and boiling over energy. I was mesmerised. A night or two later Bob suggested I went and watched a group of young dancers and singers rehearsing on the stage in the main hall at Bopp. Their front man was Samba Ndiaye. His father was their patron.

I wrote in my notebook of the day:

> Tonight saw a group of young Serere at Bopp rehearsing some folk dances and comic love songs with Tam Tams. Some of them were really very good, especially the men, all out of work aged 16-22. They are preparing an evening to raise some money. They call themselves 'Belle Etoile de Sine Saloum' — Bright Star of Sine Saloum — the pretty riverine province from which they all come. I think this is it.

It was to be the first of several visits to their rehearsals and to the compound where most of them lived. Almost every one had a story. There was Arfang, a hungry colossus with huge buck teeth, who threw himself into wild dances with total abandon. A bricklayer, he had been looking for a job for months. There was Mass Sene, as diminutive as Arfang was huge, a talented drummer though otherwise unskilled, illiterate, totally without means and suffering from a drug problem. He had never worked since leaving the village but he was the *griot* — the minstrel poet — of the group and could improvise praise songs to order. He loved city life and wore a pair of dark glasses and a golfing cap at all times as badges of his membership of the urban world. There was Ousmane Faye, older, a man of the world, a former *maître d'hôtel* in the President's Palace and now trying to put together a small fishing cooperative for the unemployed within the Serere group. The choreographer was Prosper Gding, a professional dancer who was sometimes engaged in the troupe of the National Theatre, a bluff and hearty man, a *boulevardier* without the means to indulge himself. There were a number of young women who were working as maids and had squeezed time out of their long working hours.

The possibilities of filming how new arrivals — country boys and girls with few material resources — tackled the challenge of finding a livelihood in a strange city seemed endless. Samba's group, in their search for work and attempts to raise money for their daily needs, became the subject of the film. Their attempt to

**Ousmane Faye and family, 1992**

collect a larger sum to launch the fishing cooperative by staging an evening of folksong and dance was its climax.

To someone like Samba, legatee of generations of oral history, digging back 25 years into an episode of his past was achieved with scarcely an effort. It was still fresh and clear.

'I remember when we first met at Bopp. We made the film in 1969 during Ramadan. At that time I was Secretary of the Serere Association which we had formed in Anglemousse and which contained a theatre group. I was one of the performers, not because I was any good but more to encourage the others.

'We had a mutual aid group. It brought together all the Serere migrants to protect them against misfortune and to help them develop good relationships.

'When a Serere meets another Serere that he doesn't know, they can easily get into a fight about the slightest thing. It was our idea to bring together all the Serere people in town, so that they could meet, get to know each other, pool their resources and help each other. That was our motto.

'The idea of the theatre group was to make a bit of money so that we could give a little to those who took part but lived at a distance — like the girls who were maids in people's houses — so that they would have an incentive to come back and take a full part in our group.'

## Amateur Theatre Group 'Belle Etoile de Sine Saloum'
**Members of the Group with jobs:**

| | |
|---|---|
| Samba Ndiaye | Maintenance at SENELEC |
| Sombele Diouf | Tailor |
| M'Baye Gueye | Mason's labourer |
| Prosper Gning | Theatrical dancer |
| Madadi Diouf | Fisherman |
| Bakari Sarr | Fisherman |
| Issa Sarr | Tailor |
| Doudou Sarr | Garageman |
| Doudou Diop | Waiter at High Court |
| Lamine Dior | Fisherman |

**Members of the Group out of work:**

| | |
|---|---|
| Mamadou Ndiaye | Doyen |
| Mass Sene | Drummer |
| Waly Niane | Former soldier |
| Arfang N'Diaye | Mason |
| Amath Marone | Cook |
| Ousmane Faye | Maître d'hôtel |
| Alioune Ndiaye | Apprentice mechanic |
| Sacoura Badiane | Cook |
| Pierre Dior | Teacher |
| Issa N'Daw | Greaser |
| Mamadou Sene | Greaser |
| Abdoulaye Dioune | Cabinet maker |
| Gorgui Thior | Tailor |
| Mamou Thiare | Tailor |
| Sitapha Thior | Wrestler — fisherman |
| Ousmane Sarr | Photographer |
| Lamine Boikhoum | Labourer |
| Ousmane N'Diaye | Labourer |
| Babou N'Diaye | Typist |

**Girls in the Group — all working as maids:**

| | | |
|---|---|---|
| Daba Diouf | Fatou Ndour | Sigua Diouf |
| Nidiougue Diouf | Marie Mibam | Germaine Gualch |
| Moussou Samb | Yande Faye | Grane Faye |
| Bernadette Thiaw | N'oone Thiaw | Oumy Sall |
| Codou Tinn | Coumba Faye | Fatou Fall |
| Oumy Diop | | |

Opposite are the members of the group in the shanty town of Anglemousse in January 1969. Not all of them lived in Mamadou Ndiaye's compound.

According to my notebook: the wages of a maid in 1969 varied from 200 to 300 francs a day (about 30-40 pence) and their food. The monthly wages were between 2,500 (less than £4) and 7,000 francs (just over £10) plus food. A girl of 15 or under, who would do all household chores except the ironing, might earn 2,500 francs. 7,000 francs was the rate for a young woman of 20 or more who had experience and was able to do every household task asked of her.

The subscriptions into the Serere Solidarity Fund were 150 francs a month for those in work, 75 francs for the workless.

David MacDonald

**Mamadou Ndiaye ('Serere'), 1969**

As I sat with Samba in 1992, I wondered whether my memory was correct that the group was unconnected to political figures.

'In Senegal,' Samba answered, 'when you want to bring all the Serere people together in one association you have to keep party politics out of it. If you don't, there will quickly be opposing factions and the whole thing will blow apart. We wanted to support and celebrate our own regional ethnic character and customs. We are related to the Pulaar speaking peoples in the north. Sadly, my children hear Wolof everywhere and don't like speaking Serere. We have had to get used to the idea. The doyen of the group was my father. He was also our patron. He was a whole-hearted Serere. That's his picture on the wall. You probably recognise it.'

A large black and white portrait of Mamadou, wearing the fez without which he was never seen, had been lovingly framed and placed in a position of pride on the wall of the living room. It had been taken by David MacDonald, my cameraman, in 1969. It caught the air of determination mixed with a gentle piety which were strong marks of character in him.

'Even when he spoke Wolof,' Samba continued, 'it was clear from his accent that he was a Serere. And he was nicknamed Mamadou Ndiaye Serere because he loved his Pulaar name so much. It was he who thought it was important to re-unite all the Sereres. He was even congratulated by Bonafin Diouf, the former Minister of Labour, for his efforts. He's dead now but my mother is still alive and lives with us.'

'What about some of the others in the group. Where are they?'

'Ousmane Faye, who you remember left a good job as a *maître d'hôtel* in the Palace, found work in a tourist hotel in M'Bour and is now running a restaurant in town near the National Assembly. He's doing really well. His family is with him. You must go and see him.

'Abdalou Ndiaye has managed to make a living out of radio repairs. Waly Niane found work in a factory making electrical wiring. Arfang, who was one of our unemployed builders, went to Gabon and has worked there for 10 years. He came back for a while, couldn't find work and returned to Gabon where his bricklaying skills are properly valued. Mass Sene, the little drummer who was in the film, died tragically young. Prosper joined a big African touring theatre group called the Sacred Forest and left them when they were performing in France. He married a Spanish woman and now teaches folk dancing in Spain.'

Samba laughed. 'He has done very well and has had a large house built in his native village Ngueniene in the Saloum, presumably for his old age.

'Both my brother and I married girls in the group. Both were working as maids. My wife was earning 5,000 francs a month at the time — about 150 francs a day. The younger ones were paid between 500 and 2,000 francs per month.

'All the girls who danced in the group have become wives and mothers. They have done very well for themselves. They have become very successful teachers. You see, there was a whole ferment going on inside our theatre group. The girls were part of that. When they came to us they were without education. They knew nothing. When they joined the group their horizons were immediately broadened. They awoke to all kinds of new possibilities. Now they run their households well and are influential in their communities. The group was a good school.'

I had made the following notes in 1968.

> The girls in the group all walk to work or in search of work. Some go into town, others try their luck in the new and neat housing estates built for civil servants and minor officials. The exploitation of the girls is quite shocking. The humiliations endless.
>
> There is also a *marché aux bonnes*, a maids' market behind the UN office on Independence Square. Those seeking work sit along the wall of a side street from dawn hoping to attract the eye of an employer. The morning I walked through, there were about a hundred girls and women of all ages. Potential employers are of all races. A maid is so cheap almost any housewife can afford one. Madams come and look them over and occasionally one is chosen. But you can wait a month. At midday those who have no work trudge home and try later or stay in town and rest through the midday heat. Later, I am told boldly by a trio of girls in the group: 'It is better than staying in the village. All things being equal we do better than the Serere men and we can afford the kind of little luxuries which make Senegalese town women so chic — scarves, earrings, a pretty *boubou* or two.'

The maids' market still exists at the corner of the Rue Assane Hamidou Ndiaye and the back of the Protestant Church. There seemed to be three or four times as many young women offering themselves, crouching in scraps of shade, some of them carrying their babies. The process is certainly no less humiliating than it ever was. One has to believe that the ladies who come to look them over, whether African or expatriate, are looking only for the cheapest bargain and the least commitment.

My 1968 notebook again:

> There is an employment exchange but it doesn't seem to have any clout as far as jobs are concerned. I went to see its director, a Monsieur Ba. Yes, he said, it is the law that potential employers should let us know the jobs they can offer and it is the law that the unemployed should register with us though there is no dole money. We have 40,000 job seekers listed. But things are tough. We could only find work for 1,000 during the last three months.

This is how we recorded the episode in the film.

> Waly Niane has gone to the Employment Exchange though he has no confidence in it finding work for him. He sits patiently for an hour and eventually gets to see a lethargic clerk who sits behind a huge desk while Waly stands at attention before him.

**CLERK:** This is the paper you were given before, is it?

**WALY:** Yes.

**CLERK:** [disgustedly] Ugh! A bit old and torn your paper, isn't it? When did you come and see us last?

**WALY:** Three months ago.

**CLERK:** It looks like it [gazes at the paper for a long time]. Well, there may be something for you eventually. Work is a little thin on the ground at the moment. If everybody without work was to use our services there would be half a million people at the door, you understand? So if you want work we must ask you to come and see us every day... you have a right to...or, failing that, at least once or twice a week. [Hands him back the frayed scrap of paper Waly had given him] Your paper — alright? Now look after that paper of yours, won't you. [Shouts] Next!

It's a long time since the dance troupe met and Samba is some 25 years older now. Sitting in his house in Guedeiwaye, I asked him about his career and what he had been doing.

'When I went for my first interview in 1968 they gave me a test and the personnel manager said I had done so well they couldn't give me a labourer's job, they would see if there was anything doing in the office. There I saw the chief accountant who advised me even if I was only offered a labourer's job to accept it because I was sure to get promotion. That is how it began in June that year. After I had worked for a year I was invited to compete for a post in machine maintenance. I was successful and was trained to become machine inspector. My job was to spend my shift going round the machine room checking that all the generators were running smoothly.

'After four years the management chose the four best inspectors to go on a six months course to learn how to be a control room supervisor. So that's where I now work. We control everything to do with the working machinery in the generating station. Well, I've now been there 23 years. I got my 15-year medal, and my 20-years service medal.'

'It's a long way from the hard times in Anglemousse. I gather it all ended suddenly with a fire. Were you involved?' I asked.

'Ah yes the fire! It was in 1972. I had been working. I came home at eight o'clock in the evening. I told my wife — she was very pregnant — that I was going out to see a friend who lived close by. While we were chatting there we heard cries and shouts of 'Fire! Fire!' I dashed home to find that all the Sereres in our association had rallied round to save our possessions. We got everything out but all the shacks were destroyed. The whole district was gutted. As you will remember we were like sardines. The alleyways were very narrow. The fire jumped across easily. The fire brigade couldn't get in.

'That night someone lent us a couple of rooms near by so that we could work out what to do the next day. The next day the housing chief from the council came and told us not to try and rebuild. "We are going to shift you all to Guediawaye," he said. They gave us nothing but a plot of waste ground. We knocked up some rooms for my parents. My wife and I stayed close to Anglemousse for a couple of years in rented rooms but it was too small for a growing family and eventually my father insisted that it would be much more convenient and a whole lot cheaper if we joined them. There was plenty of space so we built three new rooms and moved in 1974. We have been here since. When we have been able, we have rebuilt in brick and stone.

'At first there were only my father and mother, my wife and I plus the two children, Fatou and Ousmane, whom we brought from Anglemousse and a third born in Guediawaye in 1974. Now we have eight children. We lost one. He was sick. He had whooping cough. He had been vaccinated but I don't think we were told the whole story. I think he died for some other reason. Anyway, that's the end of our family. We have agreed not to have any more. I am very sentimental and I don't want my own flesh and blood to suffer.

'We are ambitious for the remaining seven and will support their efforts as long as we can afford the costs in each new school year. The older kids are very ambitious. I am very happy about that. They are working hard to succeed. I shall do all I can to encourage them. All my children attend state schools. There have never been any fees to pay, but books and materials have to be paid for. A good exercise book now costs 700 francs (over £2) and I had to buy four of them the other day. Older children need good clothes and shoes. That's where the costs of education mount up.'

Samba thought for a moment. 'We have been fortunate,' he

Christian Aid/Derrick Knight

**Samba Ndiaye in 1992, aged 47**

added, 'but it doesn't mean there have been no hard times. It is impossible to please the family completely. You see there is not only my own family here. There are other families. There are the sons of my grandfather. There is the daughter of my grandmother. I cannot provide for all their needs, I can only do my best as an African and a good Muslim.

'At the end of each month I have to buy almost 150 kilos of rice, at 150 francs a kilo, 25 litres of cooking oil and 25 kilos of sugar at 325 a kilo. This costs me some 60,000

francs (£138). I buy two large tins of Nescafe and a supply of teabags. For breakfast I buy four kilos of bread a day.

'We eat a lot of fish. There are all kinds of fish available. I like to buy big fish. I go to the shore and I buy directly from the fishermen as they land their catch. I spend 8-10,000 francs and when I get the fish home I cut them up and we freeze them. I do the same with the meat.

'Nevertheless we cannot afford to eat rice every day. I only eat meat on Saturdays and make up with lots of potatoes. We need four kilos of meat every Saturday and a big bag of potatoes. That's because of the number we are expected to feed.

'My wife makes cakes and ice creams and sells them in the neighbourhood. With her freezer she can make things which bring

in 20 - 30,000 francs a month. What she makes goes into the family
kitty. All this is necessary to give the family a minimum of luxury.
When it comes to clothes, I pay out every three months. I give my
wife 15 - 20,000 francs for the children's clothes.

'Another thing. I don't have any outside help. No relatives I can
go to for a handout in an emergency. I have only one retired
grandfather who has younger brothers. He was a police driver and
he owned an HLM [government pre-fab] house. He sold that and
bought a cheaper place in the country where he stays most of the
time. But he comes calling now and then with financial problems
and I am obliged to shell out for a 50 kilo bag of rice or something
similar.'

'Samba, when we came to film you in the compound in
Anglemousse in 1969 it was towards the end of Ramadan and your
father was worried about the cost of a sheep for the Fête of the
Tabeski. He bought one for 6,000 francs. What did you do this
year for Tabeski?'

'I bought a sheep for 70,000 francs (£152). It wasn't even the
best quality animal. The best sheep were selling at between
115,000 and 200,000. I was ready to pay for the more expensive
animal but I decided to spend a lot less and help a relative who
could not afford his sheep to get one. If you have the means you
have to do it. It is not a Senegalese custom, it goes back to
Abraham who had promised God to sacrifice a sheep if God gave
him a son. When God had given him a son and he had to fulfil his
promise, he couldn't afford a sheep. Instead he prepared his own
son for the sacrifice but God sent him the Archangel Gabriel with a
ram. That is the obligation.

'It's part of the faith. There is not a great deal of difference
between the vision of Mohammed and Jesus Christ. At the
Tabeski, if you have the means, you have to sacrifice a sheep. But
if you genuinely cannot afford the cost, then you are freed from
the obligation. I remember one year during the great drought
when people were so poor that the Chief Imam decreed that the
Tabeski should not be celebrated that year. It was to help people
get back on their feet at a particularly hard time.'

'I see that the district here has filled up a lot since I was here 10
years ago. Is there overcrowding on the level of your old days in
Anglemousse?'

'It has filled out but there is space here and the roads are much wider. I like it here. I am surrounded by family and we all live as a traditional Senegalese community. It wouldn't suit you Westerners. In the SICAP estates, which as you must know are separate two-storey European style houses, everybody lives apart and keeps to themselves. There is no neighbourly contact. But in African towns there has to be a real sense of community.

'Having said that, I am not at all pleased with the way things are going. I see my neighbours struggling and at their wits' end. When we buy our food supplies we are forced to bring them into the house at night. We cannot eat during the day because there are people living next door who are without means and if they smell cooking... well, it just becomes impossible. If I had my way, everybody should have a reasonable job and fair salary.'

Whatever Samba said about the neighbourhood, when I left him the streets of Guediawaye were bursting with people as if it was a national holiday, but a holiday which nobody wanted. Not only the paths but the streets and side-alleys were blocked with pedestrians, teenagers mainly, out of school or out of work, restless, watchful, gesticulating, chatting, dancing, playing, squatting, leaning, dozing, arguing, shouting, accosting strangers, telling tales, greeting neighbours — sharing a joke, a cigarette, a drink can, a torn page of newsprint. Market stalls everywhere. Temporary displays in front of wooden stalls, street vendors competing with shops. Crowds and more crowds. Ancient nags, ancient carts, sheep panicking, skeletal dogs scavenging, rusty Renault buses, held together by layer upon layer of thick blue paint covered in Islamic symbols and prayers.

Guediawaye was one of the satellite townships established on distant sand dunes to relieve the pressure on the city of the crowds of rural migrants attracted to Dakar to build, they believed, a modern and model African society. Since then the flow of migrants and their families from the rural hinterland has been relentless and overwhelming; the story of the Sorcerer's Apprentice without any magic recipe to halt the tide.

Like the 'Bright Stars' to which Samba belonged and who acknowledge a debt of gratitude to the Centre de Bopp, the Centre itself has grown and evolved through the last 25 years, its fortunes rising and falling depending on who was in charge, how the programmes were funded and the covetousness of a government minister or two who wished to limit its independence or claim its successes as their own. It was always ambitious but tightly constrained by the modest funds it could attract and its lack of space at Bopp. In 1990, its name was changed to the Centre Ahmadou Malick Gaye (CAMG) in memory of its former president and benefactor. It now links up with training programmes in other townships and in the provinces.

The local management increased the number of vocational courses available to young people. The trainers took on more counselling of the young who were mentally and spiritually disoriented. The dream of every country boy was a well-paid office job, but such jobs were out of reach of the uneducated. So, too, were most trades if the applicant did not have at least an elementary school leaving certificate.

In response, part of Bopp became a miniature technical college called CEVA — the Centre for Vocational Education. It offered crash courses on such useful trades as plumbing, domestic electricity, technical drawing, bricklaying and pottery. For the women there was sewing, crochet, hairdressing, soft toy-making. These offered immediate home-based opportunities of earning. For girls with secondary schooling and without family ties or religious taboos, Bopp offered basic commercial office skills.

But CEVA's resources were always modest even when it evolved from a 'mission' into a locally directed and managed charity without religious ties. In the Eighties the state 'disengaged' (stopped funding) education and abandoned industrial subsidies as part of the IMF/World Bank Structural Adjustment Programme. Private and charitably funded industry training schemes were dealt a mortal blow. Instead of the state and private industry each sharing the burden for the training of the young to meet an increased demand for skilled employees, the effect was a dramatic shrinkage of any training in vocational courses.

So CEVA is seen as a lifeline in a perilous situation and demand has far outreached possibilities. This is well illustrated by an informal weekend conversation I had with a group of ceramic workers and teachers in their studio at CEVA. It harshly exposes the obstacles, ambiguities and contradictions facing them, even when highly skilled, in their wish to build a small ceramics business for which they can prove a real demand.

I spoke first to Ismaila Sy who was chosen by his colleagues to talk about their problems.

'When I left school I didn't have ceramics in mind but a teacher at the school ran a pottery course here and he brought some of us to see whether we might be interested. Since then we have become more and more involved. We learnt the trade, we then became trainers of new recruits and we also started a small production line.

'Today is Sunday but here we are. We need the work but we also love it. At the moment we have an order to satisfy. During the week the teaching timetable makes it difficult to produce much. So we need to catch up. We have to come in on Sunday when there are no interruptions.

'CEVA as a whole recruits some 50 to 60 young people into its courses. They do a general introduction course for three months and then join specific trade workshops. We get our quota of five or six which is as many as we can take, given the lack of equipment and the confined space we have. It is sad because as long as we are doing training it would be good to take as many trainees as possible.'

I asked if they considered themselves fortunate to be able to earn something as trainers and be able to sell their products as well even if only on a small-scale.

'Fortunate? Well I'm not so sure,' answered Ismaila. 'Perhaps in comparison with other trades but not in terms of what could be done if we had the means. The market is wide open but we are stuck in a small artisanal frame. We cannot meet the thirst for pottery work because of this. There is a whole field of architectural pottery as well as the retail trade in decorative work. If we were able to equip a real workshop to take advantage of the market which we know exists, then perhaps we might be counted as fortunate. The trade is there for the taking and nobody is exploiting it. All those things which we import and could stop importing if we had the means. There is the makings of a real Senegalese ceramics industry here which would provide jobs for many workers.'

I wanted to challenge what sounded like an easy answer, so I brought up the matter of factories closing and the freeing up of the import trade. Wouldn't that mean fiercer competition for any local industries?

They all shook their heads and Ismaila replied.

'The problem of developing countries is that they always have to negotiate a transfer of technology and since they have little to offer in return it is a bad handicap. If each country took in only that technology which really suited its level of development and its needs — its real needs, then I believe that extraordinary benefits might come out of it.

'Just take the example of pottery. The raw material, clay, is here on the spot. The human potential — trained potters — exists. We might only have to import certain special enamels and the electric ovens which have a working life of some 10 to 15 years. So the import costs would be small and the country would also save on the import of basins, lavatories, floor and wall tiles and other household items which we can make here.'

I asked what was stopping them from starting up somewhere else rather than sticking to the small CEVA workshop with its obsolete equipment. Firstly, they had no capital and it would have to be found. The enterprise would have to be properly equipped. It would need an extended credit which they were unable to get without collateral or a sympathetic donor.

'We are unable to make any substantial savings. All the training personnel are virtually voluntary. They only get travelling expenses. The work is regarded as charitable. What we earn is from the sale of pottery. We are entitled to 50% of all monthly sales. It is not much. It depends on the season. Some months it's quite good. Other times it doesn't work out. It enables us to survive, just about.'

Mamadou Camera was another of the veterans of the pottery workshop, now in his mid-thirties. I asked him about his situation at home. Was he a family man?

'Not yet,' answered Mamadou. 'Not married either, but it doesn't mean that I have no dependants to worry about because I have my mother and father and all the other relatives that are at home.'

It is always difficult to get the Senegalese, indeed most West Africans, to talk in concrete terms about their family matters. It is not in the culture. The relationships of the extended family are so complex that however willing, an individual will need many hours, even days, to explain them. It is much more difficult if one is a stranger and a white, even coming as a friend.

Ibrahima, another of the group, took up the subject.

'I have to provide for my parents at home. They depend on me

**Mamadou Camera, ceramics teacher at CEVA and master potter**

completely. I am obliged to work. If I die here I don't know what will happen. I feel ill but I have to go on working. I am exhausted. I have to rest. I often get dizzy spells.'

Mamadou spoke up for him. 'He hasn't got the wherewithal to go to hospital. To go to hospital one must have money. At the hospital, if you haven't money you can die — oh yes! — in the present system. Life is too costly here.'

Mamadou again: 'I have two children to feed. I have my wife to feed. My wife also has her family who often have money problems and come to me for help. How can I help them? We spend the day here with only a roll of bread and a few peanuts to sustain us. It's grim.

'We are almost a family here. We have been together for nearly 20 years. We have the same ideas, the same worries about the future. We desperately want to break out of a working life of bare survival. We know it is possible but there are obstacles. There is a saying that one should teach a person how to fish rather than always give him fish to eat. It is our case. All we need is the necessary means to enable us to work independently.'

Where did they think the money was going to come from? I asked. 'Who is going to provide you with the means if not yourselves?'

'We have the good fortune that there are NGOs in Senegal run by Senegalese and working in Senegal,' he answered. 'I am convinced that those people are best able to help us. They have been doing it for 20 years or so but we have our own ideas too which are, what? — in short, to liberate ourselves. The NGOs are best placed to approach a foreign donor on our behalf. If they could get us a grant then we could set up elsewhere and leave the space to new people who, when qualified, may join us or go their own way. To them it is only a little and it would free us. That is our one concern. The need always to ask foreigners, to depend on foreigners, that is what we wish to avoid. It is vital that people should be enabled to run their own affairs.

'There's plenty of enterprise here. Take the way we sell our production. There are young students, young unemployed men who come here every day with a small sum of money of say 5,000 (£10) or 10,000 francs with which to buy pieces. They then resell them wherever they can, in the town centre, in the suburbs. It is their only way of making money. They have no other source. Going to school serves no purpose. They have nothing. They are doing nothing. In a sense we are providing about 20 youngsters with a lifeline. That's good.

'We've seen a kid come in first time with only 5,000 francs who now arrives with 100,000 to take his pick of pots. 100,000 is a big sum of money these days. And we know that if we had the materials and the equipment we could find work not just for 20 kids but 100 or 150. There are so many who would like to trade but we do not have the goods.

'Most of these kids come from families of 15 or 20 in which only one is earning a salary and has to support the rest. 50,000 francs (£115) goes nowhere. They are the only member bringing in any money when the father has been laid off or is retired. In Senegal we live in tight families. It is very important to us. One is obliged, forced to play a part in the continued well-being of that family. It is very hard to save in our society. There are always problems needing money to solve them. One earns a little but one doesn't eat. One lives from day to day. I am talking of the bulk of the population. If you go into the townships you will find people who are really suffering. They have nothing. They cannot even buy food to eat. They have too many problems. Yes, things have broken down in town. That is why we are anxious to hang on to the little we have, even the little workshop. We want to do all we can to keep it going. It's all we have.'

Mamadou Camera added: 'What is so frustrating is that the potential is enormous. At present we just have to turn down any big orders. We have made out our case to CEVA. At least provide us with a new oven, a mechanical clay puddler, some more potter's wheels, a greater range of enamels. With these we shall make more money for all of us. We are waiting.'

'At least we can live on hope,' said Ismaila. 'We never get the chance to talk to an outsider from the funding agencies which support the centre. If we see them at all it's on a working day and they are shown the techniques and what we make. There's never a chance to discuss our problems. Perhaps you can make a stronger case on our behalf than we seem to have made. Please try and make others understand how we feel.'

PART TWO

# JOURNEY TOWARDS DEVELOPMENT

# CHAPTER THREE

# ALONG THE FLOOD PLAIN

*I have not yet cut the umbilical cord which ties me to Mother Nature.... I never take nourishment from her breast without first asking forgiveness, trembling. I never cut down a tree, needing its trunk, without asking a brotherly forgiveness. I am only the extremity of the being whence all thought springs.*

**from *The Ambiguous Adventure*, by Cheikh Hamidou Kane**

The River Senegal is West Africa's equivalent to the Nile. It flows in a huge upwards loop some 1,700 kilometres long, from the mountains of the Fouta Djallon in what is now Guinea, to drain gently into a massive many-channelled delta before reaching the Atlantic at St Louis. Though it lacks the monuments of old civilisations which make the valley of the Nile one of the wonders of the world, the Senegal valley is rich in history and in heroes. In the past it was a crossroads of many cultures. It does not take much imagination to visualise the massive trans-Saharan caravans bearing salt, crossing the river bed in the dry season on their way south to exchange it for Ashanti gold, or to conjure up the vast markets in which the goods of the Middle East, North Africa, the Atlantic coast and the Bight of Benin were traded by people of a hundred tribes and languages.

This was where Islam met and converted great swathes of West Africa. This was a rich area of agricultural production included as an outer province in a succession of West African empires at the

time of the Middle Ages in Europe — Ghana, Mali, Songhai. Its
people provided warriors for those empires and set up warrior
kingdoms along the valley of the Senegal in their own right until
the French forced them into its colonial territories.

The Toucouleurs, the Soninke and the Peulhs who settled in
the river valley have played a prominent part in the shaping of
society in West Africa and dream of reclaiming that influence in
modern Senegal. The language of the Peulhs, Pulaar, is one of the
most important national languages spoken in Senegal and is
understood by communities of common ancestry as far away as
Nigeria. The people who speak it are known as Halpulaaren. It is a
matter of great pride.

The Senegal River valley communities are once again in a
melting pot from which they will either emerge as the engineers of
their own destiny, or as another group of victims of the

**The Senegal River valley**

David MacDonald

**River Senegal near Matam, before the droughts killed the fish**

miscalculations and lack of judgment of distant economists and politicians who see 'development' as a formula.

One of the main reasons for the uncontrollable growth of Dakar and its ring of breeze block and timber suburbs in recent years has been the failure of the government and its international bankers and advisers to create a prosperous agricultural community. The impoverished villages have sent their sons and daughters into exile in the hope that they will be able to earn a living elsewhere.

Traditional West African societies in the past hardly concerned themselves with money. They used complex barter arrangements between families, neighbouring villages and castes of skilled artisans. Then at the beginning of the 20th century the French colonial power needed cheap labour for its major engineering works and plantations, so they levied taxes in cash from the people in all the territories that they had conquered. Villagers were forced to find the money somehow. So began a seasonal migration of the young and able-bodied peasant farmers, coming

particularly from the villages in the remotest and poorest parts of
the country, to hire themselves to colonial farms and to colonial
businesses. Even at the miserable rates they were offered, they
were able to pay the family taxes and to buy a few presents and
consumables for their loved ones back home, found in the new
shops and market stalls offering European mass production goods
which were flooding into Africa to the ruination of local trades.

When independence was won, the new national leaders should
have recognised and given priority attention to the outstanding
contribution which the peasant farming community was capable
of making to the fledgling state. There should have been a master
plan for its development and resources to implement it. But the
Senegalese politicians who led the first independent government
were gifted intellectuals who had been brought up in the cities on
a strong diet of French culture and social values. Their political
strength lay in the cities. They spoke highly of the gallant efforts of
peasants and pledged substantial backing but did little for them.
They commonly used then, and still do use, the scathing French
word 'brousse' — the bush — to denote everything provincial
outside the cities. It is a word which has strong overtones of the
primitive, the wilderness, the unknown. For a school-educated
civil servant, to be sent 'en mission' and 'en brousse' is seen, not
just an adventure but a sacrifice, even a punishment.

There was no lack of advice and warnings from both European
and Senegalese experts during those first years of independence.
It seemed obvious. If the agricultural community could be moved
out of its traditionally cautious subsistence agriculture into the
modern market economy, and if it started to provide surpluses for
the cities and towns as well as feeding itself, the country would
have a solid foundation for growth and prosperity. The farmers
too would prosper. More important, a prosperous farming
community would provide a market for the fledgling industrial
sector and give it a chance to grow and find ways to break into
world markets.

Instead the farmers were fed fine sentiments in five-year
development plans; incentives to go on growing raw materials,
like cotton and groundnuts, which the former colonists had
exploited. They ignored warnings about a saturated world market
and plummeting prices.  They embarked on a series of training
and credit schemes for peasant farmers, never properly funded,

frequently aborted, destroying government credibility.  There was little encouragement to diversify and food began to be imported in ever greater amounts to satisfy the more sophisticated tastes of the citizens of the towns and cities. It was easier and cheaper for the government to import 300,000 tonnes of cheap broken rice from South-East Asia than to devise and carry through a thorough-going agricultural reform. The country was drawn into heavier and heavier debt because of the neglect of the one part of the economy which might have been expected to provide an income.

Statistics are not a very reliable guide to the situation in countries such as Senegal where neither the budget nor the machinery to collect regular records exists, but they do show existing trends. Although almost 90% of the population still lives in the countryside, World Bank figures for the last 20 years show a steady decrease in per capita food production. Population regularly outstrips output. The share of agriculture as a percentage of the GDP has fallen from 30.2% in 1977 to 22% in 1989. Senegalese agriculture now provides less than 50% of the country's needs even in a year of good rainfall. Some provinces are the victims of food shortages which have to be covered by imports or even by food aid. Food imports rose some 40% between 1980 and 1990, even though structural adjustment programmes were being implemented.

Of course it is not only the failure of leadership which has produced such poor results. Senegal, together with many other African countries, has suffered a long period of drought years, some of which have been years of environmental devastation and famine.

Senegalese farmers along both sides of the *fleuve*, as everyone calls the Senegal River valley, have always been harnessed to the annual cycle of rainfall. The agricultural calendar has been planned for centuries to get the best out of a modest but regular rainfall, and to exploit the wet, freshly silted land left as the waters of the annual flood recede. The river may skirt the desert edge for most of its journey but it rises in the spongy tropical mountain forests far to the south where the rainfall is normally abundant and prolonged.  But when the system failed, as it did dramatically at the start of the Seventies, it was a disaster.

The drought years of the Seventies caused widespread damage to farmland and animals, destitution of communities in the most vulnerable regions, desertification and other damage to the environment. They undermined food production and speeded up migration. In Senegal, the worst hit region was in the north, along the *fleuve*.

In those years, many European aid agencies became involved in emergency programmes for the victims of the drought. Once the immediate crisis was over, several remained in contact to provide support for local development efforts — a continuing but more modest aid programme designed to underpin the rural population of the region and to help it rebuild the community and prepare for the inevitable changes. Such an aid programme was the Integrated Programme of Podor (PIP), supported by a consortium of European church-related aid agencies including Christian Aid. The PIP and its staff of trainers and teachers is presently accompanying scores of village groups, especially women, in their efforts to gain control of their own lives. For many, these links with independent aid bodies provided the first real step on their journey towards development.

A further hammer blow was delivered to farming communities in the Eighties by the series of structural adjustment programmes imposed by the World Bank and IMF, some of whose conditions involved the running down of all state enterprises including those which provided subsidised fertilisers and other agricultural inputs, the withdrawal of training and counselling cadres, the imposition of a free market philosophy and the privatisation of health and educational services.

Contrariwise, as Tweedledee said, and against all logic, the main engineering work of a huge internationally funded project for the damming and controlled irrigation of the River Senegal basin, shared between the three countries of Senegal, Mauritania and Mali, was completed in 1992 after 25 years of work.

The lives of one million farmers and their families in Senegal are bound up in the scheme and will have to conform to a rigidly financed, dramatically different package of farming techniques generically known as the *Après-Barrage* plan. The people most affected have not been consulted in any meaningful way and they are ill-prepared for the change. They are increasingly aware that they may be not the beneficiaries but the involuntary victims of a gigantic economic disaster. The dawning of such an awareness is doing wonders for the growth and consolidation of grass roots organisations.

Midway into the Nineties, agriculture is once again at the top of the national agenda. Having squandered every other opportunity, the government may wake up to the fact that there is no other part of the economy with a potential for growth which might save the downwards spiralling economy.

But is there time to bring about a meaningful change?

In these chapters local people express themselves as they wrestle, on the one hand with saving what is good from the legacy of a traditional society, while on the other with the pressing need to come to terms with the modern world beating at their doors. Their thoughts about past and present have been pulled together to make a sort of litany on the theme of communities facing change.

Scratch any proud Toucouleur and out bursts a flood of stories and legends of the old days. There may be little surviving written history, but oral memory is a special and cherished gift of these people. 'When an old man dies, a whole library burns down,' Hampate Ba, the great Peulh scholar of Bandiagara was fond of saying.

**Aboubakary Deme,** *a former agricultural trainer*

'Across the river is the ancestral village which was once one of the cities or "Foutankesse" of the kingdom of Tekrour. There were many capitals of kingdoms. There was Guede, Godo, Timbo, Tuabou. All strategically sited. Famous places. Defendable against attack by traditional arms. Guede is a rich village with good community and collective lands. Now, with the new laws about the ownership of land, the introduction of mechanical irrigation and the cuts in government services to farmers, the old village is about to be abandoned because the villagers no longer believe they can survive there. They want to be near the road.'

**Thierno Ba,** *a farmer's son become director of a non-governmental rural development team*

'The problem of the Senegal River valley is very specific. I was born in the valley. What one finds in the valley can be found nowhere else in Senegal. When one says that the valley was the granary for the whole of Senegal it is because of the geographical feature which meant that in the past the rain fell in the Fouta Djallon, far to the south in what is now Guinea, and the bed of the river filled. There was a whole stretch of the river where it flooded

Christian Aid/Derrick Knight

**Guede — ancestral village threatened by modern irrigation plans**

some 25 kilometres on either side and then the level fell gradually, leaving a damp soil perfect for the cultivation of many crops. So the inhabitants of the valley who mastered annual floods were also unlike other people.'

**Hacchim Ndiaye,** *a former village health worker, now trainer in village water management*

'The region between Matam and Podor is a region populated mainly by the Toucouleurs, a very conservative farming community. From time immemorial until 1970 their way of looking at things was very simple. They depended entirely on the river. Their whole lives were controlled by the river, by the rainy season which brought the overflow which fertilised and irrigated the land for their basic crops.'

Cire Boccum

**Cire Boccum,** *farmer*

'The Toucouleur is very attached to the traditional crops. They provide security. The Toucouleur saying is that the sheep destined for sacrifice at the Tabeski fulfils two conditions which comple- ment each other. First you have the manure and maybe the milk while it's fattening. Then you have the meat for the feast of Tabeski. The natural flooding of the river provided sufficient humidity for the cereal crop and the falling level of the river provided the chance of growing further crops of tomatoes, potatoes, chick peas, onions and peppers.'

**Thierno Ba**

'One of the deeply ingrained customs carried from one generation to another is the contract with the land. When we were children and played out of doors, we were told to take a mouthful of earth and eat it. With that you have entered a contract with the earth and whatever height of scholarship you attain, wherever you go you will think of this soil and you will want to return.'

## Hacchim Ndiaye

'The local society could evolve gently at its own pace. It could ignore change. With such a lifestyle it didn't have much need of schools either. Education had been provided by the old men in the villages.

'And there was a family pedigree and a caste system within the clans. There were closed family circles of Toucouleurs within which authority was wielded by the head of the family, obedience to whom was unquestioned. There were the 'nobles', the 'slaves', the blacksmiths, the fishermen. Families were not allowed to marry out of their social band. There were the age groups, especially important for children and young people,  and there was the strong influence of Islam which was also conservative. All of this was very precise and very coherent.'

## Thierno Ba

'Knives, forks and spoons existed here before. They were made by the blacksmiths, the leather craftsmen. They worked with traditional means and materials. The cloth for dresses were made in traditional ways and it meant that people grew cotton and used it themselves. There was a sharing of skills and processes among these producers. Some grew cotton. Others harvested it. Others again carded the cotton and made it into thread and later into cloth. There was a whole chain of work and the kind of solidarity we talk about yearningly today was a reality then.

'I believe all these links which existed then meant that 'solidarity' was not just a glib expression but was the very stuff of daily life in the community. In real terms, everybody depended on another. The farmer farmed. It was his whole life. He used techniques he understood. He had resources. He had experience. He had the knowledge so he was the best person to do it. The herdsman prepared physically for his work from an early age. It was no accident that he drank milk and was thin so that he was able to trek with the animals. He had a mass of useful information on grasses, on trees, on land routes across the desert or the savannah which were safe to follow at certain times and certain seasons. He was best prepared for this kind of work. The fisherman on the river had his skills and experience. All this made for a genuine solidarity. The farmer needed milk for which he offered millet in the market. The herder needed millet. The fisherman needed milk or rice. In those days there were traditional bartering arrangements. Money did not come into it.'

**Aboubakary Deme,** *farmer and marabout*
'I have pupils, called *talibes*. I teach them the Koran. In the old days that was all they did. Now they go to the French school in the morning from eight to midday and at six in the evening they come and learn the Koran. On Saturday afternoon, too, they learn the Koran. Children today see things differently from the way we saw them when we were young. Now people are much more aware of what is real and what is not. They do not believe that God decides everything one does or doesn't do. Beliefs are evolving.

'In the old days if you told a child the devil did this or did that, it would believe you. Now most children don't believe in devils. In the past, it was taken for granted that the devil could make a person mad, change them into some other creature. The old generation still thinks so even if the young do not. One's imagination was full of such things. Even I believed them. I used to see all kinds of phantoms in the woods coming after me.'

**Thierno Ba**
'We identify strongly with our families, with our villages, with our districts. Before saying I am Senegalese, I say to anyone that I am a Ba, from the family of Bamababe, and that I come from Ouressugui in the *waalo*. I believe all the inhabitants of the valley are profoundly attached to their land and it means that the relationship between one who is born in the valley and his land is like that between the herdsman and his herd. The herdsman sees little difference between the value of one of his children and a calf. Both are part of the same system. It is the same for a man who lives by what grows on his land. That land passes down from generation to generation. It is where the ancestors are buried. There is a saying which is that the land doesn't belong to only one generation. It was passed on to the present generation and it has to be preserved and well prepared for the next.'

**Salimata Olel Ba,** *president of the village women's association of Nenette*
'In the old days when everything bloomed and grew in the

Salimata Olel Ba

abundant rain and there was lush grassland, the cattle were contented and the Peulhs found it so alluring that they wanted nothing better than the chance to be in it and delight in the beauty of nature and sing about it. It was the same down in the *waalo*. When the water rose after a good rain, trees flourished, grass grew and it was beautiful. We are old enough to remember the beauty of nature.'

## Thierno Ba

'The hold the elders have had over the community is vanishing as it becomes clearer to more and more people that they are no longer in touch with the times and that even their expertise on the environment is proving worthless as the climate, the rainfall, the flow of the river, fail to respond to known patterns of the past.

'The old men looked at the trees and saw that the birds were building their nests lower than usual and were able to interpret this as a sign of coming drought and that this year they should cultivate in the valley bottoms and low lying areas. Another year they saw the birds building much higher and this meant a good flood was likely and it would be possible to cultivate fields in drier places. We, the young men, didn't know this but they had the experience. We were told that these elders had spiritual guidance.

'Cattle was another indicator. The elders noted the dates when the cattle crossed the district with their herders en route to the grasslands. They listened to the mooing of the cows. They understood the meaning of the herders' law of the three sevens: the age of seven when a child should know a certain minimum about herding, 14 when he will already be expected to have an expert knowledge of the types of animal, ailments, diets, the best grazing places. Then the age of 21, when he should understand the language of the animals, their treatment, their care, everything.

'But if the cattle disappear from the district, if traditional agriculture disappears together with other signs and symbols, the experience of the old which gave them their power will disappear and the elders know it and are fearful. You see how village problems present themselves. They are very difficult ones.'

## Hacchim Ndiaye

'Then came the moment when that regular cycle of rains and floods was interrupted. The water failed to overflow across the village fields. The rains could no longer be relied on to water the *djeri*, the fields above water level. So as grain stocks vanished, the only marketable goods were the riverside condiments — tomatoes, peppers, squashes. OK, they still could be grown and river fish could be caught. Herds of cattle and goats could be pastured. They lived on that for a while. Money has never been important in this society.  In the years of drought from 1970, all this traditional system started cracking. It happened in all kinds of ways. People began to make decisions on their own. Individualism took over. The most respected and prosperous heads of families found themselves unable to meet the demands made on them by dependants and began to lose power and prestige. Now, unable to give their children the things they want, they cannot stop them following modern fashion or behaviour or prevent the girls from making themselves beautiful in their own way, even if it is contrary to religion and custom.

'In the past it was possible to have a large family and satisfy all their needs because there were family fields and other economic resources. Now they do not exist and the young are going their own way ignoring the old disciplines. It is a tragedy for family values and it is hastening the decline of the agricultural economy as the young migrate elsewhere to try and find the lifestyle they think they deserve and which their fathers cannot provide.

'All the young and able-bodied men who were meant to cultivate the *waalo* and the *djeri* fields suddenly had nothing to do. So there was a rural exodus towards the cities and to other countries.'

## Salimata Olel Ba

'When there is lots of rain and the wet season is fruitful, grass grows high and trees flourish. Then we have no problems. Even if there are strong winds, they don't do any damage and we don't

Christian Aid/Derrick Knight

**'There's no grass and the trees have gone. There is nothing but sand now.'**

feel them too much. However if it doesn't rain and the grass doesn't grow then the sandstorms come early and damage the crops.

'When there were big trees and huge forests we didn't have any trouble with high winds. Now that so many trees have died in the drought there is a lot more wind. In the past we knew exactly when to expect a period of sandstorms, now we cannot predict the arrival of winds with any certainty.

'Where we have a windbreak of trees, the winds are reduced. Where we have fruit trees around the house, we don't feel the wind. But in the desert of the *djeri* there is always a wind because there is no grass and the trees have gone. There is nothing but sand now.'

## Cire Boccum

'Land ownership is a hot potato. You see, the new law says that land titles should be given to the users, but in this part of Senegal not all the users are the real owners. Many of the owners are government officials or party members and of course they don't wish to lose their traditional rights which have allowed them to keep land in the family and get a share even when they are away. So you see it's an impasse while those gentlemen are still in power.'

## Thierno Ba

'The bond between the inhabitants of the valley and their land goes a long way back into the past. Newcomers cannot have the same feeling for it. An outsider or an agribusiness will only try and make it yield as much as possible and one risks another disaster on the lines of the groundnut basin. Someone who is a native of the valley has such a close relationship with the soil that he would try and talk to it, to care for it, to share his joy when he sees a tongue of water spreading over it and it flourishes, to feel the pain when it cracks open because there has been no flooding that year. He is free to decide whether to plant or not, to lop branches off one tree and not another because it is forbidden or because it is the tree under which he has rested for years and years. It is that sort of relationship.

'There are some local places, some local features which are intimately linked to the lives of the inhabitants of the valley who have their own special vision of the land which is difficult to explain to an outsider. An outsider looks at a field and sees a hectare of land to cultivate. The local farmer also sees it as the spot where one of his children was born, where he sat to ponder some crucial decision, where he first heard the news that his wife had given birth, all of which shows that the links between agricultural practice and land are different here and economics, culture, social relations and magic come into it.'

## Cire Boccum

'The farmers are completely disheartened by the present Land Law. The local people along the river have no intention of giving up their land on the instruction of anybody who is not one of them. There is already an outside property company going about boasting of having millions to invest in farmland. There are local men who have lands along the edge of the main road who won't give them up for any reason. If they can't work the land themselves, they'll get relations to do it because of the threat by the state that if the land is not in use then it can be sold to outsiders. But that would lead to conflict. No stranger will step on to that land alive.

'If businessmen think they can come here they will have a fight on their hands — it will be a real war.'

'The farmers are completely disheartened by the present Land Law.'

## Thierno Ba

'There is a word for land in Pulaar which is '*djori*'. *Djori* is the
monument to tradition, a historical monument, a monument
where people go with their insurmountable problems and take a
little soil with which to wash themselves to make themselves
stronger and get in touch with the secret associations, because in a
village there are always two sorts of association, those that are
visible, like women's groups, productive groups and so on, and
the secret associations which are those which preserve the
mysteries of the land. That is why some are prepared to die to
protect their land because it is so important to them.'

# CHAPTER FOUR

# RICE AND BE DAMMED

*We do not have an agricultural system in which it is normal for its farmers to have their feet in the water.*
**Thierno Ba, director of the PIP, Ndioum**

Some 900 years ago the Arab historian Abu 'Ubayd 'Abd Allah b. 'Abd al-'Aziz al Bakri described the special features of the agriculture based on the seasonal flooding of land in the Senegal River valley. The farmers, he wrote, sow their seed twice a year, first when the land is damp when the water begins to recede and later when the water has fully receded but the banks are still moist.

The inhabitants of the valley have successfully farmed the flood plains and neighbouring land for hundreds of years using a complex system of collective land management based on clan and castes within society. The traditional cereal crops are millet, grown on the rain-fed sandy fields away from the river (the *djeri*), and sorghum on the flood plain (the *waalo*) as the annual flood recedes. Maize and various vegetables and condiments are grown out of season as the banks of the river dry out. In good years they have managed to put aside surpluses of cereals which see them through years of drought and occasional plagues of grasshoppers, locusts or grain devouring birds. In the past the economy of the valley was almost self-sufficient. The river provided abundant fish which bred in the flooded inlets and creeks when the waters rose and thrived on the nutritious silt. Nomadic cattle herders pastured their animals in the harvested fields and watered them in the creeks or uncultivated stretches of the river banks, providing milk, meat and manure.

When the Sahel, including Senegal, was hit by a series of disastrous droughts climaxing in 1973, the loss and suffering was so great that the whole world became involved in a rescue campaign. The event forced the villagers along the river valley, hitherto dependent on a good seasonal rain for their main cereal crops, to worry about the future. Various organisations began to provide equipment to develop rice paddies as a possible safety net for villagers in drought years. Groups of farmers began to tinker with small enclosures flooded by diesel motor pumps from the main stream of the river. The aid agencies were keen to provide some of the capital costs but nobody at the time seems to have done the rigorous calculations necessary to see whether rice could be a viable crop in the long term or whether the community could obtain credit or had sufficient skills to manage the maintenance and replacement costs which such undertakings required. Many villagers with access to aid funds drifted into rice cultivation with less than total conviction.

Meanwhile the government of Senegal and its international advisers had decided to gamble the country's agricultural future on a scheme for a vast irrigation programme covering the whole valley. It was to be shared with the two neighbouring countries of Mali and Mauritania. The plan was to build a system of dams to harness the river waters to enable farmers to convert to modern techniques within large managed irrigated fields and to produce vast amounts of cheap hydro-electric power to stimulate industry, supply the needs of the farming community and the towns. The seasonal flooding would cease and outdated traditions would vanish. So, said the wise locals, would the woodlands and savannah which depend on the annual flood to replenish the groundwater which keeps the trees alive, and so would the game which sheltered in them. There would be no firewood, wild plant foods and remedies used in traditional medicine.

The costs were shared by a consortium of foreign government and institutional backers and the bills were postponed to a distant future. The costs for the major dams alone were in excess of three and a half billion French francs (about £350 million). But those were not the only costs. Every hectare of land prepared for irrigation would cost a further £5-6,000. The target of 60,000 hectares a year until the end of the century required a further budget of some £15 billion, a vast sum far beyond the resources of an already debt-ridden and crippled economy in which few wished to invest. The scheme envisaged most of those hectares as growing rice.

It is not a plan for which the blame can be laid on the IMF or the World Bank but they have become embroiled. Their advice was that the country should feed itself by increasing the growing of traditional cereals, millet and sorghum, on farmland which need only be irrigated when the rains failed. This was a good deal cheaper and easier for the farmers than growing rice. The Bank argued, however, that some rice should be grown and sold in Senegal and the country should stop importing it. In this crucial case its advice was ignored. In parallel however, as part of the structural adjustment programme, the Bank had insisted on the dismantling of the state agricultural advice and management services which had provided subsidised supplies of fertilisers, equipment and training to farmers and farming cooperatives throughout the valley. The farmers have been left without support at precisely the time they needed help and training.

Behind the scenes the master minds of the river basin scheme, the OMVS — Organisation for the Development of the Valley of the Senegal — and its financial backers were determined that the population of the valley should be weaned away from the idea of cultivation based on an annual flood and that the flow over the dam in the upper reaches at Manantali would be closed to build up a huge reservoir to generate electricity and to secure a constant depth of water in the river so that it became navigable all the year round.

In this arrangement the farming communities were the almost inevitable losers. The high tension electricity cables would eventually pass over their heads towards the coastal cities on both sides of the river. There would be no cheap electricity for the farming communities as a rural electricity grid would cost too much to justify for scattered villages with few potential customers. The freshwater fish which had been an essential part of the local diet seemed doomed by the new system. The pastoralists would not be welcome on the enclosed *périmêtres* for fear of damaging the dykes and channels. The farmers would have to pay for the water used in irrigation and had no guarantee of getting a good price for their rice.

The people of the valley at the present time are not accustomed to the disciplines of rice growing, nor are they sure that the change will be economically viable. Are they destined to become the victims of a grandiose and unrealistic *Après-Barrage* scheme which becomes a major planning and environmental disaster or will they be the first generation of modern farmers with all the economic benefits that are promised? Like all such questions in Senegal the answers are very ambiguous.

Some independent economists have compared the costs of rice growing in South East Asia with African experience and have concluded that Africa can never compete on an equal footing.

In a world economic climate favouring the freeing of all trade it is difficult to see how expensively and artificially produced domestic rice can possibly compete on equal terms with an Asian variety produced on natural wetlands.

Whatever the truth it is clear that those most involved have been least consulted. They are confused and unsure of their rights. Changes in the legal ownership of land have added to the difficulties of a deeply traditional society which feels itself threatened by predatory outsiders. It is not to say they do not have strong views about the changes being foisted on them. They say they find it difficult to make themselves heard by 'the authorities in air-conditioned splendour', who refuse to listen because they are convinced that they are right and because the farmers know nothing of value to tell them.

My visit was at a moment when the old state-managed systems were breaking down and the new market-led private companies were proving even less reliable and trustworthy. There was a lack of authoritative information. The interviews which follow reflect the pessimism which such a situation engenders.

'Ask yourself,' said one farmer weeding a healthy crop of maize on an irrigated plot, 'whose approach to development it is which decrees that the only reason for irrigated agriculture here in the valley is to grow rice? Why should we grow rice? The answer seems to be because it has become an eating habit. And it is an important factor in the stability of the urban population. There is a well-known saying in Senegal that the best way to trigger off a *coup d'état* in the country is to make rice disappear or to stop the cultivation of rice and to ban its importation.'

**Cire Boccum,** *a middle-aged farmer in the village of Mboumba*

'I was born here in 1926. I have never lived anywhere else. Apart from the time I was in the army I have always been a farmer. During the Second World War I was in the Senegalese Regiment and spent the time in St Louis as a quartermaster. Then I was drafted into the colonial administration. The time came when I was sent upstream to Podor by my French boss, Monsieur Vedenne, to find uses for a stock of ploughs, agricultural equipment and fertiliser which the French had imported to give a boost to rice production. They did not know how to go about it. There were problems galore.

'Later I was asked to take charge of the training of the peasant farmers in the area who had never grown rice. So I was ordered to teach them how, make sure they understood and watch them do it. It didn't take long for them to grasp the essentials. The farmers were paid wages to prepare the paddy fields. They were also able to harvest the rice and be paid for it. At the time such a thing was unheard of. The farmers were very enthusiastic about the experiment. Looking back, those were golden days.'

Christian Aid/Derrick Knight

**Aboubakary Deme**

**Aboubakáry Deme,** *a farmer and marabout from Mery; a man of 55, bearded, stocky, apparently contented. He makes his living by farming, by teaching the Koran and religious law, and by using his skills in the interpretation of dreams.*

'I was born in the district of Matam in a village called Foume Hara Demboube. I spent seven years in the Koranic school. We were all Muslims and farmers. When I was 11, I left the Koranic school and went to the French school. When I was 20, I left my native village to go looking for work. I was the eldest in a large family. I had big responsibilities from an early age. I met another member of the family who had the same name, Aboubakary Deme, who was working as an agricultural extension worker in rice cultivation at Louga. This was in 1962 and I joined him as a young trainer at Podor. I was given two villages to work with. They wanted to be able to plant rice. They knew nothing about it. They needed to know about seeds, fertilisers and so on. It was a simple small *périmêtre*. No motor-pump, simply a channel from the river into the paddy field which filled during the wet season when the river rose. When the seedlings began to grow the channel was sealed and the rice continued to grow for three months and then it was harvested. There was only one crop in a year during the wet season using the natural flooding of the river.

'Later I returned to Kanel and cared for a mixed herd of cattle and sheep for my mother. But in 1973 there was no rain and no flooding of the river, no grass. We lost many cows and sheep. Only the goats survived. In 1975 I decided to look for work in the Ivory Coast. On the way I again met my relative Aboubakary in St Louis and he again enrolled me as a village trainer.

'I taught rice cultivation in a number of villages on the road to Matam — Mery, Mboumba, Takayoune. This time we used motor pumps. I acquired a plot of my own at Mery and eventually settled there with my third wife. I have 10 children, the eldest is now 20. I went back to herding and have a paddy field of two ares of rice. If you maintain it properly it gives you 16 sacks of 100 kilos, at the worst 10. With that one eats and sells. If you have cash in hand you buy millet and fish to eat. You don't sell your rice at all. It isn't enough to make ends meet. I also have some goats for their milk and a small herd 100 kilometres away to the south where there is pasture and water. We used to keep our animals here. There was grass and everything they needed.

'In the past there were very few paddy fields. Now there are many. There are all kinds of new organisations coming into the region. Things are beginning to change.'

**Imam Mamadou Diah,** *a Peulh in his thirties, handsome, penetrating expression, short-haired with close-cropped beard.*

'I remember when I was 12 years old and still a *talibe* in the Koranic school being sent to buy rice at 35 francs a kilo. When I was 18 it had risen to 75 francs. It was all imported rice through the Compagnie Française de Commerce Morel et Prom, the

Compagnie Française de l'Afrique de l'Ouest (CFAO), and several others. Later the price rose to 100 francs and now it is 135 to 140 francs a kilo.

'The variety of rice which is preferred in the region is one which is grown here, the Chaya (or Jaya) because it is soft and mixes well with crushed millet to make *couscous* and different sorts of cakes. It takes six months to grow to maturity. Those who live in the cities prefer imported broken rice. But in this part of the country where we grow and eat millet, especially to make *couscous*, any cereal which can play a similar role is preferred.

'Many of the more settled Peulh herders have irrigated paddy fields. But they will tell you that they took to rice cultivation like a drowning man seizes a floating branch. We seem to be in a situation where it costs almost as much to grow and harvest as the sale returns. The costs eat up some two-thirds of the revenue you hope to receive. Then you have to count in seed and labour. You are lucky if anything is left for the family. If you make a mistake you may still have all the expenses and end up in serious debt without a proper harvest. If you are illiterate you may be unable to make the right calculations or to stop your supplier from swindling you. That is why our people are now beginning to realise the importance of reading, writing and numbers.'

**Thierno Ba**

'The matter of cereal production and rice has become very ambiguous. Take the present price of rice or of millet. Who fixes their prices? It's the government. But what criteria does it use? I often say to farmers who come to see me, you have a kilo of rice to sell, set your own price. I am certain they are not going to use the same criteria as the government.

'I was talking to a farmer the other day about the pros and cons of rice and millet. He said: "If I have a kilo of millet, I winnow it. I remove the bran and I give it to my goat who will give me milk in return. I leave her to grow. Next I put the millet into the mortar and crush it. It can be used in two ways. Crushed small, it can be cooked and eaten at midday. Crushed roughly it can be made into *couscous* and eaten at night or for breakfast before going to the fields. But with a kilo of rice there are not the same possibilities."

'So for that farmer a kilo of millet is more attractive than a kilo of rice. But what is going on? In the market a kilo of millet sells at

20 local francs (4 pence), perhaps up to 40, while rice sells at 130 local francs (26 pence) a kilo. Why cannot millet be sold at 130 francs or 150 francs given the value of the cereal. These are some of the things which ordinary people do not understand and which are the result of the so-called free market economy that has its own rules and other controls which are different from those by which the farmers would normally be guided.'

### Hacchim Ndiaye

'I cannot see at present how the Senegalese farmer can grow and sell rice to compete with the imported rice which sells in the shops for 150 francs (30 pence) per kilo. The farmer cannot wait. He has to maintain his agricultural calendar of planting and harvesting in order to meet everyday needs and demands. He is forced to sell whatever he has to offer, at whatever price he can get, so that he has some money to live on. Now we have a situation where there are merchants with well-stuffed wallets who force the price of rice down and can afford to store it and husk it at their leisure, waiting for the price to rise later in the year when there is a shortage. The farmer who sold his rice at 40 francs finds that he has to buy it later at 150 francs. That is the problem. One sells now to become indebted later.

'The Senegalese agricultural policy needs to be revised drastically. Surely the high price of fertiliser should be lowered? By itself that would make a big difference in the standard of living of agricultural communities. So many things depend on the stuff. If it came down significantly it is possible that farmers might even begin to be able to produce and sell rice at a small profit...or the rice market has to be rationalised. Instead of buying rice from abroad a priority should be given to the purchase of locally grown rice at a good price. That would also help. Something urgent must be done to help the peasant farmers. It is important.'

### Cire Boccum

'Now agriculturally speaking we are limping badly. The SAED, the government body from which the farmers got their farming supplies and whose task was to improve the livelihood of communities in the river valley, has suddenly pulled out. It was as if you told a child who hadn't yet learnt to walk, "Go ahead, try it," and the child falls flat on its face. That was our problem when the

SAED went. It took all its stocks of material. It cancelled all credit schemes. It no longer counselled the farmers. It told them to go out and buy whatever they needed. But the farmers don't have the resources to do that.

'I know many good farmers who until this year had always sold their rice directly to the government through the SAED. They paid back any advances for supplies which they owed to the SAED in kind at harvest time and were paid promptly for the rest. This year the farmers have not been paid. They are crippled.

'The peasant farmers have been left empty-handed by the government's action. They came through the drought years by selling off whatever possessions or livestock they had. If they had unexpected expenses in the rice-field or other debts, they sold animals. Now they have no livestock. They have been abandoned without means. They are on their backs! Before? No problems. One sowed at the right time. One held the government in high regard. One harvested correctly. One paid one's debts fully. One took what was necessary to start a new growing cycle and went ahead with confidence.

'The cancellation of state support and the way it has been done has taken everybody by surprise. I'll give you an example. We have a big 276 hectare village *périmêtre* here at Mboumba and there are four organised groups of farmers using it. A group of 120, another of 65, a third group of 60, and a group of 45. Men and women. This year only one of the four has been able to get going. They are going to harvest their maize in a week or 10 days time. The other three have money problems and cannot get going. They haven't even cleared the ground.'

### Hacchim Ndiaye

'We are seeing a strong advance of malaria. There is the effect of the dams on the river which allows water to stagnate and to breed water-borne diseases such as bilharzia which has already spread into existing paddy fields and is bound to spread further as irrigated agriculture takes over from traditional forms of cultivation. Paddy fields will also become breeding grounds for mosquitoes. So what is being done to fight malaria? Well, there is the mosquito net dipped in insecticide. It is proving very effective in killing any mosquito which lands on it but it is by no means the answer. Many people don't use it or cannot afford it. On the other hand the mosquitoes have become resistant to well-established drugs so that even where families could afford to try and protect themselves it no longer works. So malaria is claiming more victims.'

## Thierno Ba

'At Guede Chantier there is a large irrigated *périmêtre* which is being completed to grow rice. The irrigation channel crosses the village and that is where people wash themselves, clean their cooking pots and children swim. That channel has the highest incidence of bilharzia in the whole district of Podor. And that is only the beginning.... People are not used to taking precautions. One of the first steps should be a campaign to make villagers aware of the dangers and precautions to take. We do not have an agricultural system in which it is normal for its farmers to have their feet in the water. Now with the advent of irrigated plots that is what is happening. It is clear that there will be a terrible human toll. Yet this is not taken into account. It is not being discussed. And when one brings up the subject one is told that one is being alarmist.'

**Bokary Lou Ba,** *a farmer in his mid-forties, member of a village cooperative. He was a tall sinewy man, confident and direct. He came straight out of the field with mud drying on his legs and sweat soaking his singlet. We stood on the edge of a vast area of what looked like a man-made desert but was the preparation of a new irrigation system. As we talked, a bulldozer was ripping out the roots of old trees.*

'I live in Guede village and this morning I went to my paddy field to put fertiliser on it. The seedlings were bedded out a fortnight ago. It is now September and we expect to harvest in January.

'My paddy field is in a *périmêtre* that we have made ourselves. All we have to do is syphon water into it with a length of pipe. It's a well thought out scheme which needs precisely timed care. My plot is 80 ares. I put aside 40 for rice and 40 for tomatoes.'

I asked what his harvest was like last year.

'I had 22 sacks of 100 kilos, which makes 2 tonnes 200 kilos for the 40 ares. That is not a good yield. The reason was that there wasn't enough fertiliser on it. We did not have the right information. We didn't have enough money. It's hard to get any credit at the

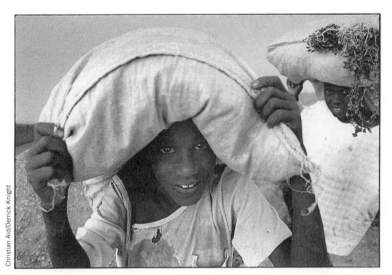

Christian Aid/Derrick Knight

**Carrying rice to the factory**

bank. In fact there are too many difficulties facing the farmer.

'Everything is now on the farmer's back. If you grow rice and you deliver it to the factory, they don't pay you properly. You get no cash. Not until the next season. If you have no other means you can't buy the materials for a new planting. The delay in payment makes it impossible for us to finance ourselves.

'The price of fertiliser is now 100 local francs a kilo. It used to be around 30-40. In the past we made a part payment when we bought the stuff. Now the system is privatised we have to pay it all at once. Fertiliser is very important in getting a good rice harvest. It has to be used at the right time.

'The big problem for us cultivators at the present time is how to plan our agricultural calendar correctly. And how to sell one's production and recoup its value at once so as to be able to start a new cycle. Can we really hope that things will be sorted out?

'If we had been paid for our production, we were going to grow maize. Now we have little hope of getting anything from our *waalo* fields. There has been no flood on the *waalo* this year and now it's too late. Few of the normally flooded inlets and ponds have had any water. What has caused this is beyond our understanding but we believe it has to be the new dam. Since the dam closed the fish have gone. Since the dam closed there has been less sorghum and there is less grass. It's one hell of a mess.'

**Mr Babali Sall**, *farmer. A tall lean man in his fifties, deeply wrinkled by wind and sun, wearing a shabby indigo under-boubou and a peasant's woolly hat.*

'It's a sad state of affairs we are in. The traditional farmer is very dissatisfied. Rice is all very well but there is only one dish that can be made with it. But our millet and sorghum can be used in many ways to give us a varied diet. Even if we have to grow rice, we might be able to get by if it was possible to sell the rice crop at a fair price as the government has promised. But it hasn't worked out. We delivered our rice to the processing factory at Dagana last year and we are still waiting. We haven't received anything. The tomatoes we sold last season, the same story. Nothing! Right up to the present time. Our green peas also went to market and we haven't been paid either.

'We have the receipts but what use are they? It's the merchants. It's the factories at Dagana. It's the SAED who took our rice and paid us nothing. It is essential that when we send our rice to the factories it is paid for immediately. But it doesn't happen. The situation is impossible.'

## Bokary Lou Ba

'You must understand that we are scattered populations of the wretched poor. We live off what we can grow and the sale of our surplus products if we have any.... We cannot live by rice alone!

'We know that we could grow other crops more profitably, but they tell us that we cannot grow millet and rice together in irrigated *périmêtres* and we cannot safely grow cereals elsewhere if neither the natural flooding of the land nor an artificial flood can be guaranteed.'

I asked what they had done to protest about it.

'We have done everything. We have briefed lawyers. We have sent a delegation to see the Prime Minister, another to see the Minister for the Rural Economy. They all made promises that it would be sorted out and our money would arrive but it hasn't. The other day a delegation representing some of the 30 villages who are in the same boat, came to see me and said they couldn't wait any longer. What else can we do? We have already made one protest march to the factory. We want to make another. We told the prefect of the district and he told the Governor. The word came back to postpone the protest and they would send a high-powered delegation to talk to the companies in-volved. They promised that all would be settled within 10 days at the latest. It is now 20 days and we are still waiting.'

Christian Aid/Derrick Knight

**Oula Ba**

**Oula Ba,** *an elderly farmer, member of the Guede Cooperative*

'It's all very well growing more rice but it's all a waste of time if the factories refuse to buy it from us. What are we supposed to do?

'It costs a lot of money to grow rice and we need to sell it at a good price. It is the same for tomatoes. There are no subsidies any more. We have to grow rice here. We have no other option. If the government is serious about raising agricultural production it must make it possible for farmers to buy their materials cheaper. And when you have paid out all the expenses and you try to sell the rice at a fair price, what happens? They make you wait nine months!'

'Could you abandon everything and work elsewhere?' I ask.

'And where do you suppose that might be? We are skilled farmers. We want it to work smoothly. If it doesn't, there's no alternative but to pay up and start again.'

The traditional cereal crops of the region are easy and cheap to grow. Rice requires constant attention and regular dressings of fertiliser, pesticides and herbicides. The paddy fields are hosts to several water-borne diseases. As one of the interviewees said, the main reason for the race to grow as much rice as possible seems to be to satisfy the eating habits of the people who live in the cities. The cost of carrying out a rice revolution in the Senegal valley seems to be beyond the wildest dreams of the government and its advisers. The time chosen to make it clashes disastrously with the sweeping budget savings forced on the economy by the IMF and the World Bank which include the dismantling of technical services and credit schemes designed to help agriculture. There are too few private enterprises in the country to pick up the pieces. The farming communities are struggling on their own to develop their own associations and sources of credit. What is clear is that there can be no return to the past. The dams are a fact and the community will have to find ways of adapting to them or building up enough social pressure to force the management to take notice of their wishes and needs. If not, the margin between recovery of the agricultural community and a disaster will be a dangerously slim one.

# CHAPTER FIVE

# NOMADIC HERDERS — A lost cause?

*I am convinced that soon there will be nothing and nobody left in this part of the country.*

**from *The Ambiguous Adventure* by Cheikh Hamidou Kane**

Among the distinguished looking elders who called in at the compound of the PIP at Ndioum was Monsieur Ousmane Ndombo Ba, a Peulh chief. He was a giant in every way. He towered over his companions and he was as broad and muscled as a bull. Even seated cross-legged on one of the mats which served as mobile offices he was an obvious potentate. He sat upright, calm and every inch a leader. If one had wanted to cast anyone for the part of a feudal king, he was perfect. A powerful neck supported the sort of head of which sculptors might dream. His dark eyes flickered beneath trimmed bushy eyebrows. His head was both close-shaven and polished, emphasising a weighty and magnificent skull. He had the profile of a figurehead on an eighteenth century man of war. On the chest of his fine cotton *boubou* he wore three medals for services to the state. But now the state had abandoned him and he was disillusioned and fighting mad. His people were being tricked out of their livelihoods.

'If you can get him to talk to you about how the herders and their families are doing in the current economic crisis, he knows more than almost anyone,' whispered a local. 'He knows everybody, has seen everything'. So I politely dropped a hint. He turned his hooded falcon's eyes on me and considered whether I was being sincere or momentarily curious. He saw that I meant it.

'If you want to know about the economic problems of the Peulh herders and pastoralists I will invite you to come and spend a day with us at Mafre where we are settled at present,' he said. 'Let's say the day after tomorrow.'

You swerve off the main road a few kilometres beyond Guede and turn south between a line of stunted trees and look for the track which leads to Mafre. The country is hilly, bearing in mind nowhere in Senegal is above 300 metres and here we are talking of hillocks of some 20 metres above sea level, a height that the annual flood never reaches and which defines it as *djeri* — the dry rain-fed land.

The elderly little 2CV belonging to my veteran guide and mentor, protested the gradient and the soft sand. There were a few trees and scattered thorn bushes embedded in red sand and more red sand. This year the rains had stopped further south. This year there had been no '*hivernage*', as the three months' wet season is called, turning on its head the French for winter. It was in fact both hot and humid. Here only some 4 to 12 mm of rain had fallen, a twentieth of the normal. Little more could now be expected. It was a disaster for rain-fed crops. Grass seeds lying dormant in the sandy soil had not germinated. Everything was bare.

It is some 19 kilometres from the tarmac to Mafre, a small Peulh settlement, not yet on any map. The track is sometimes visible and sometimes not. The driver searched like an Indian scout for the least sign in the softer soil. There was not a hint of animal or human life until, breasting the last low ridge, we saw ahead a collection of houses and sheds, straw huts and the yellow concrete tower of a bore well set into a grove of eucalyptus trees. Under the trees a dozen cream-coloured long-horned cattle sheltered. We drove into a large enclosed compound with several solid single storied buildings, our host's home.

Monsieur Ba greeted my companionable guide as a 'son of the soil' and ushered us into a darkened room whose walls and floor were covered with rugs and carpets. It was in effect an exclusive men's reclining room for rest and conversation. We were asked to relax like potentates on mattresses and leather cushions seductively arranged for comfort. Our host shouted a few instructions and settled himself cross-legged, with one elbow on a huge knee in a natural pose like a thoughtful Buddha in a precious Japanese carving. 'We shall just quench our thirsts,' he said, 'and then I shall tell you about the difficulties in which we are trapped at the present time.' He wore today a fine white cotton under-*boubou*, the very lightest of woven muslin worn in folds and allowing air to reach the skin.

One of his wives, to whom, as usual in the more con-servative families of these male-dominated

**Ousmane Ndombo Ba — Peulh chief**

Christian Aid/Derrick Knight

societies, we were not introduced, brought in a tray with a large bowl of slightly sour diluted milk with sugar. This was her house. Later we were welcomed and ate lunch in a marginally less grand second house across the yard belonging to a second wife. The chief poured a large glass each. We slaked our thirst over short speeches of welcome and thanks. More milk went down.

Another tray was brought in. This also bore gourds of warm milk. This time with *couscous*, cooked cracked millet over which milk is poured. It is then topped with a small ladle of cow's urine before it is stirred and drunk like a weak porridge. Locally it is highly prized and it is almost an insult to refuse a second or a third helping on these sorts of occasion. It is not yet half past eleven and despite the open windows, it is like an oven indoors. The refreshment is capped with a large bowl of fresh, frothy warm milk straight from the cow.

'In the past, when it rained properly and there were annual

river floods we had practically no problems,' the chief began. 'At that time any assistance we were given was quite unnecessary. But when the rains 'failed and now when the rains have failed again, we must get help.

'The Peulh without cattle is nothing and is no longer a Peulh. The Peulhs' traditional resources are cows, goats, sheep. The whole of their society and livelihood, their customs, their ceremonies, their joys, their sadness, everything revolves around and is met by the sale and use of their herds and flocks.'

The chief poured out his lament in a deep resonant voice as if in verse in his own Pulaar language. I was listening to the living spirit of a people. It was translated immediately by my guide into French and though he is expert in both tongues, one instinctively knows that there is a loss. There is a further loss when I translate it into English.

'For the last three years we have not been able to bring back any of our animals from the south because it hasn't rained. There is no grass for them. There has been no pasture on the *djeri*. There has been none in the *waalo*. What are we to live on at the present time? We are in the hands of God. We are part of his secrets.

'All we have been able to do is bring back a small herd. We have some milk and from this we can take a little pleasure in life. It at least allows us to join in spirit with our large herds in the Saloum to the south. I am truly ashamed not to be able to show you some of the magnificent animals that we possess.

'I'm now 72 years old and during my life I have known all the great men of our people. I have been decorated by President Senghor and by President Diouf and I'm still in good health because the climate seems to have suited me. What wealth my family has acquired I have often shared with my people and have struggled to establish their rights when it appeared that the Peulhs were being forgotten.'

In the overpowering heat of midday we felt imprisoned in the luxurious inner sanctum to which we had been taken out of courtesy and we asked to be allowed to move into the shade of a large open-sided hangar or shelter in the middle of his compound. Here there were various bamboo beds and mats on which a group of elders and relations were gathered. There was a lot of banter in Pulaar between them and my 'son of the soil' before we continued. The pain of the heat was somewhat lessened.

The chief went on. 'I'll explain what I mean when I say the Peulhs are forgotten. The farmers of the Fouta Toro have always lived off the crops grown during the rise and fall of the river. We Peulhs fitted into that way of life because we took our herds far away during the growing season and brought them back later. It suited the farmers to let our animals graze on their fields after the harvest in exchange for the manure they left behind. There was always plenty of unused riverbank for us to bring our cattle to water when they needed it. In the dry season we took our herds south into the *ferlo* [the vast empty grass and woodlands of the interior] where there were permanent ponds, wells and natural fodder.'

The telling became a litany to which the assembled company either nodded assent or made little noises of appreciative agreement. A sort of 'Amen to that'.

'But now,' the chief said, 'the lands along the river valley are being turned into big irrigated zones and allotted to villagers. We find it more and more difficult to find watering points. We are not represented in their village associations and have no say in what decisions they make. The state is not interested in us either. We have no effective lobby in government circles. The new agricultural strategy offers us nothing. Cattle farming does not feature in the government plans. I have led delegations to meet with ministers but they have achieved nothing. What we have managed, we have done with our own resources.

'The plight of the Peulhs is starkly obvious when they come and ask to be given some land to cultivate. It means they despair. It means they can no longer prosper in the pursuit of their special skills with livestock and in the way of life which is part of it. They need land to grow crops in order to survive.

'I am speaking in the name of all Peulhs. If at least some of them are prepared to settle and cultivate, perhaps the others will be able to continue working with livestock.'

Ousmane Ba reminded me of a king of the forest, the head of an endangered species threatened by changes in the outside world that are beyond his understanding.

'We have tried to form a settlement here. The trouble is that there is not enough water. The pump on the borehole does not work properly. There is no grass because it hasn't rained. There is no back-up or expert advice to make it possible for herders to

Christian Aid/Derrick Knight

**Ousmane Ndomo Ba**

adapt to the new conditions. We had no need of *waalo* land in the past; the *djeri* was quite enough for us. But now we are forced to go into the *waalo* to get water for our herds. It goes without saying that if some animals get into cultivated fields by mistake, the owners will demand compensation. Sometimes there is even a fight. It seems the Peulhs are always in the wrong. They say that no field has moved to find the animals, it's the animals which found their way into the fields. If you look after your animals they will not do any damage, they say. So if animals stray it is natural that you should compensate us, they say, and because we the Peulhs are badly represented in the rural communities we always end up paying over the odds.'

One of the elders sitting close to the chief butted in.

'I heard about some Wolofs who took animals from a Peulh herd because they were convinced that the animals had been damaging their crop. The Peulhs demanded the return of their cattle because it wasn't them that had done the damage. The Wolofs indignantly replied, "Yes it was and you must pay us." A Peulh who wasn't directly involved came to the herders and said: "Pay what they ask, otherwise they will try and provoke you into a fight and you will end up paying twice as much." They were advised to pay 500,000 francs (about £1,000). They haggled and agreed on 20,000 francs and everybody was happy. This happened in the Diolof further south. It couldn't happen here in the same way because we all live side by side and are related.'

Monsieur Ba thanked him and continued.

'For over 40 years we never had problems. We never needed to go near the *waalo* fields. We didn't even need to cultivate small fields. Now we have to rethink. We need help and advice on land matters so that we can grow crops. We have no means to do it alone.

'The government has cut most of its veterinary service for pastoralists as a condition of its getting new finance from abroad. They have allowed others to take a large area of forest and pasture used by my people for generations in the reserved forest lands in the south which are vital for our cattle in the dry season.'

'What exactly are you referring to?' I asked. My guide explained.

'The chief was referring to the sudden deforestation in April 1991 of 45,000 hectares of officially protected forest reserves by the disciples of the Mouride Brotherhood. Someone in government had given them a permit. It seems that it was so desperate for foreign earnings from the sale of groundnuts to reduce its total dependence on financial instalments from the IMF, the World Bank and other foreign donors, that it was prepared to go against its own public policy of protecting the environment. It happened in the Mbegue forest, east of Koalack, an area of forest and scrub with a scattering of water holes and borewells which had been listed as an agro-pastoral reserve. It had been an important zone for over 40 years for nomadic herders for the pasture of cattle and ruminants during the dry season. Large herds came south from Mauritania, Mali and northern Senegal. That year there were some hundreds of Peulh camps and over 100,000 animals in the zone. It was also a vital corridor through settled farming land for their herds to reach pastures further south along the Gambian frontier. Those zones had been the subject of various protection and conservation projects financed by USAID and by the World Bank.

'Then on the 25th of April we all heard an appeal from the Grand Khalif of the Mouride Brotherhood, which as you know is one of the most powerful Islamic cults, ordering his followers, for the Glory of God to come to the village of Kelcom on the edge of the Mbegue forest with their machetes, their axes, their saws to cut down a forest.

'Within weeks a huge area was flattened and ploughed for groundnuts. Five million trees and bushes had been torn up. Many of the best water holes and wells had been enclosed. The protests of the Peulhs and their supporters which included the World Bank went unheard. Other donors in Europe kept quiet. You have to remember that Senegalese troops were part of the 'Desert Storm' campaign and they may have been too embarrassed to protest. We did not get anywhere, even though CIMADE and other NGOs took up the cause.

'The Mouride Brotherhood is immensely powerful. Some say the government majority depends on it. For years the intensive cultivation of groundnuts by its followers has progressively ruined the land and turned it into a virtual desert. Nothing will ever grow there again. Then what happens? They colonise another area. It is tragic for many reasons. The country's dependence on the export of groundnuts, a virtual monoculture, is so great that no environmental or human cost is too high to increase the possible return. At the same time the export price of groundnuts has been steadily falling so that the volume of nuts exported has continually to increase in order to earn the same amount.

'For the sake of a few million dollars for a couple of years, whoie communities are dispossessed, the farming methods are unsustainable and once again the declared policy of the government to encourage agricultural food production is stood on its head. It shows a complete disdain for the welfare of the community and care of the country's dwindling natural resources. It isn't the first time. It's been going on for years. Each time the outcome has been a disaster.'

The official protest of the World Bank in this case did not stop me from thinking that the story might have been different if the country had not been put under the stringent discipline of the structural adjustment programmes. The invariable rule of structural adjustment was — increase the foreign trading balance by whatever means was possible. In this case the damage caused was irreversible.

'Was there any case to be made for the Peulhs causing their own destruction of the protected woodlands by overgrazing?'

There was a vigorous shaking of heads and various members of the circle wanted to answer at once. My old guide listened to the opinions that were voiced and then said he would summarise the gist of what he understood and what he knew.

'No, they all refute that. The Peulh communities and their shepherds have visited and looked after these lands for many,

many years in traditional movements of people and cattle. Many of their ancestors are buried there. They follow the grass and the water. They love nature. They are very careful. They understand that the soil is poor. It can't survive regular crops. Their way of life is good for those lands. They are improving them. If only they could convince the powers that be that this was so. Now they have lost hundreds of camp sites and many ponds. There is only a fraction of land left to them.'

The second speaker was the Imam of the village, a handsome and thoughtful nephew of Monsieur Ba. The form conversations take in Senegal, where it is rare to talk to anyone on a one-to-one basis, is for each successive speaker to confirm or agree with what has just been said before moving on to new ground.

Mamadou Diah

'My name is Mamadou Diah and I am 48 years old. I thank Allah and give praise to the prophet and then wish to thank you for coming all this way to discuss with us the deep causes of our problems. For us the first and foremost concern is the care of livestock, our tradition as pastoralists. And now it is being ruined, the results are getting worse and we are deeply worried.

'We normally keep our large herds moving about in the south where we have lands reserved for our use. When the rains were good and regular, we left those lands and returned to the north to pasture our cattle here. When the rains failed and the lands became barren we had to move south again and make improvements there. The reason we are here now is that we realise we have to lay claim to our local inheritance and modernise our animal husbandry. Nobody would say that we have farming in the blood but we are in a new situation. We have to redeem our pride.

'For years we have felt able to turn our backs on formal schooling for our children. We sent them out instead to learn the skills of cattle farming as shepherds. But now a formal education has become a necessity. Any Peulh who comes back to the Fouta Toro without written proof of his right to a piece of land is at a great disadvantage. If he cannot follow the new administrative rules or establish his legal claim or argue his case before a rural community meeting, he may lose it.

'Furthermore, whenever we have organised a local assembly and prepared a list of reasonable requests with which to petition the authorities, it always seems to get stuck somewhere because we don't know how to deal with modern officialdom.

'We have now to try to catch up and repair the damage. We have recently re-established ourselves here in Mafre. Our forefathers abandoned an earlier and well-established settlement here in favour of living on the move with their herds. When times were good, they preferred that way of life. But that tradition has been under attack for many years now. Nowadays there are few rich Peulh families. Herders are scraping by on small profits. Nobody can afford to support large numbers of dependants as was the custom. We have decided that we may have to invest in irrigated fields to give us the means to support our passion for animal husbandry. We are looking for a way forward.'

A thin elderly man, who had followed closely and nodded agreement to many of the points, wanted to interrupt.

'We have the feeling that much of the aid from abroad is going astray. When we see bags of red millet and other foodstuffs with foreign language messages on them, they are always being sold in the market, whereas we are convinced that they were sent as a gift. That is why we prefer to meet donors face to face, to share our ideas and try and work out ways to struggle against our apparent destiny.'

The Imam broke in.

'There is also the question about our borehole which my uncle mentioned in passing. It is a real matter of survival. The sides of the well joined to it collapsed when it was being deepened and the well-digger had to be pulled out. Now the water from the borehole is so dirty that you cannot wash clothes with it or water the vegetable garden. It's vital for us, otherwise we shall not be able to stay or if we do we shall be eating stones. It can't go on.'

Another man joined in.

'It's not only the problems of agriculture and animals. It's our health, and the teaching of skills to our women that we are missing out on.'

The Imam took up the point.

'The priority is certainly the health of the community. If one is not in good health all the rest is worth nothing in comparison. What we want is the means to turn an empty roofless building that we have here into a health post. At present, if someone is ill or if a woman is having a difficult labour, we have to take them down to the nearest health post, a distance of some 25 kilometres. We can keep the sick person or the woman here until they either recover or die. We can also call in one of the traditional women healers who might be able to use her skills. Others die through lack of care.

'We need a vaccination enclosure so that our animals can be treated on the spot rather than having to take them a long distance, cross the main road and risk having the animals scatter in all directions. We want to be self-sufficient in health matters.

'As far as the women are concerned we already have a literacy class in our national language — Pulaar. There are even children who can read and write in it now. All our herd boys and shepherds attend the Pulaar school because they are sure it is the right thing to do. We want that to continue, because we realise it is improving their chances of getting work and it helps them understand the modern world. But the women also want classes in needlework, in embroidery and in leather-work and they want a building of their own where these things can be organised when it suits them best. Training is the key to so many things.'

Another man joined in, energetically using his prayer beads to punctuate his short thought.

'Our only training school at the moment is our Pulaar school which was built by some other donor agency than the PIP. We have never had any other school. Before that of course there was a Koranic school, the school of the *talibes*, the school of the poor. Now we are aware that it is the Pulaar school which contains our future.'

The Imam disagreed.

' To know the differences between Islam and Christianity, and to understand the way the world is moving, you need to go to either French, Arabic or English schools. If we had had a French school here our journey would have been shorter and less painful. The children here are very intelligent. Even our shepherds, if they had the choice, would put one child in the French school and another in an Arabic school to have the best of both worlds. If they lived together each would contribute his special knowledge. Peulhs who have accepted training have understood the value of knowledge. They learnt it late. Proper schooling will get them over their present obstacles. They are convinced of this. However rich you are in animals, in hard cash or whatever, without knowledge you cannot be certain of anything, you cannot preserve, maintain and manage your affairs, but with knowledge comes enlightenment.'

The old chief returned to the discussion.

'A perpetual movement of people and animals in search of water and pasture is no longer possible. If you see a Peulh building a house in brick it shows that he is having to settle down. He now needs training so that he can develop. It is really the Peulhs' best political option.'

After this we broke for lunch. My guide and I followed the chief into another house which made up the south side of the inner courtyard and sat on rugs, to be served a delicate aromatic lamb stew with rice, milk and *couscous*, followed by a basket of small bananas. The chief and my equally venerable guide talked in their own language. We then strolled back to the shady central shed to find the larger group digesting their meal and beginning their siesta. It was clear that nobody had any intention of moving for the next two hours until the heat of the sun had diminished.

When one is given the privilege of sharing time and experience with such a group, it is only polite to let events take their course, not to be impatient. They do not understand what a European is doing visiting remote villages unless it is to verify that foreign aid is getting through. The Imam voiced his own opinion thus.

'The reason the donors want to make contact with the population directly at the grass roots is that they suspect that their funds and support may not be getting through to the people for whom they are intended or that agreed plans are not being carried out. We are comforted to know that there are people who really care what happens to their aid. We can have confidence in people like that. We are clear that northern donors show their real concern by leaving their pleasant climate and coming into the blistering heat and discomfort to check the projects they support are working out and to correct any deviations.' He was being perfectly sincere.

The light beyond the shelter was white. The air was still. The temperature back in the mid-forties. It was time for the first afternoon prayer. After the prayer there was silence for a further ten minutes or so while some of the group counted off a quota of personal prayers on their beads. Then more mattresses and pillows were brought out and we all reclined comfortably on the ground. The chief dozed off on a platform bed. After a while his first wife came out and started giving him a gentle and loving back and neck massage. My guide in the meantime got into a spontaneous theological discussion with the Imam over the Five Pillars of Islam about which my guide had written a book. It went on with appreciative and good-humoured help from the rest of the group for the best part of an hour. There was no attempt to translate for me, nor did I ask.

It was when we began to discuss the costs of basic commodities and the difficulties of buying and selling that the economic contradictions within the country were vividly underlined.

The Imam began. He had a good memory.

'I remember when I came back from school that a two kilo loaf of local sugar cost 125 francs. It quickly went up to 300. Now it is priced in the market at Dagana at between 900 (£2) and 1,200 francs. But contraband sugar floods the market and prices out the local kind. A 50 kilo sack smuggled from Gambia for 7,500 francs is now sold here at 15,000 francs, a good deal cheaper than locally made sugar.

'25 years ago a four kilo measure of millet cost 200 francs (then worth about 30p) or 50 francs a kilo. Now it has risen to 400 francs a measure or 100 francs a kilo. This is the basic cereal which is grown locally and sustains the population. But there are stocks of millet being dumped on the market which come from overseas donors and are intended to feed the poor in bad years. Now they are being sold to provide some ready cash for the government in order to keep itself going. It has to be a form of fraud.

'Animal prices rise too. When rice was sold at 50 francs a kilo and millet sold at 30 francs, the cost of a fat sheep was 1,000 francs and that was a good price. Now that a 100 kilo sack of rice sells at

Christian Aid/Derrick Knight

**'Time for afternoon prayer...'**

14,000 francs, a 15 kilo sheep sells at 15,000. The price can go as high as 25,000 francs (£55). If we had the means we might be able to buy three month old lambs and raise them until they were six months old and sell them at a good price. We could do good business with other animals, too. A lamb taken out of the herd and fattened in the household with scraps and leftovers for a year will fetch 15-20,000 francs. Do it for two to three years and the price can be as high as 30,000.'

The group was coming alive. Several men wanted to pitch in. This is what they knew about. They were on firm ground.

An emaciated elderly man on the edge of the group had been nodding vigorously and now chipped in.

'I agree that my friend's small lamb taken out to the field, brought back, fed on good straw fodder, cuddled, will fatten nicely and will sell at 15,000. It shows that if we went into the business of fattening sheep we would improve their quality and do good business.

'Now, nobody has so far mentioned fish. I don't know much about it but someone here must be able to tell the stranger what goes on.'

Indeed, another man who had not yet spoken was eager to talk and was given the nod by the Imam — who seemed to have become the chairman while the old chief enjoyed his continuing massage in the background.

'River fishing is finished. All we have left is saltwater fish. When saltwater fish comes on to the market we buy it because fish is part of our diet, but it would never be our first choice. I'll explain. Since the time when the river ceased to flood the plain in a proper manner, the fish have not been able to breed. In the past river fish bred in vast quantities in the flooded side streams and inlets along the valley. The river was rich in fish. Local people ate fresh and dried river fish. They preferred it to all others. It suited their tastes. But since the river water has gone bad, smells rotten and doesn't flood the ponds and creeks, there are no longer any little fish. The water from Manantali is a stagnant water, a rotten water and is worthless. Water does not like to be imprisoned or kept in the same place for long. It loses its vigour and freshness and its value diminishes.'

These Peulhs of Mafre are among an increasing number who have been forced to experiment with mixed farming. They accept some of the blame for ignoring economic change in earlier years but they also blame the failure of the government to maintain a progressive policy to protect the fragile environment against deforestation and desertification which was agreed by them and backed by international aid. They are not convinced that either the government or anyone else has properly costed or worked out the consequences of the move into large-scale irrigated agriculture for the population. In this they are not alone.

The complaints poured out.

'People are used to working out prices but may not be used to working out the exact repayment of advances made. If they don't know the exact figures then they will be forced to accept what they are told and keep what is left. It is a handicap. There isn't precise information at each level to show how much you owe. If there are suppliers who say you owe so much for seed, so much for fertiliser and so much for irrigation costs, you know what to expect. But if a cultivator doesn't know whether the supplier should take 10, 20 or 30 sacks, he cannot argue if he has nothing left. That is the importance of literacy.'

At the end of the afternoon there was time to make a short tour of the settlement. Three young men, nephews of the chief, took me across a parched sandy field to the damaged water pump where the small herd of long-horned cattle were waiting hopefully for a drink. I understood that water was coming by cart from a neighbouring village.

We walked across a large communal and fenced vegetable garden which at this season was neither dug nor planted. It was divided into family plots of about six metres by four. Scattered lemon and lime trees were flourishing. This year, work in the garden would depend on the repair of the pump which was the source of water for everything. The chances didn't seem to be good. On our way back young girls were pounding millet outside temporary straw houses. Only the chief's house spoke of permanence. The rest signalled that they might just be passing through. But were they?

# CHAPTER SIX

# THE WOMEN'S CHALLENGE

*I have asked the women to come to this meeting today.*
**from *The Ambiguous Adventure* by Cheikh Hamidou Kane**

In 1969 it was hard to organise village women because of the narrow social traditions of the riverine communities and the threat women might pose to the strict patriarchal rule of the male heads of families. In Dakar, however, the head of the Department of Rural Animation was encouraging his staff to promote women animators in those villages which had successfully organised the men. 'Was it a real initiative?' I scribbled in my notes at the time, 'or was it a bit of window dressing?'

In the Rural Animation Centre (CAR) of the district of Matam, the chief professional animator was a young woman, Fatou Bathily, 22 years old, married, born locally but brought up in Dakar. After failing her degree course, she had answered a national appeal for able young administrators to go into the field. She had been signed up. In Senegal civil servants go where ordered. She had been sent to Ouressugui near Matam. Her husband remained behind in Dakar and only saw her during the holidays. She was a militant and lively person with an attractive outgoing personality, but she felt she was fighting an uphill battle.

'Here,' she said, 'men are dominant. Women can do nothing without their husband's consent — spending money, buying clothes for their children, visiting relatives, taking a bus to a local market in a neighbouring village, joining a sewing circle, from the most trivial of decisions to the biggest ones.'

Her main concern was mothers and children. There needed to be a revolution in the way pregnant women were treated, the way a child was born. Mothers needed to be educated to accept better and more hygienic methods, to understand the risks of infection, childhood illness, tetanus and to end all kinds of superstitions in infant feeding.

'Most villagers,' she said, 'are suspicious of me because I am on my own. Wives are jealous of their husbands talking to me. Men are worried that I am turning their wives against them. Mothers question the value of my advice because I have no children of my own. All this tittle tattle and superstition has had to be met and overcome before I can be of use re-directing the energies of women in the villages.'

The resistance to women having individual voices and a power of decision in village and family groups began to crack during and after the big drought of 1973. As the younger men were compelled to migrate in search of work, more and more women became acting heads of families. They had to make decisions, be responsible for the planting and harvesting of the family fields, debate issues in productive cooperatives, decide how and when to sell any surplus, above all keep alive the family networks which were an essential part of the fabric of Toucouleur society.

Today the status of women in the Senegal River valley has changed dramatically. There are hundreds of women's groups and associations in the villages engaged in all kinds of activity. Women are the active agents of change. There is still resistance among members of the older generation, but while they may still be able to exercise some control over their wives, they can no longer order around their daughters.

Two conversations give a flavour of the full extent of that change and of the passing of a society that only privileged old men regarded as ideal.

Away from the river, on lands on which no self-respecting crop farmer could make a living, is a Milky Way of hamlets and villages, most of them too small to be on the map. They are used as staging posts by the Peulh nomads and their herds during the three months wet season. It is the season when even deserts flower and normal rains produce a short-lived but lush crop of sweet pasture. Water in temporary pools and ponds is within walking distance.

The Peulhs, who have spent the rest of the year on a trek or, in the technical language, on *'transhumance'* far to the south in the Saloum or the *ferlo* where grasslands and water can always be found for their animals, return to their ancestral heartland. Here they refresh and fatten their herds, renew family contacts with their cousins, the settled Toucouleur farmers, and bless Allah for the beauty of nature.

One of these villages is Nenette, 33 kilometres south of Ndioum.

At first sight it is no more than a scattering of wooden framed mud houses in a wilderness of sand, but near by is an oasis of greenery — a borewell, a small woodland with a cool micro-climate and a luxuriously green vegetable garden. Nenette, with a population of about 1,700 people, is famous in the whole river valley for its dynamic women's association and the programme of change which it has pioneered in the teeth of the economic crisis and the destructive effect of years of persistent drought.

Christian Aid/Derrick Knight

**Fatimata Dia**

**Fatimata Dia** is a handsome, sparkling and outgoing woman in her early thirties who is a part of this revolution.

'My name is Fatimata Dia. I am the health worker in the village. My main concern is to help the community keep healthy and to look after childbirth. I have been doing it for 11 years.

'My daily routine goes something like this. When I wake up in the morning I first take care of the kids. I give them their breakfast, then I go to the well to fill my water pots. I then prepare whatever I have decided to cook for the main midday meal. Afterwards I go to the health post. There I am ready to deal with any health matters which may arise. Everything I need is at hand there and I treat the sick who come to the post to the best of my ability. I do what I can. If it is beyond my scope I make every effort to get the patient to the hospital at Ndioum.

'I stay in the health post until midday, then I shut up shop, return home and finish getting lunch. I do not have anyone to do it for me so I do it myself and serve the meal — just me and my small children. You see, my husband is a cattle trader. He's in Dakar at the present time. He keeps cattle and moves them from place to place far away in the *djeri*, in the Fouta and around the big ponds, depending on the season and the pasture. He sells in town.'

During the calamitous drought years from 1969 to 1974, the whole area became a virtual desert. Woodlands died, thousands of animals perished, food aid and charity became a necessity. The scars of those years still show in the landscape. Dead groves, vast swathes of red sand, abandoned villages. In Nenette and elsewhere the young and active men left home to look for work in less difficult environments — in the city, in neighbouring countries or by migrating to Europe. While some of them sent money home, many vanished. The women and children were left behind at the mercy of their better-off relatives or of hand-outs by aid agencies.

It was at this time that the PIP, with its support group of mainly church-related European donors, took root in the region to bring aid to the victims of the drought and help train people to survive in what had begun to look like a long cycle of poor rains and climatic change.

A reliable supply of water to drink, both for people and animals, was the urgent priority. Some well-meaning foreign aid programmes installed new wells and deep boreholes, many of them with expensive motor pumps or solar power systems which soon broke down, leaving villagers bereft. The donors had not taken into account the need for them to be run and maintained by trained mechanics or village managers. PIP too, with its limited funds, had a modest well-digging programme at this time but saw the real need as enabling the people of the region to achieve greater economic independence and to take a greater part in running their own affairs. Since so many of the younger men had migrated and since the old men, the elders, tended to be stuck in the past with traditional thoughts and ways, PIP believed it should encourage and support the burgeoning women's groups to become new poles of development in their communities. A programme of training was begun to meet the needs of village families and to find new opportunities of earning some money. The women led, the young men who remained had to follow. The old looked on.

The PIP encouraged villagers to organise around vegetable gardens as a way of improving a thin diet as well as of earning a little money. At Nenette the women formed their own association to develop one. Brought up on milk, meat and millet, they had to learn gardening skills. Soon they were highly successful, spreading into many other activities and winning their financial independence from hand-outs, whether from absent husbands or outside agencies. By 1989 the association had been able to improve the well-being of the population of Nenette to such an extent that they asked PIP to reduce any help it was giving it and to allocate its share of support to other villages who needed it more. More important, the men began to return and families were re-united. The dispersal of the Peulhs beyond the region ceased as new opportunities offered themselves. Now there is a big garden which has generated the revenue to finance many of the other activities in the village including the building of the three-room health post. With the guarantee of security for their families, the men can once again return to herding as a way of life.

Fatimata again:

'I don't usually go back to the health post in the afternoon because I have other jobs to do. I have the family field and I share the work in the collective field run by the woman's association of Nenette. There may be visits to make, such as a trip to Ndioum to get advice on some problem. It depends on the priorities.'

I asked what sorts of sickness she had to deal with.

'In the morning,' Fatimata answered, 'it's mostly cases of malaria, diarrhoea and conjunctivitis, there are also bad coughs, chest infections at certain times of the year. I also treat cuts and wounds. Every morning brings three or four different sorts of problem.

'I also attend to births. If there are risks, I have to send the pregnant mother to the hospital at Ndioum. If the mother is in another village I reach her by horse and cart. If she has to go to Ndioum hospital, it's the same. We only have carts.'

'What sort of training have you had?' I asked.

'I was chosen by the village to go for a period of training at the hospital at Ndioum. A course lasting six months.'

The hospital at Ndioum was built and is maintained by the French charity Terre des Hommes, with help from UNICEF. The care it is able to provide is exemplary but because of the government cuts following the terms of the World Bank and IMF structural adjustment programme, the Senegal Ministry of Health slashed its countrywide health service and might have been forced to close it altogether if its upkeep depended on a government budget. It even has difficulty finding the salaries of the chronically underpaid and increasingly rebellious junior staff. The health care network was in bad shape before the structural adjustment programmes were imposed but the demands of the IMF and World Bank broke its back. The staff in the health union UNSAS at the hospital at Ndioum were holding a token strike in protest during my visit.

Fatimata moved her blooming and chubby 18-month-old son from one arm to the other. I wondered why she thought the village had chosen her.

'I can't say really. Perhaps because as village midwife, I had never made a mistake and the women took this into account. It was no big deal. It is voluntary and unpaid. Any donations by patients go directly to the village health committee. It is they who manage the affairs of the health post. Only fees for midwifery come to me as of right. The new mother or her husband give me 1,000 francs (about £2), sometimes 1,500, and on the day of baptism a joint of meat, a bar of soap, something like that. That's the only money I see. The rest is handled by the management committee.

'My first medical kit came from the hospital. Now we get a supply of essential medicines through the health programme of the PIP. It's not a gift, it's a revolving loan. I use dehydration kits donated by UNICEF.

'My main problems are the treatment of the many types of sickness which I see. I am concerned in particular about the number of children who are ill because malnutrition has weakened them. The level of malnutrition is worrying and I make sure I stress these cases in my reports.

'The malnutrition has a direct link to the family budget. It can be the result of the ignorance of well-off families who don't look after their children. But it's usually a result of the tight money situation. In my village, at least, it is not a problem of weaning.

'Talking of the economy of the village, it is mainly the women who work because they are engaged both in agriculture and in vegetable gardening. Most of the problems we have are the result of government actions. We women keep in touch with the world outside. We are actively involved in the development of the village. We want to show our neighbours how important it is to break away from old traditions, become independent.'

Fatimata spoke animatedly. Her youngest child bounced on her lap as she underlined her points with a strong arm.

'It is over 10 years since we formed a women's group. It was our own idea. We dug a well and organised a vegetable garden. With the money it generated we were able to do other things. We organised ourselves more formally and sought advice from the PIP and had a deep borewell put in so that we could increase the scale of our vegetable garden. Now we manage the garden, the well, the health post, a flour grinding mill and a centre where the women meet to talk, hold literacy classes, and learn crochet and cloth dyeing. The women have shown a great enthusiasm for the improvement of the village and are prepared to work hard to get it. Over 50 women have been taking literacy classes in Pulaar and we reckon that three-quarters of all the women in Nenette can read and write in Pulaar. Many can keep accounts.'

Thierno Ba told me later that Nenette was a veritable oasis in a desert. He told me a local anecdote about the women's enthusiasm for literacy. 'When a woman in Nenette urgently needs a cup of salt or some other household item, she now sends a small child with a note to a neighbour so that the whole village doesn't get to hear about her housekeeping lapse by having it parroted aloud in the street. The Nenettoise, I often say, has become the symbol of cleanliness, wisdom and openmindedness.'

'Fatimata, what sort of water supply do you have at Nenette? '

'We have a good borewell and our main problem is the cost of diesel fuel for the motor pump and the fees of the mechanic who looks after it. There are no other water sources. It is good drinking water but I am so nervous about keeping it that way that I have the lab in the hospital at Ndioum check it regularly to make sure no dirt is getting in.

'In the old days it was tough living in the *djeri* because it was necessary to raise livestock and to cultivate millet to subsist. We were cut off from other communities. As the traditional life became more difficult, water got scarcer, the rains didn't fall when they should, the able-bodied men left to find work wherever they could find it. The women left behind took stock, and found that they were not alone in their problems and that there were organisations prepared to support them. Little by little they discovered how to work together, hand in hand, share experience. We made up for our lost education by joining literacy classes. We worked hard, we trained ourselves in new skills and, by using the facilities offered by PIP for the promotion of women in the villages of the region, we were able to become part of the modern world.

'Now we are well motivated, well trained, and we have a well run organisation independent of our menfolk. They have nothing to do with it and no say in how we spend the money we have earned. In the old days a woman could not make even 1,000 francs a month, now there are few who don't always have spare cash in their pockets. It's our own property. We do with it what we like.

'At the present time, because the rains are so poor, we are having to grow different crops which need special watering. With the new techniques we have learnt from various outside agencies, we have mastered the art of growing more and better. We grow onions, cabbages, tomatoes, potatoes, and so on. We do very well with them. We eat them ourselves and we sell any surplus onions to the processors. The main problem is that the market for our surpluses is often saturated so we end up with rotting vegetables. We are handicapped because we are far off the track and nowhere near the main road. We haven't got any means of preserving and processing vegetables. A reliable market is needed. It doesn't exist.'

Finally I asked Fatimata about the environment. Did it worry her?

'Yes. Take firewood, which we cannot do without. In the old days there were no problems. There was as much as one wanted in the woodlands all around. But since the desertification, there is no firewood near by and one needs a cart to fetch dead wood from a distance of many kilometres. If you have no cart you have to pay a high price for the wood you need for cooking.

'The environment worries us sick. We have a local committee to protect the remaining woodlands and undergrowth against bushfires and the anarchic killing of wild animals. Our men remain herders and have many animals. Now that the government has withdrawn its veterinary services, they have had to build their own vaccination enclosure to protect the herds. The government does too little to protect the environment. There is a law against the cutting down of trees in the *djeri* but there is nobody to police it. We regret that the PIP doesn't do more for the herders. We raise the matter with them every time we have a chance.

'We would like to plant fruit trees but they need lots of water and we can't do it. We don't have enough from our one deep well. But the men have planted drought resistant shelter trees like prosopis and eucalyptus and have helped by building fences for us, even though they remain herders at heart.'

Madina Niathbe is a large, busy village about halfway between the towns of Podor and Matam. It is on the south bank of the Doue, an arm of the river Senegal and therefore in the *waalo*, the alluvial flood plain. Despite this the village is surrounded by sand and suffers from it. Much of its protective tree belt died in the Seventies droughts. From Madina, a hand-hauled ferry carries vehicles and people over to the long island of Morphil and its closest village of Kas-Kas. A tongue of tarmac leads off the main motor road from St Louis to Matam towards Madina as if the intention was to build an all-weather road into Morphil to open it to regional and national markets. The goodwill and the money ran out within sight of the motor road.

Madina is an old village full of tightly packed buildings and narrow winding lanes with well-kept mosques sticking out here and there like gold fillings. Its one novelty is a high yellow concrete water tower and a deep borewell. The village has clean drinking water. Nevertheless a villager said: 'Some people living close to the river, being both lazy and ignorant, cannot be bothered to use the taps but scoop water straight out of the river which is seriously contaminated. "Our mothers always did it, so why shouldn't we?" they say when one mentions it.'

There is a busy weekly market selling all kinds of household goods, animals, firewood, a variety of locally made pots and local grown produce. There were tinkers and medicinal herb sellers, dried fish and butchery to order. Madina is one of the few links between the agricultural gluts of Morphil and the rest of the region. The market is an important barometer of the economy. For many local farmers it is a first and last chance to sell their surpluses. It is also one of the few outlets for the produce from the island of Morphil across the water.

As with so many villages in the region the effect of the years of drought was to scatter the most active younger men to seek work throughout West Africa and in France. The elders, the women and the children were left behind to tend the family fields and to wait hopefully for the monthly postal order. Many women became acting or permanent heads of families. It was the start of a social revolution. The women began to organise to earn their own money and so free themselves from the monthly agony of not knowing whether they would have money for food.

Madame Djieynaba Ouman Ndiath was a disciple of my friend Hacchim Ndiaye, a former state nurse whose personality and ideas about raising the standard of living of villages has had an impact on many communities. His own story features in a later chapter.

Djieynaba and the women of Madina had been challenged by Hacchim to improve their health care, their children's diet, their clean water supply, their money-making activities and their trading. She was now the president of the women's association.

Djieynaba Ouman Ndiath

Christian Aid/Derrick Knight

The interview was not easy. I was forced by circumstance to visit her without an interpreter. She spoke Pulaar with a few French words, but she was an enterprising woman and she mobilised two young schoolboys to help. One was a secondary school boy who happened to be on holiday; the other an 11 year old Koranic school pupil, self-taught in French but of sharp intelligence and intuition for the spoken word. He reminded me of Samba Diallo, the boy hero in Cheikh Hamidou Kane's novel *The Ambiguous Adventure*. He could have played the part.

The two boys formed a double act and translated both my questions and Madame Djieynaba's answers in a sort of relay, filling in each other's gaps, passing the baton when one was tired.

Madina is at the traditional and conservative heart of the middle region of the river valley. It is against custom for a woman to talk to any man outside the family by herself but I had used the introduction from Hacchim to plead a busy schedule to avoid a clan gathering being called.

'The problem of water...'

We talked in the enclosed yard of her house in the middle of the village at the end of the day and in the gathering dusk. Fearing problems of translation with abstract ideas we stuck pretty much to the core of everyday life.

'I work every day in the communal field with other women, growing vegetables. I have been doing that since 1979. I work with my hands and a *daba* (short-handled hoe) because I have no machines.

'We have two problems. The problem of water and the problem of selling the produce, because we have very few customers. We do market gardening. We grow onions, tomatoes, aubergines, cabbages, carrots, potatoes and so on. Some prefer to sell to each other, others use the weekly village market.

'It is often hard to sell vegetables because all the women grow their crops simultaneously. They eat what they can and then try and sell the surplus in the market. Sometimes there is too much. There are 430 of us on a small communal field of three hectares. Each woman has a small plot.

'We have our association of women. I am its president. We do sewing and other economic activities. We are all agreed about our aims. Development is part of my work. The women are taking literacy classes in Pulaar. I have done the course already. It is the women here who are determined to reinforce the speaking and writing of Pulaar before other languages spread to this area as a result of the building of the dam at Manantali. We want the smallest children in the village to know about their ancestors and their culture. I personally dislike them learning other languages. I do not want our language to be drowned. Now that the dam has been built, all kinds of new people about whom we know nothing will want to come and try their luck along the river. We shall be swamped if we are not careful. That is my worry.'

'What sort of problems do you have in making improvements?' I asked.

'When Hacchim was here we discussed our lack of machinery. A motor pump for instance. We can borrow one from time to time. We talked about organising ourselves better. Now that Hacchim has left, we find that his replacement gives us no advice and tells us nothing about certain illnesses. He gives us no help about health in the home.

'When Hacchim was here we paid the 100 francs subscription and were treated free. The new nurse also charges us a 100 franc subscription fee, but asks another 50 francs for a consultation and we also have to buy any medicine prescribed.

'When Hacchim was here he used to organise cooking demonstrations and taught us the value of different foods. He taught us how to choose foods to give a balanced diet to our children by using the colours of the Senegalese flag — reds for proteins, meat, fish, eggs — yellow for energy, cereals, fats — green for fruit and vegetables. You see I haven't forgotten.'

Djieynaba smiled and inclined her body towards me as if I was already an old friend sharing in her complicity.

'And it worked, because our children began to put on weight and they were not ill so often. But,' she added sadly, 'he's gone. Another problem is that Madina is quite a small village and doesn't have much good land. The gardens are small while the number of women wanting a plot (48 square metres) is very large. There is a shortage of agricultural land and we have problems with sand. We cannot expand our garden easily. We have to get our water directly from the arm of the river. We need a flour grinding mill, new hoes, and metal fencing so we don't have to cut branches from living trees. People ask us why we cannot save up for our mill like some other groups seem to have done. We cannot. It is too expensive. We hope we might get some help from abroad. We used to have links with the PIP but today these no longer exist. In the past one of their agents came to talk to us about our problems but he has been sent into the *djeri* and he has not been replaced. We need help to develop ourselves — to have *bamtaare*.

'Besides, we are not the only association. The youth association has a vegetable garden too and there is an association of migrants who funded the building of the clinic and a new post office so that their families can receive the money they send from abroad without delay. It cost them 25 million francs (£55,000). The government wouldn't help. There's a group of potters who make very good pots but they can't get their trade going outside the village because there's no transport at a fair price. It's worse with perishable vegetables because there are times of the year when there is too much of everything in the local market and we have to sell at any price or watch it decay.

'We find it hard to agree with other groups on how to avoid having too many tomatoes or too many onions to sell at the same time. There's nobody to organise our trade. We are a long way from the coast where the best markets are to be found.

'In general though the village is quite up to date. The PIP built a cereal bank and our women's centre. There's a number of village savings banks. There's a good dyeing cooperative. There's a theatre group.'

'What about firewood?' I ask.

'Firewood is very expensive,' replied Djieynaba. 'Three pieces of wood cost 50 francs (9p). I have had an improved cooking stove since 1986. You can see it there in the yard behind me. With that stove, three pieces of wood will do two meals, whereas with the normal three brick stove they only do one. But any source of firewood is now so far from the village that it is necessary to buy it from traders who carry it in carts to the village market. All my women colleagues in Madina also have to buy their wood.'

'Finally,' I ask, 'Is there anything stopping your women's association forging ahead?'

'We are not sitting still,' she said emphatically. 'We all know that *bamtaare* consists of three things — good health, good understanding, which includes literacy, and a mastery of cultivation. If we do well with our garden perhaps we shall be able to afford our mill and other things.'

The traditions of a male dominated society which kept women in their place as submissive, obedient and on the whole silent servants of their fathers, husbands and male relatives began to take a buffeting in the winds of change which blew across the river valley in the post-independence years. The women really began to assert themselves in the years following the drought of 1973. This revolution was even taking place in remote and isolated villages.

Kas-Kas is an old village on the island of Morphil, a low-lying and fertile sliver of land 100 or so kilometres long, a result of centuries of rich silt deposited in the flood plain of the River Senegal. It is cut off from the rest of the country for several months a year. Yet it survives and somehow thrives.

To get to Kas-Kas you get on to a rutted track beyond the village of Madina Niathbe and down to the water's edge of the Doue, a wide arm of the river. Some years ago a Dutch aid project whose aim was to end the isolation of Morphil built a causeway across the Doue but every time it rains it is breached. The alternative is a hand-hauled chain ferry and then a twisting track east across deserted fields and treeless mud flats. The driver, with one eye on dark clouds far to the south — because this is supposed to be the rainy season — and thinking of home, reminds you grimly that the track becomes quite impassable when it rains or when the river rises. Only last week some friends of his were marooned here for five days. He makes it sound like a prison sentence.

Kas-Kas, like all the villages on Morphil, is raised above the flood level — an island on an island — and is surrounded by a strong protective dyke. When the river floods the only way out is by canoe. Kas-Kas was built on the very edge of the mainstream and literally on the frontier of Senegal. On the far bank is the country of Mauritania. In good times this meant nothing because the people on both sides of the river shared a common heritage and were often parts of the same family.

In 1989 the people of Kas-Kas were horrified and fearful as inter-community conflict flared between the two countries. Beginning with some minor incidents of trespass upstream, it turned into a full scale expulsion of nationals in each country. On the Mauritanian side however it became the pretext for a violent ethnic cleansing and expulsion of black riverine communities by the dominant 'white' Moorish government whose supporters had become increasingly covetous of agricultural lands in the river basin. In 1989 the dams had been completed and the value of valley land would be multiplied by the irrigation schemes and cheaply available hydro-electricity.

Mauritanian soldiers and police pillaged properties and villages on their bank of the river and forced large numbers of 'black' Mauritanians to flee across the river to safety. These expulsions created intense fear along the river and laid a heavy burden on Senegalese villagers who felt obliged to provide hospitality to their fleeing relations and neighbours as long as it was needed. Even after official help was available the burden remained. The dark clouds of the conflict still hang over the region. Officially there is peace but the victims remained in limbo, stripped of identity, property and livelihood, most of them still in camps in Senegal with bare rations and a sense of abandonment.

The conflict increased the isolation of villages like Kas-Kas because traders added the excuse of personal safety to that of distance as reasons for shunning Morphil. Teachers, nurses and administrators stayed away for the same reasons. As they came mainly from the large coastal towns they regarded the prospect of Morphil as a Muscovite might fear a tour of duty in Siberia. In addition the distrust between the two governments resulted in a freeze on all joint development work along the river basin —the so-called *Après-Barrage* plan which was to follow from the completion of the dams and closing of sluices in the same year.

Nevertheless the actions of the women's association at Kas-Kas are one of the real breakthrough stories of recent years. They were the first in the valley to have an irrigated *périmêtre*, managed and successfully farmed solely by women.

About 100 women and small children turned out to greet the delegation of women from European donor agencies supporting PIP, who had come to see and encourage this initiative on a fine day in September 1992. I happened to be there at the same time.

When an elder infiltrated the formal greetings and took it on himself to welcome the visitors, the women's president, Madame Bineta Ba, without a trace of customary reticence firmly stopped him. 'Sit down, listen and keep quiet, old man,' she said firmly. 'This is our show. It has nothing to do with you. These are our guests. We want to tell the story of our achievements ourselves.'

She led the group out of the village along raised pathways on dykes protecting the land and the village from flooding. Crossing an area of sun-scorched fields in which nothing had grown this year, we arrived at an enclosed area bursting with tall ripe maize. Close up, we saw that the maize was inter-cropped with low growing squashes, *gombo* (ladies fingers) and beans. The dykes, water channels and fences were well maintained.

'Soon we shall be harvesting the maize. Later we shall be growing vegetables, peppers and tomatoes in the dry season,' said one of the women leaders.

Bineta Ba

**Bineta Ba** eagerly explained the history of the Kas-Kas women's group.

'In the old days, the story goes, Kas-Kas was divided into quarters. In each one there was a small garden in which women grew a few household extras — sorrel, groundnuts, herbs. After the 1973 drought, when most families were going hungry, onions, lettuces, vegetables were added. It was at that time that we heard about PIP, a group at Ndioum who were trying to help communities to survive the drought. It looked as if we were in for some bad years.

'The PIP staff encouraged us to cultivate garden plots on land outside the village in the dry season, that is after the main cereals had been harvested and before the hot season set in. We prepared a plot and learnt the techniques of market gardening. It was during this time that the Dutch aid project came to the village but they only wished to work with the men. They had money for an irrigated *périmêtre*, the water to be drawn from the river by motor pump. The men's group chose some land and went to work levelling and protecting it. But at this point the work stopped. Some of my sisters here reckon it was because many of the men were suspicious of the new project and of the extra work they would have to do.

'We had already had years of experience with gardens,' she continued. 'We decided we would like to take over the abandoned *périmêtre* and cultivate it. That was how it started, first with a 20 hectare plot for household consumption and then with larger and larger areas to grow crops for the market.

'We asked PIP to help us. We wanted training in how to manage a bigger effort than we were used to. We had to have a motor pump. There were costs to be met. We had to contribute 500,000 francs (£1,100) and PIP would give us a loan for the remaining balance of 300,000 francs. We would have to put money aside to pay it back over four years. We were able to agree together and begin work.

'First we planted maize and followed it with *gombo* and sorrel between the plots. As we went along we all became more confident and got good results. We felt we could do more. We persuaded our men to help lay out a new *périmêtre* and then another. We moved from crops for our families to crops to sell. Even with the distance to markets, we made money. We put some aside for other activities — a women's promotion centre, a health post.'

Firmly secured to the river bank was a large diesel motor pump with its heavy plastic pipes climbing up the bank into the enclosure. 'Who looks after the pump?' asked the Swiss delegate.

'We do,' answered one of the women. 'There's a team of women who manage and run the pump. She is our engineer,' she said, taking the hand of a bright-eyed young woman in a resplendent blue gown and pulling her forward. 'This is Djenaba Diallo and she is teaching others who would like to learn. And she,' pointing to another of her colleagues, 'is the leader of the team who have learnt to draw up new plans, decide which way the water should flow and that sort of thing, the topographers. We have colleagues who have learnt what we need to know about plants, their health, the costs of fertilisers and insecticides. We needed to ask the PIP for some help to start literacy classes to show us how to keep records of our finances.'

It was with the growth of literacy that the women were able to run what became a very professional operation. 'Now,' as Thierno Ba explained later at Ndioum, 'the group are able to run their affairs entirely on their own; our PIP staff only make friendly visits. The women enjoy a good discussion about technical matters from time to time. We ourselves are now learning from them how to manage irrigated *périmêtres* on different kinds of soil and we encourage other groups to arrange visits to Kas-Kas to catch some of the enthusiasm of good organisation without reliance on outsiders.'

'PIP sent us a *monitrice* for a time to set us on the right road with literacy work.' said Bineta Ba. 'Now we have a place to meet, to welcome visitors, to store our produce and equipment, to hold classes. Can you believe it? Some of the men want to join the courses. They regret saying no to the project when they did but they give us some help in doing the heavy digging and levelling of new plots.'

The women of Kas-Kas have money in their pockets. A growing number are learning to read and write in Pulaar, their mother tongue and can keep records, do accounts and write their own letters to absent menfolk and even to district officials.

'*Bamtaare?* It begins with us. It's our future. We are just beginning,' shouted our hosts as we left. Their example is being talked about enviously throughout the region: if they, why not us? Now women along the valley are becoming managers, literacy teachers, mechanics, village agronomists, *animatrices* of many activities, in other words leaders in their own development and that of their communities.

# CHAPTER SEVEN

# WORKERS ABROAD —
# Villagers at heart

*The vibrant image of his own country was there in his moments of doubt to prove to him the reality of a non-Western universe.*

**from *The Ambiguous Adventure* by Cheikh Hamidou Kane**

Moussa Ndiaye, a tubby man in his fifties, the local public letter writer, sat on a stool behind a little desk in front of a small kiosk in the market place of Matam, close to the post office. His father now 83, and almost blind, with nowhere else to go, sat cross-legged on the counter inside, wearing a loose white under-*boubou* like a local Mahatma Gandhi.

'I do on average some five letters a day. A good letter in my best longhand takes between two and three hours. The minimum cost is 25 francs but the customers are expected to give more. My best customers are the wives and mothers of migrant workers abroad — in France, Abidjan in the Ivory Coast, Congo Brazzaville where men work in the diamond fields, lots of places. The commonest letters are requests for help to meet day-to-day difficulties, making ends meet, but also for a sudden illness or burial. The peak time for such letters is during the wet season, when last year's harvest has been eaten and the next one is still growing. I can supply love poems and personalised sentiments and I am discreet.'

Moussa clearly enjoyed being asked by attractive young women to express their secret emotions to absent lovers. He wore a strong scent, his slim fingers were heavy with rings.

That was 25 years ago. There is no public letter writer in Matam today. Moussa retired to Dakar, a rich man. The phone and the fax have replaced his flowery formulas. It is less romantic but more efficient. The absent migrant workers are now highly organised in associations linked to the development and welfare of their villages and use modern technology to achieve their aims.

Young and able-bodied men have been leaving the Senegal River for several decades in search of work, first in Dakar and other Senegalese cities, and then abroad. At first the exodus was seasonal, during the dry season when work in the fields had ceased. Then the last 20 years of drought resulted in the speeding up of widespread desertification and forced almost all the young and active men from the valley to seek work elsewhere. As the migrants went further afield, they stayed away longer. Soon it ran into years. They sent money home for the family or to prepare for their eventual return. When they came home they were given certain social privileges, they brought home foreign currency and for two or three months they were the cock of the walk. Then suddenly the money had gone. They realised it had been largely wasted and they had to start all over again. They often found that the money sent to their families had not always gone to their loved ones but had been kept for the personal use of the patrician head of the family through whom it had been channelled. This led to family quarrels.

Then the migrants began to organise ways of making sure the money was better employed. They created new social organisations to help their families and the communities in which they lived. They became a motive force for the development of the valley. Without them many villages would have disappeared.

Throughout the Senegal River valley there are now hundreds of such associations. During the years of drought their contributions have taken the place of crops in the fields which the villagers have lost.

One such body is ADO, the Association for the Development of Ouressugui. I met its president, Elajh Dia, at his lodgings in Paris. He may have been a well-paid and renowned pastry-cook in his part of Paris but like all the migrants I had met over the years who intend to return to their native country he lived in puritanical simplicity, the bare furnishings of necessity. The migrant who intends to go back cannot allow himself to live like a westerner *and* maintain the steep payments he makes from his earnings to the village where his family remain and his dreams lie. One or other has to give.

Elajh may have lived in Paris for 18 years, but his quarters were still 'temporary' — an attic room in a nineteenth-century block close to the Gare St.Lazare. He half-jokingly called it a *studio*, the French euphemism for a cramped bed-sitter. It was late afternoon. He had worked all night, snatched a few brief

Elajh Dia

Christian Aid/Derrick Knight

hours until I called. He was a bear of a man in his late forties, at ease with himself, with a deep-pitched voice which one sensed could be either eloquently persuasive or sharply demanding. He was clearly used to dealing with strangers seeking information and using up his precious leisure moments. He was both patient and good-humoured about it.

The two of us filled most of the uncluttered space in the room. We sat on hard metal chairs, the only seats. His mattress was on the floor, his cooker was a two-ring Calor gas burner in a dark corner. The one luxury was the telephone, necessary to him as the doyen and spokesman of a network of migrant workers. With the phone he was better informed about events in Senegal than the international press. The France of the Nineties had become increasingly hostile to outsiders. He had to be on call.

I said I had first been in Ouressugui in 1968 as a guest of the CER — the Rural Expansion Centre, the then lynchpin of the government rural development programme. 'In fact,' Elajh chuckled, 'ADO has its offices where the old CER building stood. And,' he added, 'what's more we're doing their work for them.'

The new laws in France may have consolidated the rights of existing migrant workers and given them the benefits of minimum salary protection, but they had closed the door on an older system. In that system, migrants could effectively pass their work permit to another member of the family when they wished to go home for good. The family continued to benefit from the overseas income. 'Now that door has been shut,' said Elajh, 'I am one of the generation of Africans which has been sacrificed, but we don't want or expect to die here. We still feel the pull of the land. We are farmers at heart.

'I go home about once every two years. My wife, children, the eldest of whom is 12, remain in Ouressugui. I have been here long enough. It is time for me to return, but if I do so, the income I contribute will stop. The family cannot survive without it in the present economic climate over there. It is the same for hundreds of other migrant workers. So what do we do? One of the things we have to do is devise ways of making the village more able to support its young men and women of working age without them having to leave.'

I said I understood he had founded ADO.

'Yes. The Paris wing of ADO was founded in 1982. It was the dream of myself and a taxi-driver friend, Amedy Diawarra, also from Ouressugui. We had come to France, unschooled, understanding little. We worked hard and because of our jobs we learnt French quickly. Because our French was better than some of our colleagues, we were asked to help with their problems at work or with the authorities. In short, we got hooked into the legal and social problems that migrant workers have. Eventually it seemed better to organise properly.

'We had friends among a group of farmers near Limoges and others in the Drôme who were keen to help us organise, raise funds and visit the village. To cut a long story short, we now have 164 members in France, 537 in Dakar and 625 elsewhere in Africa. All contribute to the village projects fund. In France we also have a solidarity fund for emergencies among our group — illness, a funeral, that sort of thing. We are in touch with each other all the time.

'Almost all of us are sending money back to the family. So you can say that we divide our salaries four ways. Money for the solidarity fund; money for the family in Ouressugui; money for the village projects fund; and money we keep to live on.

'I am certain that the North wants the undeveloped countries to remain that way. We are squeezed in all directions. We cannot export our goods at a fair price. Rice imports into Senegal are subsidised so that Senegal farmers cannot sell their own at a decent price. The Mauritanian conflict in 1989 was a terrible blow to the communities in the river valley and still festers. There must have been some sort of international skulduggery going on because the French didn't then, and hasn't since, used diplomatic muscle to resolve the dispute as she has in other West African disputes in the past.

'Our people have given up expecting anything from the government. They are now resolved to run their own affairs. I will give you some examples. ADO has taken on the challenge of re-organising the local health service because the state has abandoned the rural communities. It is ironic, perhaps, that ADO has been helped by French and Belgium funding as well as the savings of ADO members.

'ADO has funded and built a new school at Ouressugui so that all its children have the chance of an education.

'Because the government has been closing post offices, which are vital to our families if they are to get their money orders when they need them, ADO has devised another way of getting funds quickly from its migrant worker members to their families back home. It involves a deposit and account number in Paris and Dakar, a local representative and the cost benefits of being able to make large collective orders. It uses the existing cereal bank and turns it into a reliable shop for essential food and other basic necessities.

'We have organised or taken part in local meetings about the so-called *Après-Barrage* scheme for the development of the Senegal River valley. So far it hasn't worked to our benefit. The population along the valley were not consulted before, during or after the building of the two big dams and the closing of the sluices which stopped the natural seasonal flood. The electricity which is supposed to be one of the benefits of the scheme to the farming community is indefinitely delayed because of the recent Mauritanian dispute. The main power lines were supposed to go downstream along the Senegalese bank and have branch lines into Mauritania but after 1989 Mauritania feared that these lines might be cut should another conflict start. They have now insisted on a parallel line from Manantali through Mali and along the north bank, a scheme both expensive and impractical. I doubt we shall ever have cheap electricity in the valley itself. It will all go to the cities.

'There has been a complete breakdown of government agricultural services. Their ideas for big rice-growing *périmêtres* have proved more of a burden to the villagers than a way of securing a decent livelihood. Take the *périmêtres* being built at Podor. They have stripped the area of trees and bushes. It is entirely open — an invitation for the Harmattan winds to slice across and make agriculture impossible for much of the dry season. The running costs are enormous. In contrast, our members in Ouressugui have made a practical small-scale irrigated *périmêtre* 10 kilometres from the river, fed by a borewell 80 metres deep with its own motor pump. The scale is more appropriate.

'There is still no secure market for any surplus that the villagers produce. When you go to Senegal you will hear about last year's tomato crop which was exceptionally good but could neither be sold because the market was saturated with cheap imports from Morocco nor converted on the spot into paste or sauce because villagers did not have the technical skills.

'ADO has expanded beyond Ouressugui. Every village in the middle valley has its association of migrants working overseas who send money back — 400 of them, all told. It would be a disaster if they didn't — the drought years caused much hardship and loss for their own families, and the income from overseas prevented the worst effects of the drought. Each association is a lifeline for its village of origin. What our communities fear most is the invasion of agribusinesses, with lots of money who will take our traditional lands.'

Elajh works long hours. He has short rest hours and his members are very demanding of his time. The president of a prominent migrant association, like ADO, is in demand for all kinds of reunions and public meetings. I asked his blessing on my proposed visit to Ouressugui and hoped to see him again.

'Thierno Ba at Ndioum is a highly respected brother of ours,' he said. 'Put yourself in his hands and he will arrange for you to meet our people when you are there.'

Thierno Ba, speaking to me weeks later under the palaver tree in the PIP project centre, didn't disagree with what Elajh Dia told me. 'But I am not a leader of ADO and don't speak as such,' he emphasised. 'I was one of the founder members of ADO in France because I was studying there at the time. I have never wished to be on its council. I have never been an official of ADO either in France, or Dakar or in Ouressugui. I have always preferred to be an active but independent member and I believe that is what has given me the chance of being heard. I have my own vision and my own beliefs about what should happen in my own village and I can say things without risk of being disciplined. I bring to any discussion my experience of development and I am deeply committed to my home and to its active development.'

'How important is the impact of the migrant workers contribution in the Senegal River valley at the present time?' I asked.

'It is less important up here in the district of Podor than it is around Matam and down towards Bakel. In the Matam and Bakel districts I did some research which showed that almost 80% of the money families had to spend came from abroad. What this means is that if the families of migrant workers do not get their expected money order at the end of the month they face grave difficulties.

'Take the example of the small irrigated village *périmêtres*. There have been many debates about their unprofitability, but what one has to take into account is that they are underwritten by migrant workers abroad. It is they who pay for the planning and laying out of the area, for the fertilisers, insecticides and other running expenses. It is worth asking oneself whether, if the migrants had not continued to subsidise the running of the *périmêtres*, the families could have fed themselves through difficult years. So many of the traditional farming activities, those of the rainy season, those of the traditional flooding of the alluvial plains, the freshwater fishing, have failed in recent years, that the cash contribution of the migrant workers has become vital to the community.

'It is not only a question of what kind of work is going to be available to those who return from years of working abroad, but of finding work to occupy those who have remained in the villages. That is why all the development projects supported by ADO and other associations of migrants in other villages are so important. What projects? Literacy classes for women and young people, cereal banks, agricultural projects. ADO is experimenting with ways of growing crops midway between a fully irrigated system and the traditional crop cycle linked to the annual flood. The idea is to develop a suitable piece of land of some 30 hectares in which to invest heavily — a deep borewell with a good pump, for instance — where it will be possible to grow wet season crops and if the rains fail at a critical time to pump water from the borewell for immediate irrigation. The borewell will only be used when the lack of rain is going to cause damage to the crops. This will save water, diesel fuel and be cheaper to run than a full-scale irrigated *périmètre* which demands water all the time.

'The migrants are gradually changing village life and customs, both for good and for ill. They may initiate important local works and projects for the collective benefit of the village but at the same time they are concealing the way they are having to live abroad. They say nothing about the economies they are forced to make and the difficulties of living decently abroad. So when they come home on leave with a few savings, they are forced into all kinds of extravagances. Before their time is up, they will have nothing left and may even have difficulty in travelling from their village to Dakar. Luckily for them they will have to have bought a return ticket, otherwise all would be lost.

'Migrants seldom think rationally about the life they lead abroad. They thankfully leave Senegal behind with its problems and its minimum of comfort and amenities and they believe that they have stepped into a world of luxury. Little by little they realise that the new life is not so easy. They may be packed into communal hostels where men sleep for four hours and have to give their bed to another. There is no comfort. I have witnessed my countrymen living in terrible conditions and when they come home they do not explain these things to their young relatives who continue to live for the day when they, too, can get away and live the high life. When they do, it's a brutal shock.

'I have often said to my European colleagues that if their compatriots were not so impatient, there would be no more migration. They tell me that is not possible, that barriers or no barriers, people will still get into Europe.

'France introduced the *carte de séjour* [temporary residence permit] in 1974. What happened before that? A fellow went to work in France with a work permit. After a time, years perhaps, he wanted to go home and gave his work permit to a young brother or other close relative. It was quite acceptable. Some family cards passed from father to son over several generations. That's how it worked. But as soon as the residence permit came in, it put the holder under pressure to seek to bring his wife and family to join him and have other children in France who would have citizenship rights and form in their turn a second generation. The village has lost people it needs to be able to grow; the French have made it more likely that existing migrants will not feel able to go back but bring over their nearest and dearest instead. It is no solution to the problem. There has to be a better, more honest, answer and the associations of migrant workers in France are in a strong position to negotiate with the authorities there.

'There are also differences and difficulties when the migrants try and control what goes on in the village. When they left they lost some of the power they might have had over those who remained. At the time they may not have had any political anxieties, but there were others who remained in the village, elders perhaps, who promoted their own particular interests. Eventually there came a time when there were misunderstandings.

'At Ouressugui, there was a moment when the village was due to be given a new status as a rural council. The old political leaders argued that as they had been campaigning for 25 years, it was up to them to nominate the leaders of this new council. The members of ADO said that as it was a dynamic new community, it would be both right and proper for everyone — the young, the old, the migrants, their families who remained, everybody together — to take charge of the new situation.

'Well at first it was the old political guard which campaigned for "*Sopi*", the ruling party slogan meaning "change", but they soon realised that they would get nowhere without the support of the young generation. The young generation also began to understand that they could make no progress without an accommodation with the old guard. Now that the electoral system has been altered in Senegal to allow Senegalese migrant workers to vote, I think positive changes will start to happen more quickly. I think the government of the day will take more notice of them and the amount of currency that they are contributing to the national economy.

'ADO has opportunities that other villages may not have. It certainly isn't the overseas groups who dictate to the village what they should do. The migrant workers went away leaving a bad situation and they are trying to put it right. I have always said about ADO that it has three main pillars. There is the social pillar — the village which is at the receiving end, which knows its own way of life, its own organisations, its values. There is the administrative pillar which is at Dakar, where the leadership deal with all problems of administration, negotiating with government departments, banking matters, communications between groups in different countries. It is they who meet returnees, those travelling outwards from the village and see them through the formalities. They also look after visitors from France, partners, the media and take them to the village if required. There is also the economic pillar. That mainly consists of those who are abroad. There are sections in Paris, Gabon and wherever there are more than two migrant workers to form a local cell. They all make regular payments.

'However, one should not go away thinking that it's the money which carries the most weight in making policy. The hub of it all is the home village, because everything and everybody goes there. I believe that ADO should be working towards a point where its programmes can become productive and self-financing. It should be working towards a time when it can manage its own social problems without relying on outside funding. In five or six years, it should have reached a position where it has real independence in economic, social and cultural matters. That is the dynamic of ADO and I think it is well within the bounds of possibility.'

Very early on a September morning one or two days later, I drove the 350 kilometres empty tarmac road upstream to Ouressugui and Matam to visit what Thierno called the 'social pillar' of ADO, the members of the village community.

There was a serious drought in the north of the country around Ndioum and Podor. Most villagers had been unable to plant their traditional cereal crops. They were tightening their belts and hoping to salvage something from their plots in irrigated village *périmêtres* or market garden plots in the coming months. It was going to be a long dry year until the first rains in May.

Most of this once lush countryside was now a devastated landscape of withered thorn bushes and vast stretches of land turning into permanent desert. Further south, there had been some rain. Close to our destination, there were shallow ponds and grass. A scattering of cattle and sheep fed energetically and splashed in

Christian Aid/Derrick Knight

**'A devastated landscape of withered thornbushes and dead trees....'**

the shallow water, sharing it with small naked children. To our left where the river lay, pale silver streaks under an early dust haze were evidence of some flooding. Here and there a solitary peasant woman toiled with her *daba* on a plot where she would replant some seed in the hope of saving something from the bad season.

The years of drought quickened the exodus from the valley of the young and active to find work elsewhere. This had effects on the way of life in the river valley which were both positive and negative. Negatively the loss of labour reduced the extent of farming activity; positively, their contributions to the family income from their salaries abroad enabled those families to subsist and often to prosper.

As we approached the village of Agnam we appeared to cross a boundary line between a traditional Africa and a new Africa of modern housing in brick and wrought iron, many with domestic solar power plants and TV aerials on the roof. This was the direct result of migrant worker income on the community. From Agnam, through Thilogne, Boki Diave, Nabatji to Ouressugui, the same signs of good fortune were apparent.

It was 10 years since I had been in Ouressugui and 25 since I had first visited it for the UN. It used to be no more than a crossroads of two all weather gravel roads — one along the *djeri* from St Louis on the coast to Kidira, on the Malian frontier, the other from Dakar to Matam across the flat central plain. The local colonial HQ had been at Matam on the river's edge, reached by a high causeway. At Ouressugui there were a few local government offices, an old colonial army barracks, a filling station and a vigorous street market. Off the road was a scattered huddle of village housing. But Ouressugui was already chosen for greater things. The two main roads would one day be tarmac and important commercial arteries, while the old centre was almost an island. It led nowhere and it had no space in which to grow.

Already in 1981 when I returned, Ouressugui was expanding fast while Matam remained dormant. The market had grown. Substantial shops and local trades had developed. The main road from St Louis was a wide tarmac highway. The bus station was a riot. In 1992 it was once again barely recognisable. Its public face featured a two-storey hotel, an endless street market, a scatter of motor mechanics and second-hand tyre dealers, a rowdy bus and *taxi-brousse* junction, scores of solidly built open shops. There were still huddles of mud brick houses but beyond were districts of new, even elegant cement and brick houses and gardens, presumably built with migrant earnings. The population had risen from some 6,000 in 1960 to over 14,000 now. It was a human hive, a boom village metamorphosing into a boom town.

In the newly built offices of ADO in an ample compound, one of the local coordinators of ADO projects, Mamadou Diga Seck, sketched an outline of recent successes.

'ADO here has many projects. We have a collectively run field of some 35 hectares. We have a flour grinding mill which is managed by a committee of 15 women. We have a collectively run vegetable garden of two hectares in the *djeri*, for the dry season. We have a social centre which is managed by a rural *monitrice*. We also have offices and meeting rooms to run and care for. We have our own cereal bank.

'Each of these ongoing activities run by ADO has its own leader and supporting committee elected by the people involved. My job is to watch over the work of those project leaders to see that everything runs smoothly. We may not have enough money to do everything we want but we have the muscle and the will to work.

'We have just built a large new school. The state refused to provide funds to build one so our members decided for their children's sake that ADO should do it. We prepared a plan and a budget with our brother members working in France. They and other friendly organisations there found the money. Now the Ministry of Education has promised to assign three teachers to us at the beginning of this school year. Everything is ready for them and we expect to be open in a couple of months.

'We in ADO have one cause, the fight against the exodus. We aim to halt the drain of emigration, to find rewarding work locally for our sons born here. This is why we are concerned about the employment strategies of the government. While it is true that migrant workers abroad are better paid, it does not satisfy them at a deeper level. It is better to remain in one's homeland.

'In Europe there are storms coming for foreigners. There will be fewer trade openings. Every one of our migrant workers either in Europe or in another part of the world is thinking about returning. One of the reasons for this is the way the *Après-Barrage* strategies are developing. I am convinced that it is necessary to organise the proposed changes in steps and to prepare each step carefully.

'One source of conflict is the splitting up of land among three competing groups. There are the inherited rights of the local population. Secondly there are the agribusinesses seeking land. Thirdly, there are all the other outsiders who want to settle here to exploit the land. My worry is for the small farmer who has a field of less than a hectare and finds himself unable even to afford the expenses of cultivating it. Won't it be natural for him to think of selling it to an agribusiness with lots of money to spend and who will eagerly mop up such plots and exploit them commercially? This will leave the farmer without the land which he inherited from his ancestors and his life will lose all its meaning.

'There is no problem if the local population is well educated and well trained. Our people must be well prepared. They must have proper access to the benefits of the dams.

'But to return to ADO, we need to fight unemployment and to create good jobs for our young adults. We have had several successes. In the building trade, for instance. When we decided to build a cereal bank, a group of our young men had the foresight to learn how to make compressed bricks out of clay and cement. Now we have a team of specialists in this method of construction who often get commissions from other agencies. This is very important because now these young men have a proper training and can earn a good living.

'There's the mill. It is managed by a committee of 15 women. At the end of the month these 15 women share a sum equal to 10% of the receipts. With that they can buy their own soap and have a good feeling about working together. At present they employ a miller who is also the maintenance man. He gets 20% of the take each month. When we train someone to do a job, we try and find him or her a modest salary each month so that they can stay in the village without hardship.'

I asked about the finances of ADO. How are the contributions from overseas managed? Mamadou Seck, a trained accountant, was in his element.

'First of all I have to say that it is very well managed. It is very difficult to withdraw funds from ADO's account without cast iron reasons. The treasurer is elected and he is at present an old stager who knows his job thoroughly. He has worked as a civil servant and he has all the right qualifications.

'It also helps that he knows all about the legalities and formal regulations concerning village development associations in the Senegal River valley because he has been a development worker in the region. Yes, our finances are well and tightly managed.

'Each year a full set of accounts is prepared and explained to the local community as well as to our kindred groups in Paris and Dakar. This has meant that more and more members join because they can use our financial facilities with an easy mind. They appreciate the open and honest dealing which we insist upon.

'You see, when someone contributes, he wants to know how his money is going to be used. Every two months we call a general meeting to tell the community in Ouressugui how much is in the kitty, what projects are being financed and what is lacking. This has also led to an increase in membership and commitment. Only last week we organised a street cleaning campaign by members. We also planted trees all round our centre. There's a lot of goodwill, especially among the young at the present time.

'I haven't talked about the financing of major projects. There is a continual follow-up of existing projects. We are now launched on a major literacy campaign....'

I remarked to Mamadou that overseas worker groups in the

past had to take steps to see that the money they wanted to send to Ouressugui got through to the people to whom it was intended. The post office was often unreliable.

'In the past the migrants did have problems,' he replied. 'The families of the migrants who remain at home were often kept waiting for the monthly payment in order to buy food. For example a worker in France, or the Ivory Coast or Dakar, might send a monthly remittance of 50,000 francs in good time which was then deliberately held up at the post office. A member of the family received the *mandat* — the money order which should be immediately cashable at the post office. They went to the post office and were told that there was no money for withdrawals at the moment. It was very tough for people in desperate need of the money with which to buy food. You go today, you go tomorrow, you go the next day, still no money! You were even using money that you hadn't got to travel to and from the post office, which is 10 kilometres away in Matam. It was very hard when the family in the village was dependent on that monthly money order in order to eat.

'As a result, ADO's Paris members took the initiative of adding a further service to the village cereal bank which was already supplying basic foodstuffs. Instead of sending money through the post, they organised a simple and foolproof system. Once an amount of money was deposited by a member in the ADO account in Paris, the local treasurer could write, telephone or fax Dakar to instruct the village cereal bank that so-and-so had transferred 50,000 francs to be used by his family to buy food. Our Dakar office rang Ouressugui to say, please supply immediately to such and such a family, two sacks of millet, two sacks of onions, and so on up to the sum of money agreed. It has proved to be very effective. With one telephone call, the manager on the spot is able to supply the family at once, avoiding any official bottlenecks caused by government penury.

'We turned the cereal bank into an ADO shop. The new system has given it a fresh lease of life. You see a cereal bank run by an association like ours cannot give credit to its customers, but shopkeepers and merchants in the village can choose to do so. In the past customers hesitated to buy cereals from the ADO bank for fear of alienating their favourite merchant who gave them credit when their money orders didn't come through. As a result the cereal bank stock went stale, termites got at it, there was waste, there were losses. Now all that has changed. We have become specialists at stocking grain and because we are able to act swiftly for our members, the turnover has increased. Now we are discussing working together with neighbouring villages.

'It seems that ADO is carrying out duties which ought perhaps to be performed by the state,' I commented. 'You said it,' he replied tartly. 'Let me tell you about the hospital of Ouressugui. The hospital is in principle open to all Senegalese citizens but it is meant particularly for those of us who live along the river valley. It is a long way, over 1,000 kilometres, to evacuate a sick patient to Dakar especially without proper transport. So it was in 1988 or early 1989 that we started campaigning for better surgical facilities.

'All round Ouressugui are small villages where the maternity care is not very skilled. If there are problems at birth, it becomes necessary to bring the woman here on a cart. So we campaigned for an ambulance, a better equipped operating theatre and experienced staff. ADO made a substantial contribution to these improvements. The hospital is virtually a regional one now. It works very well. Almost every sort of treatment which once needed the facilities of Dakar can now be handled locally.

'If the hospital cannot provide the right drugs then they can be bought with the help of ADO or the French *coopération* overseas aid budget. To guarantee the availability of proper medicines, we built and now run a well stocked village pharmacy. We keep the costs as low as possible.'

While we waited for the two women leaders to arrive we went out to look at the new school building financed by ADO members. It was simply and well built within a generous area of space for a playground and vegetable garden. The problem of keeping the interiors cool in the invariably hot weather had been solved cleverly by using false bamboo ceilings.

When we got back to the ADO offices, the young women leaders had arrived. Both of them were beautifully dressed, as is the custom. They were glad to talk. Monsieur Seck, who spoke a precise but rather dry French, translated their Pulaar. It is rare to get the chance to speak to women in village communities without a coterie of minders. Many men still see themselves as the only true mirror of local opinion, custom and behaviour. It was good to see another large crack appearing in that mirror.

I asked both to give me a summary of their daily routines and responsibilities within ADO. The first to reply was Madame Fatou Keliba.

'I have a very busy day. As soon as I get up, I sweep my room, clean my pots and pans and go and fetch water and fill my *canaris* [pottery jars]. I then grind millet to use later and go to the market to see what I can buy for the midday meal. I return home and begin cooking. I serve the midday meal and later I start cooking again for the evening meal.

'In my family it is the head of the family who keeps the housekeeping money and hands out what he thinks is necessary to do the shopping each day. My husband is here at the moment. I grow groundnuts on a plot owned by the head of the family. They are for eating at home because I cannot grow enough to sell.

'When ADO was first launched in Ouressugui, the migrant workers from France who were on leave invited me and others to a meeting to explain why it was important to have such an association. We understood that it was important to do something to develop our lands and improve our way of life. So we took up the challenge. At first there were only a few of us. People didn't understand. But when they saw what it meant in concrete terms, everyone joined in. Without *bamtaare* nothing can progress. This is why so many women have come together to work to satisfy their needs. The women are so numerous, they cannot be counted. They take part in the management committees. They have no problems with the men.

'We have a mill which we manage, and we have a collective garden near the *djeri*, run for and managed by all women belonging to ADO. We have a sewing workshop. There are 75 women learning to sew. They work in the centre on different days. Some will be coming later today, some tomorrow. We are overcrowded. Many are learning to read and write the Pulaar language.

'Before we had the mill we were all very tired. First thing in the morning it was necessary to grind the millet by hand. It was hard work. Now you take your millet along early and it's done very quickly. The mill has removed a heavy and daily burden of work.

'Before, we had no practical expertise in any craft. Since the centre opened we have learned how to sew and the clothes we make we sell to local women at cheaper prices than those on the stalls in the market. What is sold on the stalls for 200 francs, we sell for 100. We specialise in dresses for small children. The money we make remains our own. It's nobody else's business.

'The vegetable garden is cultivated in the dry season when the rains have finished and the main cereal harvest is in. We grow various vegetables and sell them locally. We have one or two tanks which can be filled directly by a pipe from the well. We fill watering cans from the tanks to water our plots.

'We cooperate with the hospital. The hospital agreed some time ago to employ a nurse who would be responsible for all primary health care but he has not yet come. So at the basic level of health education there is a huge gap. There used to be a woman health worker who looked after the matter but she was seconded to Matam. We are waiting for the new arrival so that our training can continue. We have complained loudly and bitterly everywhere we could. We are very frustrated and angry about it. Our campaign has been widespread, both nationally and internationally.

'We had various general meetings of women so that they could discuss and draw up their demands for adequate health care and protection. We believe that our appeal was heard in the right government quarters but nothing has come of it so far.'

Madame Ramata Cy was in charge of the sewing classes in the women's social centre built by ADO and we talked about their popularity among local women.

'The women come at three o'clock in the afternoon. I show them a sample of a piece of sewing and show them how to do it. They stay till five. We only sew clothes for small boys and girls.

'At first there was an instructress from the PIP who was posted here. I was her pupil and I was able to take over from her. It's thanks to PIP that we have been able to do this training here.

'ADO pays for the cloth, the thread and the sewing machines. Whatever is made in the classroom during the classes is sold and the money goes into the ADO income. When a woman has learnt enough she can make dresses at home and sell them.

'Sometimes we put on a show during one of the big public holidays to show what we can do. It works very well because other villages in the region come here to look and to buy also.'

I wondered whether the dams and irrigation schemes would affect them. The two women went into a huddle over this question and began a lively discussion among themselves. The answer I got was a kind of consensus.

'It is indeed very important. We are very concerned about the new sicknesses which may result from the water. We took part in a seminar on the subject a short time back. It could be a good thing for us all, but it depends on the water flow and the costs involved. With a regular water flow there will be new possibilities for irrigation but we shall have to watch out for the spread of water-borne diseases, bilharzia, malaria. We have not yet organised any formal scheme ourselves. We are in the *djeri* here and most of the irrigation schemes are in the *waalo*. At Nguidjilone they are doing it.'

'Is Ouressugui an expensive place to buy food?' I asked finally.

'Everything is very dear. Every time one goes shopping, it seems, prices have gone up. It's because of the economic crisis. It affects everybody.

While the midday meal was being prepared at Mr Seck's house there was time to make a rapid visit to Matam, the old river port 10 kilometres away. I had also made this trip some 25 years ago. Matam was linked to Ouressugui by a high but narrow causeway. Then as now the low-lying fields on either side were a seasonal shallow lake dotted with occasional trees. The driver, given the chance of a straight and empty road, put his foot down. He gave no thought to what might happen if he slid or hit a pothole on the unfenced embankment. If it wasn't our destiny to be pulverised, God would protect us, he reassured me. That's what he had been taught.

Then as now, the centre of the town was dilapidated and dirty. The old market was exactly as I remembered it, a squish squash of tiny stalls and shelters close to the ferry ramp to catch the trade to and from the Mauritanian side of the river. But there had been no trade with the far bank since the 1989 conflict. Business was slack. At the top of the disused ferry slipway, the town's people had piled up their rubbish. One of my companions said, 'Watch where you are putting your feet, people use this spot as a latrine at night' — these exact words had been said to me by my local host in 1969. At that time the *pirogues* of the singing fishermen dotted the broad stream. They sang the praises of the river gods. They cast a net like a giant lasso and seldom failed to land a catch. The river supplied the whole valley community with fish. Today there is nothing and nobody on the water. The drought years scorched the ponds and inlets where the fish bred, the dams may have completed the damage. The river gods were powerless.

# PART THREE

# BAMTAARE —
# The Popular Alternative

# CHAPTER EIGHT

# THE WORLD OF HACCHIM

*We the under-developed....*

**from *The Ambiguous Adventure* by Cheikh Hamidou Kane**

I must have met and talked to hundreds, perhaps thousands of men and women struggling to achieve a better life for themselves and for others but only a few remain firmly in the mind as rounded personalities, fewer still as visionaries. These few, though, have a dream of something different to what is set down by experts in distant cities and universities. This dream is rooted in their own personal involvement and hands-on experience in the field. Hacchim Ndiaye is one of them; a state-trained nurse in a remote village on the frontier of Senegal and Mauritania who has fought all his life against backwardness and fatalism in rural communities; a modest man who has given himself fully to the cause of teaching, coaxing, demonstrating, persuading the young, the women, the leaders in such places that they themselves can be the instruments of improving their lives and controlling their own destinies.

How I discovered Hacchim, and came under the influence of his optimistic but realistic agenda for rural development of the poor by the poor, is a necessary prelude to my recent conversation with him. He has moved on since 1968, but remains a teacher, an innovator and an optimist with his feet firmly planted on the ground.

When I was searching in 1968 for a peg on which to hang a film about how villagers in a developing African country understood

David MacDonald

**Nguidjilone — Hacchim's first village posting**

and responded to the mechanisms which controlled their lives, somebody recommended the novel by the Senegalese novelist Cheikh Hamidou Kane, *The Ambiguous Adventure*. It proved to be a revelation and sure guide. The setting was a village far up the River Senegal. The time was the recent colonial past. The characters were members of a proud clan run on traditional lines. The drama was a last stand of the old society, with its customs and values fine-tuned to survival and continuity by adhering to time-honoured laws. The enemy was French colonialism, representing modern agnosticism and science. I still remember the effect of a first reading, personally living through the agony of the family which had to make a painful decision about the education of Samba Diallo, a potentially brilliant scholar and future clan leader. Whether to keep him at home under the spiritual guidance of a wise but reactionary holy man, the village *marabout*, or to send him to the French school where he would learn the mysteries of western knowledge and power. Having discovered the source of those mysteries, the clan chief and head of the family believed, Samba would return with the knowledge and power to confront and repulse the threat of modernism to his people. The risk was that, far from his native land and family ties, he would forget his roots and lose his faith.

I remember being convinced that the book spoke an essential truth. It also seemed at the time to be a beacon beckoning me up river. It was reinforced by another small but influential book available at the time by Annie Lauran — *Un Noir a Quitté le Fleuve* (A Black has Left the River Valley) — about a group of young Senegalese migrants who had left a village far up the river Senegal near Bakel to become a new kind of slave at the bottom of the labour market in Paris. In the preface, the distinguished writer Albert Memmi quoted Georges Gurvitch, one of the fathers of sociology: 'There is often more sociology in an honest description than in hundreds of specialist publications.' Memmi went on to comment that Madame Lauran had chosen to open up a corner of human reality to the reader by beginning from the inside and telling the story in the way the Africans do themselves. It found an echo in what we were trying to do in film.

By the time I was on a plane to Senegal, I was sure that our village would be found in the old kingdom of the Toucouleurs somewhere between Podor and Bakel. Because the author of *The Ambiguous Adventure* had come from Matam, which was now a government administrative centre, that seemed to be a good starting place.

In a hectic round of preliminary official meetings at the UN offices and in *Le Building,* the modern skyscraper close to the presidential palace which housed most of the technical ministries, we pinpointed a very traditional rural community upstream where a team of rural extension workers were active with women, youth groups and farmers to try and stimulate local activities and provide training which would eventually improve their environment and their standard of living. I was left with the task of visiting a string of villages from which to make a choice for filming.

The following paragraphs are taken from a notebook I kept during 1968 and 1969 and are included because, though they may seem naive alongside more mature views held 25 years later, they give a flavour of the river *milieu* before the great drought of 1973 destroyed so much of it. They also show the existence of early attempts at grass-roots development work by local people long before the theme was 'discovered' by western aid agencies.

An early morning in October 1969 — a grey day at Dakar airport. Take-off 7 am. An old DC3 flying the twice-a-week domestic service to Matam, a small eastern frontier town. A hard, young French pilot and an amused Lebanese co-pilot. On board, a white UNDP expert with black counterpart, a Frenchwoman with two young children rejoining her husband on some tour of duty, six sophisticated, suited young Senegalese men, the rest — old couples, bejewelled women returning home from visits, shopping, medical care, trading in the capital, an African bourgeoisie.

The plane flies low. The morning slips away. A series of bus stops. St Louis and then Richard Toll. The river Senegal overflowing, wandering, slow moving, many branched river; never wide — a soup of sediment. Scarcely a boat. Once a *pirogue* (canoe), one small steamer — *The African Queen?* Great areas of drowned flat fields. Little sign of agricultural activity except at Richard Toll, a factory town surrounded by paddy fields and sugar cane.

At Podor, a small river port, the rain settles in. At each stop people get off, never on. Suitcases and bulky parcels disappear. Scraps of conversation. 'Have you got my vaccine?' 'What worries me is that you have not got my mechanic with you.' 'Perhaps next time.' 'I'll make do somehow'. A big-bellied merchant receives three crates of imported French apples and potatoes. Do they really allow such luxury imports?

We scud through low rain-cloud, glimpsing vast areas of woodland and bush with glinting water-holes. Matam, or at least Ouressogui, is a couple of pill boxes with a windsock next to a hard-packed laterite landing strip. As we dip, there is the river again, wider and deeper here. Beyond it Mauritania, brown, rocky, a range of hills, another country.

No sign of anyone official. Rain bucketing down. A few small boys straggle out of adjoining fields. This is it — I thought, the end of the line. How do I get back to Soho? No plane till next Tuesday. 'All out and let's get a move on,' snaps the pilot. Just then, arrival of official car. Welcome by the prefect. Door held by chauffeur.

Instant VIP status.

Fetched at five to attend on the prefect. I remind myself that I am wearing a UN hat. Cabinet meeting at his house, the former French colonial HQ of the *Commandant de Cercle*. Now stripped of all its interior clutter. No sign of family. Where are they? I take to the man — sense of humour, revelling in the power of being a bureaucrat who is respected and obeyed, but how criticise it? He has assembled members of his staff from agriculture, water and forests, livestock, transport, that he thinks might have ideas. Those who will be my guides are present. One is Amiel Agne, a local man in his early thirties with a stern horse's face and half glasses. The Prefect reads aloud the official letters from the Ministry of Rural Development and from the UN, inviting his fullest collaboration. Tickled pink at being asked. He has a short wave radio link with the Governor's office at Bakel upstream. He uses it — to show off?

The prefect lectures on all the centres, echelons, groups, cadres, the whole run down of the administration. I get a feeling of almost complete disassociation between what I'm hearing and the warmth and eagerness to help of the people he has convened. We make a plan for the visit.

Next day. Dawn is clear and promises sunshine. From the roof there is a view across some low houses to the shimmering river and a hazy flat landscape which is Mauritania. Cattle are lowing over there beyond a screen of bush. Sound carries miles. Matam on a riverside bluff above the flood, shaded by old trees. A chain ferry big enough for lorries links the two countries.

Remind myself of my mission which starts in earnest today: to find a typical traditional village whose people are being encouraged to experiment with new ways to organise, to keep healthy, to grow better crops, to face up to the challenge of the modern world. The word used by the experts is 'development'. Must mean as much as Blackpool illuminations out here. Scared stiff of not recognising what I am looking for when I see it. A white man in a distant region like this is seen as a sort of Father Christmas. Unless he is the bearer of gifts, why is he here? Why is he asking these personal questions?

Talked to the prefect's radio operator while waiting for transport to arrive. He complains about the weight of obligation on men in extended Toucouleur families.

'If you are a civil servant, everyone expects to be kept. I have four married brothers on my back. I have the normal family obligations. The young go away and rebel against the family when they return home. I have a son at the naval college at Brest in France who crosses swords with me on almost everything. It's very difficult. I secretly agree with all of it but I'm trapped in a traditional way of life from which I cannot escape.'

Using the prefect's land-rover we go south on rough bush tracks to Ogo. At Ogo is a training centre and demonstration farm, built and equipped by various UN agencies to enable modern agricultural techniques to be taught. This is where village volunteer 'animators' come for short courses. The pasture is luxurious, the buildings are in good repair but almost every piece of equipment seems to have been cannibalised, ploughs, tractors, land-rovers, lorries. As a result, nothing works.

On to Kanel, which is said to have planned a training scheme for villagers in market gardening in January (right time for filming). Rain overnight. The bush is flat and lush green with plenty of copses and woodlands. Progress slow. Stuck in a flash stream and had to push the land-rover out. Herons by the score.

Kanel. A large village. The *chef d'arrondissement*, a kind of government mouthpiece, welcomes us. More palavers. Kanel is the hub of a group of 60 villages; 19 of them have male village animators, but no women yet. The traditionalists are resisting change. They are fearful of what disturbance it might bring. Tour of village. All the men shake hands and would engage in the full country greeting if not firmly interrupted by my guide. Women are ignored. Yet we are surrounded by them. The young ones very pretty and stunningly dressed. Elaborate gold ear rings and heavy silver bracelets much in evidence.

The clinic (step higher than a health post) is almost without equipment and medicines but there is a lively young assistant. Malaria is a common illness, especially during the wet season. Waterborne diseases — bilharzia, worms, open festering cuts, eye problems. Only one dead child at birth in six months. A local woman is trained as a midwife and paid by the family.

The market is set out on the bare ground. The sellers crouch. Millet, fresh and dried fish, various herbs, dried goods, flour, rice, tea, soap. Reasonably clean. Animals forbidden.

A grand old man, a former municipal councillor from Thiès and Bakel, is brought out to greet me. We sit in his compound. The local family consists of some 60 people, all his responsibility. He speaks for all of them. Despite what he says about the 'good' old days when the old people made the decisions and the young carried them out, it still seems a very live issue today. 'We are trying to change but...', said the chief.

We meet the man locally responsible for water and forests. He has organised the planting of acacias and limes in the village to give shade and improve health. Kanel has a fine scattering of old trees along the streets giving good shade under which the old men — the 'notables'— sit and palaver. Seem to be a lot of retired old boys. Kanel not what I am looking for. Too conformist.

Sunday morning. Depart in a northerly direction. The track is worse than yesterday. The country is different. More open. A view across a gentle slope towards the swollen river. Crop looks good to inexperienced eye. My guide agrees but says crickets and grain-eating birds could still spoil the harvest. Families live in their fields as grain ripens and patrol ceaselessly with catapults and whistles.

Thilogne — a village of 3,000. The chief a handsome close-cropped 50-year-old accompanied by a young, bright-eyed health worker, a teacher and an agricultural adviser. The latter pair very much on their high horses. Palaver first, then a tour. The market under corrugated roof, smaller and dirtier than Kanel. Animals free to roam, goods laid on ground except the meat. Some tiny stall shops. Very little stock or range of goods. Not impressed.

Stop in Boki Diave on return trip. The chief is the president of the newly formed cooperative. He is a young and rather quick to jump on anyone cutting across his authority. He sends for the two village animators who had been chosen by village assembly to be sent for a short training course in how to stimulate, encourage, organise changes that villagers themselves could make to improve their lives. Listened carefully and was eager to meet whoever came forward.

Had heard about this ambitious scheme from Ben Mady Cisse, an impressive young planner in the Senegalese government who was responsible for an attempt to 'liberate' the deeply traditional rural communities. The plan was to create a network of local *Centres d'Animation Rurale* (CARs) staffed by professional trainers in rural skills who were to work with village volunteers or 'animators' — human catalysts who would encourage others to join them in forming cells of 'development'. Big question. What did that 'development' mean to the ministers in Dakar and the UN technocrats serving them? And what did it mean to the villagers? Was it about getting the villagers on to some national track or was it a genuine attempt to trigger off the growth of a grass-roots movement of self-help, even if watered by tactfully offered training and information. How quickly the words used change their meanings, depending on who speaks them!

Back in Matam. Short discussion. No likely village yet but the target clearer now. It is likely to be a riverside village. The prefect says, 'But my dear monsieur, the riverside roads are under water. You must take my *vedette*' — his launch.

Monday. The prefect's launch, 20 foot, half-decked, diesel engine, needs an overhaul and coat of fresh paint. Who cares? Clear blue sky, a full slow-moving river. Various extras on board — a cousin of some official, her baby, a couple of young men hitchhiking back to their village, the boatman and a mechanic to care for the oil-spewing, overheating engine. We are also delivering the post — packages of letters for different villages otherwise held up for weeks until the water recedes.

Travel downstream. Progress slow but romantic. Women and young girls washing clothes and bathing at the water's edge. Various kinds of riverbank farming. Men only. As the water drops, the upper *waalo* is cleaned and planted. Potatoes, maize. The tool is the *daba*, a short-handled wooden hoe with broad blade. Maize is sown broadcast. Later there will be places where one may walk right across the river bed. The banks are sometimes deeply eroded by water. Everything dries so quickly some farmers are burning off old vegetation, under water until a day or so ago, before planting. See sets of fishing buoys. Do they use lines or nets?

My mentor today is Amiel Agne, also called Bechir, the agricultural extension worker for the river villages we will visit. (He later became an important figure in the UN film.) More ambiguities. Amiel or Bechir? Children attending French school used to get a European name as well as the name given by their father. A form of racism. Keeper of tradition or messenger of the modern? A mass of ambiguities. Bechir is a government servant whose job is to overturn rooted agricultural traditions, but he is a devout Muslim, comes from a wealthy high caste Toucouleur family whose ancestry includes kings. He is expected to respect all Toucouleur traditions. He has two wives at present, divorced a third. He keeps servants who have 'slave' status in his household though technically free. He is leading the campaign for new methods but he cannot go too fast or he would have to break with his family. It frightens him. He married his first wife outside the charmed family circle — unheard of — she is scarcely recognised by his parents and aunts. He is known in many villages as 'El Fecce' — The King. The villagers cannot call him 'Monsieur'. To them he is still a respected member of an old royal family. Very ambiguous burden if you are an innovator.

Very dignified today, with his pince-nez, white shirt, tie and pale tropical suit. Says he is the first in his family to break with tradition in the way of dress. 'I wear a uniform to work and not a *boubou.*'

All kinds of birds — black and white kingfishers, fishing eagles, herons, seagulls which the mechanic insisted on calling *hirondelles* — swallows. A troupe of large monkeys protested our passing.

Visited a two and a half hectare collective field at Sadel with a tall crop of sorghum created by the Jeunesse de Sadel (the Young men of Sadel) in the *djeri* on the opposite bank in Mauritania. It should yield some 500 kilos per hectare, unfertilised. They reckon to be able to obtain some 36,000 francs at 18 francs a kilo which will be used towards building a health post or other community services. It took the 170 members of their youth group, whose ages range from 25 to 50, a total of two days' work each in a year. That included cleaning the field, planting and harvesting. It seemed a modest effort but it's their first experience of community work. They plan to harvest next Thursday and put it in a couple of household grain stores until the local cooperative buy it from them. Could they get a *waalo* field to work on to double their output? No. *Waalo* land was in very short supply. Nobody wishes to part with it.

Last stop; the village of Nguidjilone perched just above the water-line and protected by a low surrounding embankment against an exceptional flood. It has a recognisable village shape which instantly appeals.

We are the circus visiting town. Village so cut off, any fresh face is worth coming to peer at. Palaver in the shade of the village market, concrete base, clean, corrugated roof, might call it smart compared with others. Functions daily. Elderly *griot* sings praises of 'El Fecce'.

The village is two in one, a total of some 1,500 inhabitants. There is a three class primary school, a clinic with a recently arrived male nurse (Hacchim), a livestock centre with a vaccination enclosure because it is a crossing point of nomadic herders from Mauritania.

There is a community youth group formed two years ago and active. They have a collective field in the *waalo* partly in maize and partly in vegetables. They use the profit in many ways. They put some aside to improve their field. They organise social meetings. They distribute vegetables to encourage a better diet. They make a donation to the mosque. They also organise communal actions such as the cleaning and widening of village streets, burial of the dead. They maintain a small meeting house which can also be used for visitors. They help organise wrestling matches during the cool dry season.

This village has five male volunteer animators and two women who have all been on a training course and are supposed to organise village meetings and activities along the lines suggested in their training and by the extension workers in the CER in Ouressugui — when they can get here. Bechir Agne — El Fecce — is their link. The villagers give him respect not because of what agricultural advice he might give but because he is a specially eligible catch for any unmarried young woman. Intimate knowledge of everybody's family tree is more important than literacy and pinpoints precisely where one is in the close-knit lineage and clan system.

The two women *animatrices* have organised many of the younger village women into an association. They too have a small collective field or garden in which they grow fruit and vegetables including salad. They meet regularly with the young nurse in charge of the clinic to discuss health issues. He is hot on preventive measures which the villagers can take.

No time for exploring further but in my mind this is it. It has all the right ingredients. The people appear open to change and yet there is a deep-rooted traditional core to village society. This will provide

David MacDonald

**Village *animatrices* at Nguidjilone, 1969**

interesting tensions. Most important the people are agreeable to our proposed invasion. Am sure we can build up the portrait in the final pre-shooting period. The sun is sinking and we just have enough fuel for the return. We cast off on to a perfect millpond.

The sunset goes yellow and the reflections in the water are magnificent. Fish jump. Kingfishers dive in and out all round us. There's plenty of fish to feed on. The sky is crystal clear — all the constellations appear so sharply that one has a real illusion of perspective.

In January 1969 the film team duly arrived in the village of Nguidjilone when the land had dried out and the road links had been re-established. We filmed the farmers, the artisans, the village animators and tried to portray the reality of life, although we ourselves attracted onlookers wherever we put the camera down. We eventually got round to tackling matters of health. This was when we discovered the ways in which the young male nurse Hacchim was interpreting his role as medical worker in charge of the small clinic.

We filmed him at work and bombarded him with questions as he did so. Later we followed him as he made his rounds. It was obvious that even in a short time he had built up a rapport with the villagers, especially the women who are very normally very withdrawn in such a traditional setting. They listened carefully and the message was remembered. Hacchim was never pushy, nor did he ever boast of his knowledge or make a mystery of it. He showed the connection between cause and effect in simple visible examples. Nobody had taken the trouble before.

What follows is an extract from the script of my UN documentary film shot around Hacchim in 1969 and an audio interview made at the same time.

**Hacchim Ndiaye** pushes back the wooden shutters on his office cum consulting room, cum medical store in the clinic. It is the signal to the people of Nguidjilone that he is on duty.

The clinic is a modest, rectangular, whitewashed cement block, squatting on a low concrete plinth on the bare sand. It and the two-form primary school next door are the only modern-style buildings in the village, solidly but cheaply made from a basic kit of parts by the French colonial administration and bequeathed to the new republic when they left. They both have a wide-brimmed corrugated tin roof to provide a ration of shade and propel the short but violent rains as far from the walls as possible and prevent it splashing through the glassless windows. A ring of concrete posts mark the boundaries of the school and clinic yards; but the fencing meant to keep out wandering animals and windswept rubbish and give some privacy, has never been delivered. The posts serve the children as convenient goalposts and the teachers as laundry posts.

The two male teachers and the nurse have monastic quarters at one end of the block. Two shared concrete cells in which to live, eat and sleep. An outside cooking hearth, a latrine, a bucket and tin shower. No shortage of kids willing to fetch water from the river for a chance to listen respectfully to the battered and crackly radio which is the only luxury.

From his little office Hacchim can look out across the more or less empty quadrant of the village beyond the market and the bus stop to the low earth dyke which surrounds the village. The clinic consists of a narrow veranda giving a little shade, a treatment room for minor operations, an office for consultations, a rudimentary desk, a locked cupboard, two stools, one for the nurse, another for the patient, scant privacy.

Hacchim, youthful, close-cropped, dons a slightly grubby white cotton medic's coat over T-shirt and jeans and opens up his register. He is concern and curiosity personified. A villager limps in. Hacchim examines him.

**VOICE FROM BEHIND THE CAMERA:** What is a matter with this man?

**HACCHIM:** He has been gored by the horn of a cow. He is a peasant farmer. He comes from a village nine kilometres from here. It's called Dioul. To get there you go through two other villages and Dioul is the third.

The man's gashed leg is cleaned and bound up. He hobbles out.

A young woman comes in followed by a little girl, bare feet, age about four, matt grey skin, glazed eyes, whimpering. She looks under-nourished. While Hacchim talks to the mother the little girl hides behind her. Hacchim is gentle, a good listener, patient. He doesn't look down his nose at villagers like some state employees do. He is a man of the people.

**HACCHIM:** This girl has not been getting enough to eat She has had diarrhoea and then the wrong food. She must be fed on a diet of boiled food, eggs and milk with sugar.

Hacchim gives quiet and detailed instructions to the child's mother. She nods understanding but asks no questions.

**VOICE:** Can you get the mother to carry it through?

**HACCHIM:** Oh, yes. I often go into her part of the village to check up how clean people are keeping their homes. I can drop in to see that the girl is getting the right food.

Another mother comes in carrying a baby. Hacchim asks her to sit. He looks at the baby and takes its temperature. While he waits

**VOICE:** Tell me, do the villagers accept the need for modern medicine?

**HACCHIM:** Yes, they accept it very well. They prefer modern medicine to their own traditional kind but there's one thing I've come to understand and that is, if we are out of stock of modern drugs and I'm faced with a feverish patient, there are some local plants which are effective. They make an infusion from them and drink it. I don't know what they are called in French but I can name them in Toucouleur. Sometimes I recommend both. [He pauses to remove the thermometer.] This baby has a fever. It began yesterday, it has been sick and has got diarrhoea as well. The main reason is malaria. Right now if she has a prescription for a dose of quinoform, she'll be better in a couple of days.

Hacchim finds a few tablets left in his stock and sets aside two of them. He tells the child's mother how and when to give the pills.

When all the patients have gone, Hacchim makes notes of these consultations in his diary.

'I understand this is your first posting. How long have you been here and did you have any experience of village life before you came here?' I ask.

'Yes, it's my first post as a trained state nurse. I have been here 10 months. I came here in February. I was born locally in Matam which is near by, so I had a good idea of how to adapt myself and fit in to the life of these villages. I speak Pulaar and my mother is a Toucouleur. It would be difficult to treat the sick if you cannot understand what the patient is trying to tell you. You have to speak Pulaar here if you want to do any good.'

'Do the folk who come to you for treatment know how to explain what is wrong with them?' I wonder.

'Yes. In general, they have a lot to say about what is hurting them. They may try to explain it by comparing it with something else. For example, colours. I keep a colour chart handy. If someone says he has coughed up blood, I ask what colour it was. Was it black or red? So he is able to show me which colour it was. So I discover all I need to know.'

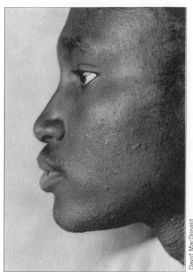

Hacchim in 1969, aged 23

David MacDonald

'So you really get on with the people?'

'Yes. Sometimes too much so, because some of them expect miracles. Take the village champion wrestlers, for instance. They seem to think I can give them an injection before a match so that they will win. Many people think injections are European magic and demand them for everything. Of course I can't help them.'

Later over a ritual mint tea in his quarters we talked again, this time about the general health of the village.

'Well,' Hacchim began, 'it's easiest to divide it up according to what people do. First the peasant farmer. In normal years, he has a good well-balanced diet. It is rich in protein, rich in energy-giving cereals, so these men are generally well-fed and don't often fall ill. They do however suffer from the hard conditions in which they work out of doors, wet, cold, extreme heat, dust, carrying heavy weights. It eventually saps their health.

'With children it is another story. Here one is often up against deep-rooted traditions and superstitions. Sometimes it's against all common sense. Parents bring in a child covered in spots. I ask them to cut the child's nails so that it doesn't scratch itself and increase the risk of infection. The parents refuse because tradition dictates that they should never do it. Or if I prescribe a diet which includes eggs for a small underfed child its parents say that it is impossible because it will result in the child speaking too rapidly. Many old traditions leave small children badly protected against sickness.

'Actually 50% of consultations concern children. They drink dirty water, they are not watched at home so they swallow all kinds of dirt, they are not protected against malaria. They often die of it in the wet season.'

'There is presumably a doctor who is responsible for the region?' I ask. 'How many times a year does he visit you?'

'It is difficult to say because since I've been here (10 months), he has only been five times. Then it was because of a serious outbreak of meningitis. This particular outbreak came from Mali. It can kill in 48 hours. Here we have no means to evacuate the patient, so we treated them in the clinic, quarantining them from the villagers. It's very contagious. In the wet season the village is cut off by land. In the dry season, one can send for an ambulance but the patient has to pay. With a serious cut, we try and deal with it ourselves and have done so successfully several times. A seriously ill person can be carried to the hospital at Matam on a cart or in a pirogue but they have very few facilities there either.'

'How do you get your stock of drugs and medical supplies?'

'We get our quota about every six months. We get a ration of penicillin, distilled water, mint syrup, nivequin, lactic acid, chloroform from which to make a liquid, then some dressings, bandages and a quantity of mercurochrome. It isn't enough and it doesn't always reach us every six months. Take aspirins for instance, they give us only 50 aspirins for six months.' Hacchim's voice rises. 'It is impossible, but we have no other means. None at all!'

'What would you need to be able to give a comprehensive medical service to your villagers?'

'Since we cannot count too much on medical supplies we should do much more health education. One should if possible prevent sickness. It would be much cheaper than trying to cure it. So we should be going out and making home visits, giving advice, recommending traditional medicines, exercises, but above all we must take health education into people's homes, encourage families to build latrines, to wash their water pots — carefully. Very important.

'Most of the villagers get their water directly from the river. Well, especially in the wet season, the flooded river washes every bit of rubbish and excrement from upstream. People and animals use it as a latrine. It's filthy. It's best to pass it all through a *canari* — a big container with a sand filter — if not the water must be allowed to settle and only the top water used. Every morning the canaris must be washed and put in the sun to dry. Then they can be filled with water. Better still is to have two canaris. One is filled in the evening and in the morning it will be quite clear and all the sediment will be at the bottom. The second can be filled in the morning and not used till night-time. That is the way that we try to work because there is so little modern medicine available.

'I do my rounds on foot to the four villages which are my responsibility. It's quite a long way, some four kilometres. I take a small medical kit with me so that I can treat any serious cases on the spot but that's not the real purpose of the visits which is the chance of giving some health education, talking to people about the benefits of having a clean village, trying to give some advice to mothers about malnourished children.

'I do a similar tour here. On Friday mornings I begin an inspection of houses. I drop in to see my midwife and we discuss any new births. She's a traditional village person but I was able to show her the link between cutting the umbilical cord with a dirty blade and babies dying of tetanus and she is now very strict about it. Now she hardly ever loses a baby.

'Afterwards I continue systematically visiting each house in every part of the village including the chief's house, to see if they are obeying the regime everybody agreed to in the village assembly. If there are any health hazards the family will be reprimanded and their name put on a list.'

'I notice that many village houses and their yards are pretty dirty. Do you find this?'

'First I talk with the old men who still have a lot of influence. I try to convince them about the benefits of cleanliness. I use the image of the large town. I say, look how our neighbour so and so left here on a journey, and then he came back. He was in good health, he was well dressed, he was clean. I suggest a comparison between these travellers and the young people in the village who don't seem to care whether they are dirty or sloppily dressed. Do you follow? It's an attempt to tell them about the benefits of keeping clean. As well as seeing the old ones, I try and talk to the women. After all, they are the ones who look after the home. If all else fails and discussing the problems doesn't

A *canari* — traditional water container

lead to improvement, it becomes necessary to use the local government system, bringing in the regional doctor, bringing charges, levying fines. I think it's wrong but it's difficult to see what else to do quickly.'

I ask Hacchim whether the local animators recruited by the government people help? His answer is unexpected:

'Well, I'm not very clear about their activities. If they really wanted to collaborate with us it would be a good thing but when they come to the village they don't come to see us so I don't go running after them. They ought to be specially concerned with our village women animators. They ought to help me by organising training sessions for our pregnant mothers on hygiene and pre-natal health matters. It hasn't happened. I have been left to give what advice I can to the village midwife.'

I kept up a continuous but casual correspondence with Hacchim through the years. I knew when he left Nguidjilone, impatient for

wider horizons in which to be active and was sent downstream to
the much bigger village of Madina Niathbe. Here he came under
the umbrella of the Integrated Project of Podor (PIP).

I didn't meet him again until September 1992 when I was once
again in the north of Senegal and Hacchim was working near by
leading a team which was training villagers how to use the new
technology of solar-powered pumps to raise clean water from
their borewells. If he didn't succeed, another well-intentioned gift
of modern equipment, like scores of others before it, would fail.

Hacchim had hardly changed. A bit thicker in his body, fuller of
face, but still restless, curious, challenging and bursting with ideas.
One knew straight away that his life had been a pilgrim's progress,
a quest yet uncompleted to find ways in which the people of the
Fouta Toro could improve their income and their well-being in a
seemingly hostile world. Senegal needed a prosperous farming
community more than ever. The paradox was that the state had
allowed itself to become virtually bankrupt and had had to give up
education and training schemes, advice services and cheap credit
to farmers just when it was most wanted. It was being left to a
motley crew of foreign agencies to pull the country back from the
brink. We talked late into an airless night outside his lodgings at
the village of Aire Lao. His wife and children remained 150
kilometres upstream at Matam.

No conversation in Senegal, however practical its starting point,
is ever a matter of getting directly between two points. Talking is
an art form to be savoured and appreciated. Time is not one of the
elements of which it is composed.

We began talking about the first village of Nguidjilone where
we first met. Hacchim scarcely needed prompting.

'I had come there straight from training school. It was my first
post. Being fit and young, I saw immediately that the young people
in the village had nothing to do when they were not working. So I
got to know many of them and suggested that we start a club in
which regular events could be organised both for fun and for
stretching their minds. That seemed to work, so I persuaded a
whole ring of neighbouring villages to do something similar. Then
we were able to hold joint events — a week or a fortnight long —
with competitive sport, football and local wrestling, music, lectures,
African literature and so on. It really made a big difference and
even today I still see former members of those groups in different

Christian Aid/Derrick Knight

**Hacchim in 1992**

offices and jobs around Senegal who say what an inspiration it was and how it helped them to see what they might be able to do with their lives.

'I tried to get the village women interested in the clubs and also to work with them inside their own associations. It quickly became obvious from my daily records that I was seeing lots of sick small children. I began to try to explain to their mothers what was making the children ill, but somehow it wasn't getting through because I remained in my consulting room. I realised I had to get out and see how they lived in their homes, what they ate, how they looked after their children, how they looked after their homes, what sort of utensils they used. Above all I needed to know where they got their drinking water from at different times of the year, wet season or in a drought because I could see that infants were dying of thirst close to water.

'When I'd got hold of the facts, I was convinced that I had first to teach the mothers in order to save the children. I began a small programme of weighing so that I got to see the infants regularly and advise their mothers what to do. After that I had to work out what could be done about the water situation. The quickest way was to try and improve the way villagers stocked water. The usual way was to keep large pottery jars in the household yard and to fill them from the river or a well, using bowls or old tins. I had to explain the link between polluted water and sickness and how to reduce the risk by using clean pots, boiling or chlorinating it.

'But I soon realised that I also had to deal with children's diet. When and how an infant was weaned was critical. So I thought that having got the young mothers to discuss their children's health we could do something more productive like starting a vegetable garden to add variety to the household meals and provide much needed elements for the growing infants.'

'None of this was part of your duties as a state nurse?'

'No. And that's where I began to ask myself lots of questions about what sort of trained persons were needed in the rural community. Do you really want a livestock advisor who can do nothing else? Or a state nurse who never leaves his clinic? Or an agriculturalist who only attends to cultivation?

'I think the state needs to make up its mind what it wants to do and then to change the training course accordingly. There's no way we are ever going to have enough nurses for every need, no way there will be enough livestock advisers, but one might be able to train a number of multi-disciplined people who don't know as much as the others but know enough to be useful most of the time in tackling both veterinary problems and village health care and giving good advice about crops or tree planting. At the moment, because there is no proper network of experts, essential advice and training in new techniques is missing. So many need training in so many places at once.'

I was vividly reminded of the small band of young government employees convened by the Minister of Planning and Development in 1968 on an upper floor of *Le Building* to whom I had outlined what I had in mind for the village film in the UN development series. The word *'animateurs'* was used to describe them. It doesn't translate but means more or less what its Latin root implies — someone who brings to life. Hence its use to those who make cartoon films.

Here we were, talking about animating the rural masses. I can hear myself saying hesitantly to a gorgeously dressed minister and his officials that I wanted to try to hear what the rural community felt about 'development' — an idea, a movement, a slogan that even then had different meanings for different people. As I said it, I realised I was speaking with a group who undoubtedly felt they had the absolute right to command whatever 'development' needed to be done in the countryside and would hear what I was saying as a critique of their authority, if not as blasphemy. Who was this foreign pipsqueak daring to suggest that there might be a point of view other than the correct governmental line on 'development'?

But the minister apparently sympathised in the end because he reined in his officials and immediately put me in the hands of Ben

Mady Cisse, then director of the Department of Rural Animation.

Ben Mady Cisse was not one of the gorgeous creatures who adorned the minister's offices, but a young technician in shirt sleeves and creased trousers in an office strewn with papers and charts. He seemed to thrive on a constant hither and thither of callers and scribbled messages from outposts all over Senegal. The proposal did not knock him off course for an instant. He was one of the strategists and boss of so-called Rural Animation. He was anxious to explain what it was all about and why it might be exactly what I was after.

Rural Animation, he said, was nothing less than an attempt to awaken the mass of the population who had remained indifferent to national development plans launched by the government. It was to give them the chance to undertake their own development from the grass roots upwards. The government had created a special budget for it — opening new channels to avoid political and technical institutions which might see it as a threat to their authority and control. They had organised a network of training centres and teams of regional animators with the ability to maintain contact with villagers and encourage them to take part in the scheme. It relied on the recruitment of village animators who would be unpaid volunteers chosen by the whole village to represent them and take part in training courses during which the new ideas could be fully discussed. The village animators would feedback the new ideas to their neighbours and then encourage them to start actions of benefit to them and to take more advantage of the range of technical and training services which were already available but under-used. It was a far-reaching and ambitious plan fully in tune with the socialist ideals for which President Senghor stood.

Recently, said Ben Mady Cisse, they had begun promoting women animators in those villages which had successfully organised the men. There were several villages in the Middle Valley with both men and women and he was sure I would find a good one with lots going on.

Now, sitting in the moonlight outside Hacchim's lodgings at Aire, I wondered what Hacchim felt he had left behind him at Nguidjilone.

'I continued to consolidate the work of improving the general health of the villages, not just Nguidjilone but of all the surrounding villages which used the clinic. By the time I left, clean villages had become the local rule. My own measurement of success was in the fall in the numbers of patients who came to be treated at the health centre and in those coming for treatment when I went to visit the other villages. Less sickness meant that my efforts were having some impact. The villagers had grasped that keeping themselves, their homes, their cooking pots, and their drinking vessels clean was important and they had also seen the value of filtering, storing and drinking clean water.

'It all fell apart when I left because my replacement did not want to do more than be on duty in the clinic and to wait until the sick came to him. All he had to do was make out a prescription or give an injection and that was that. So gradually things went backwards and a new generation grew up without getting the kind of training which they had when I was there. So now the situation has reverted. It's very sad.

'There was another government service at the time which had some good ideas — the Centres of Rural Expansion (CERs) — but were they just a pipedream? The centres had all the expertise needed for giving a real impetus to agriculture, but when it came down to it they didn't have the means, they didn't have any transport and they too sat in their offices in the town and waited until somebody came to see them. And if anyone went to ask them to come and train farmers in their village they refused point blank. It was difficult to condemn them when they had no facilities. Now that the state has slashed the budgets of all its social services they cannot be blamed for what is going wrong. But it's a shame. In its heyday, the service showed that it could provide valuable help and training for farmers and villagers wishing to experiment with new techniques. I am sorry that the state did not try to strengthen the CERs so that they could have been used as a way of promoting its agricultural policy to the whole of the rural community and in the remotest parts of the country. They have wasted a lot of money on schemes that proved useless because the people they were supposed to benefit had no idea what they were about. Much of this waste could easily have been avoided.

'You see, for me education is this. When one wants to develop something in the community and there is nobody there who can carry it out, then people on the spot must be trained. It follows that such training must precede any unfamiliar technical innovation. To rush in and hire someone who knows nothing about it — for instance, to organise cattle vaccination, supervise a tree nursery, run a pump engine — is asking for a catastrophe to happen.

'Then there are other problems. When we talk about development projects, there's the person or persons who thought of it, then there are those who are going to finance it. There are also those who are going to do the work, make the project happen. Straight away one sees clearly that there is a built-in hierarchy. There is a top person somewhere far away who does nothing except take the credit if it works, and there are those who do the real work. Success or failure depends on them. And if tomorrow the project fails, people sit in air-conditioned offices trying to work out what went wrong, but they are not personally the poorer. That's not the way to go about it at all. If one is completely honest one must provide those working within the project with the same training as those who have drawn up and launched the project. And to give them full responsibility for it. That's the heart of the training problem in the rural community. And after all these years that old problem still exists.

'For example, formal schooling. The government is having state nurses trained in France as well as doctors. They learn how to practise in a situation which is quite static. But we are in a developing country and what we need are people who can serve in our communities and know the problems of our own people. That's what is important. Or take the primary school. What is the good of the *Certificat d'Etudes* [a kind of eleven plus test]? To open the door to the sixth year? So what? It serves no purpose whatsoever. But if children were taught the rudiments of production from an early age, to have "a school for life"! That would be much more worth while. To have the basics of modern agriculture, rearing livestock, and carpentry would be of practical use. Of course some bright pupils could always go on to higher education but they would be a small number. With practical courses everyone would have something useful when they left school. That is what I call "school for life". But in the meantime all we are doing is creating a class of uprooted youngsters. A pupil with a certificate has a vision of a nice desk job in an air-conditioned office. Goodbye farming!

'And what about secondary schools? They are all in the big towns. I would like to see them spread out across the country where pupils can see how people work, can help pay for his or her tuition, become self-reliant. But at present the system favours the city. Now that scholarships and grants have been slashed and lodgings are exorbitantly priced in the city, what chance has a country child of surviving there without relations?'

I asked: 'What happened after you left Nguidjilone?'

'After Nguidjilone, I went to Madina Niathbe. It was another big village with some 2,500 inhabitants and many surrounding villages. It was on the bank of the arm of the Senegal river known as the Doue and was the ferry crossing point for the huge island of Morphil.

'By that time I was more experienced and knew what I wanted to do. I began immediately to put into practice what I had learned at Nguidjilone. I had a health centre but I was determined not to remain in it. I began to train villagers. I trained two community health workers and two midwives who worked together and were based on the health centre. They learnt how to use all the drugs and medicines which we stocked and were able to diagnose all the main diseases and illnesses from which people suffered. On this basis I organised all the villages which depended on Madina in the same way. Each one had a small health post. I visited all these villages regularly either on foot or by *mobilette* (moped). In the morning we would work in the post and in the afternoon we would gather the young mothers and have a teach-in on nutrition before putting in an hour or so on the communal vegetable garden. I knew from Nguidjilone that they must learn to distinguish the qualities of all the foods available to them and to balance their children's diet. I used a colour scheme based on the Senegalese flag to help them memorise. Red for proteins — meats and eggs. Yellow for fats and energy foods, sugar, cereals etc. Green was for vegetables and fruits. We looked at all the locally available foods, classified them and then discussed what purpose they served and how to cook them. They learnt the difference between the food needs of a man going out to work in the fields and a growing child. We did a lot of work with diet and cooking. The French NGO Secours Catholique gave us funds for a meeting place and a kitchen where we could make up all kinds of dishes.

'During some of the drought years we got food aid and it was then that we organised a number of local groups who might be able to replace that food by their own efforts. We began serious

Christian Aid/Jeremy Hartley

**Early experiments in vegetable growing at Madina Niathbe**

efforts at market gardening. We had the backing of the
government Programme for Nutrition in Senegal. That is how we
were able to grow vegetables to use in recipes in the kitchen of
our demonstration centre.

'These vegetable gardens started producing profits with which
we were able to build small health posts in many villages. The
sums of money raised were quite important. They were able to
fund stocks of essential drugs for the health centre, new materials
for the village school. They were able to put aside money for the
eventual replacement costs of the motor pump in the vegetable
garden. We were able to finance courses for functional literacy.
We had some help from UN agencies but we were also able to
start a rolling credit fund and to build a classroom for the literacy
work. Though I left some four years ago I heard it was still going
strong very recently.'

I asked whether his superiors were in agreement with what he
was doing.

'None of this work was interfering with my administrative
duties. I was fulfilling those to the letter. I also had chiefs who
were very understanding. They were also happy about the way
we had introduced a realistic and fair scheme to help pay for the
primary health service. It was a charge of 100 francs per

consultation for a grown up and 50 for a child, inclusive of any medicine. There were certain health posts which prided themselves on the amount of money they had taken to show how well primary health care was working. My experience was the opposite. As I have said about the village of Nguidjilone, a queue of sick at the health post is a step backwards. The more money in the kitty the worse the service. I told a regional meeting so and met some opposition. But I maintained that the fewer people came to the health post the healthier they were. It meant preventive actions had been successful. My chiefs understood this and let me get on with the various programmes. They didn't interfere and they did what they could to help. This was also true of the regional doctor.

'Madina was the end of my nursing service. I decided I wanted to have a break and do other things and try out different ideas.'

We had begun the conversation talking about health care in the village some 25 years ago, so I asked what he felt about the state of health care now.

'In the early years of independence it was the state which provided the staff, the medicines and the equipment and built the health posts. Later they gradually stopped new building work. Villagers who want to have their own health post now have to build and pay for it themselves to an official plan provided to them. The villagers have even found themselves paying for the equipment, the medicines and the staff. As time passed it became very difficult to get a supply of medicines. It also got more and more difficult to recruit trained health staff.

'Now there is a new government public health policy which says that health care should reach right into the most remote villages. Village health agents and midwives should be recruited to do this work and a professionally qualified worker in the larger clinics would supervise the volunteers in the health posts.

'The trouble is that state nurses, as you will remember my saying earlier, are not trained for this sort of work. The nurse is used to receiving the sick in his consulting room and the village health agents have to come to him for advice and instructions. The health posts still do not have enough medicine and the result of it is that the quality of much health care has fallen — fallen very considerably. A lot of prescriptions are written for which there are no supplies available anywhere in the region.

'One of the effects is that people turn more and more towards traditional medicine. They go to the *marabouts* who are supposed to be able to cast out sickness. They go to the market and buy charms or herbs from traditional sellers of such things. They go to traditional healers (*guérisseurs*) who have a real knowledge of natural remedies from trees and plants. These people can get good results but they can also do serious damage. In the past we knew that there were only certain sicknesses which need not be treated with western medicine. We had a choice. But now people are going back because they can't afford the high cost of modern medicine. It's no longer a choice. It's simply that people are forced back on the old traditional remedies.'

I asked Hacchim about the Bamako Initiative, a new international attempt to improve primary health care. Was it working?

'The Bamako Initiative,' Hacchim answered, 'has been talked about for over a year. The idea is that the state will provide a basic stock of essential drugs to every health post. The occupant of the health post will organise the opening of a small chemist's shop near by, managed by a village committee. This committee will be responsible for the sale of medicines at a very much lower price than that of the commercial chemist in the town. The list of essential drugs and medicines is limited to those that are the most useful and effective. All that is fine, but there are two big problems. There seems almost always to be a breakdown in the local stocking of medicines. They run out and cannot be replaced for weeks, even months. Secondly, village committees are not properly trained to control the money on which fresh orders depend. So the system breaks down. But the idea is a good one. At a time when the buying power of villagers has fallen so far, it is vital to provide medicines which are within their means.'

'Does the fall in standards mean people are dying earlier?'

'If we are thinking of statistics, the answer is no, but it's not that simple. There has been a real effort at mass vaccination of children against the killer diseases — whooping cough, measles, mumps. These diseases came and went every year and killed off hundreds. For the moment a lot more children are immune, but it depends on regular follow-up and that is by no means certain in the catastrophic economic situation of the country. The problem is that this has fuelled a massive increase in population for which there is no work and no money. That is another big subject for discussion.

'On the negative side we are seeing a strong advance of malaria and other water-borne diseases along the river valley. Then there is malnutrition. The growing poverty of people in recent years is having an effect, especially on the most vulnerable groups — young children, pregnant women, infants being weaned. I don't know what the figures are since I am no longer in the medical corps but I feel that the problem of malnutrition has not diminished over the years and at certain times of the year leaves the weak more vulnerable to other disease.

'Then there is the old problem of the motivation of trained medical staff. The kind of training nurses and health workers receive does not suit the needs of the community. It makes them unfit to recruit and train village agents who try to copy their style and turn into miniature state nurses who never visit the sick. So people have a low opinion of modern medicine. And if they ever have to go to hospital, it's worse. There are long queues for a single over-worked doctor whereas one knows that there are unemployed doctors and pharmacists in Dakar. Even if you are admitted, you have to send out and pay for the drugs which are prescribed because the hospital has nothing. Nothing works.

'Then there is the uncontrolled sale of drugs and medicines. You can go into a chemist or a street market and buy drugs which are out of date, exposed to the sun, useless, perhaps dangerous. This too contributes to the falling standards of health care in the community.

'In short, I believe that it is the community health work of certain individuals and independent groups that has led to improvements in primary health care, not the professional training in western medicine which is given to our medical corps.'

Hacchim Ndiaye left the nursing service in the mid-Eighties to work for an independent agency called SEMIS — Services for Improving the Energy Needs of the Sahel. Its driving force was Bruno Legendre, a Frenchman with a long track record of hands-on work on the economic problems of the area.

'We were very much on the same wave length,' said Hacchim. 'I found that my practical work in market gardening and local foods was a good foundation for what we were going to attempt to do.

'SEMIS' main object was to create new skilled jobs in the rural community and to make sure that the local economy was capable of supporting such enterprise. Part of that was to see that the new job holders — technicians, plumbers, electricians, maintenance engineers — were adequately prepared and trained. In the meantime Bruno was trying to raise money for a programme of community training for solar water pumps in villages along the Senegal valley. But there were delays in financing. While waiting I moved into a house in the village of Aire on the main tarmac road and we did some very interesting economic research.

'The first task was a piece of direct observation in nine villages in the district of Podor to measure what they ate, how much they paid for food, what shortages they met, and what other resources they had for everyday living or future planning like house building, maternity, travel. At the same time we noted what they grew and when, in relation to season and rainfall; and how they sold their produce, at what price and to whom. We looked at everything bought and sold in a number of villages each month and noted price changes according to season or other causes.

'It was from doing this research that I began to understand more thoroughly the real beginnings of development in a village community. For example, if one is seeking to provide evidence about how well or badly a village was doing, one would go to the baker each month and ask him how many loaves he had baked;

Christian Aid/Derrick Knight

**Hacchim at Aire, 1992**

then to the butcher and ask how many animals he had killed this month; and one immediately had a graph. Then one asked the post office how many *mandats* (money orders) they had received for such and such a village within the month. The figure revealed the support being given the village by its overseas migrant workers. One went to see the nurse in the health post and collected from him the number of consultations he had given, and the number of cases of malnutrition he had noted.

This was also important. After that one found out how many new houses had been built, how many new bricks had been made and a host of small costs and details like that. Finally one made an analysis of the situation in the village and by putting all the village results together, one had a picture of the whole district.

'Let me give you an example. When you see that the baker begins to have trouble selling his bread you know that the buying power of people has fallen. If they eat less meat, knowing how important meat is in the local diet, and are eating more cereals and beans which are cheaper, you know that there is less money in people's pockets for their food budget.'

'1990 was a drought year, which must have made it especially interesting,' I suggested.

'Exactly. Rainfall plays a big part in the situation. The river did not overflow that year. The rains were poor and fitful. Many of the fields were as dry as a bone and it was impossible to plant them. So the available income of these families fell. You have to know what their basic needs are. You have to find out whether they are buying sufficient food or not. If they are not buying food, is it because they don't need to, or because they have no way to buy it? These were the facts we needed to know. Then we could make a chart of changes from month to month.

'We published the data on behalf of the government Food Security Office in Dakar for nine months from March to November 1990. Then they ran out of funds for an independent survey and fell back on the impressions of local civil servants in the region. It's not the same thing. They hardly leave their offices. They fill in a standard questionnaire. There is a lot of guesswork. However the experience provided valuable information about the way development starts at the lowest level of the economy.

'When the money ran out for that work we tackled something which was even more practical in terms of the valley communities. It was a weekly bulletin which gave the market prices of the main crops and agricultural products of the 15 local markets in the district of Podor — cereals, paddy rice and husked rice, millet, vegetables, meat and poultry. We got together and trained a team of 12 reliable local investigators, mainly young people with sufficient education and encouraged them to form a properly constituted GIE (*Groupement d'Intérêt Economique*) — the officially recognised small enterprise group which is supposed to give access to credit and state assistance. SEMIS financed the design and preparation of the project and it was then presented to various possible donors. It was eventually funded by the European Development Fund which has some very large agricultural programmes in the middle valley.

'We began to publish the farming bulletin called *Kabaaru Njeeygu*, every fortnight from September 1990. At first we sold it on market day in the villages. Later we looked for ways of getting it more directly into the hands of the farmers and herders. There was never a large distribution, a few hundred copies only, but what it showed was the differences in supply and demand between local markets. It could be used as a guide both to buyers and sellers. If, for example, it is known that the price of a kilo of onions is 100 francs at Pete and 40 francs at Thille Boubakar, the farmers at Thille will take their stock to the market at Pete while customers wanting onions will go to Thille.

'It's the same with sheep and chickens. There are big differences between one area and another at different times of the year. It's vital for buyers and sellers to know this.

'We felt we were helping the local farmers to make money. They needed all the help they could get. I'll tell you what happens. At the beginning of the growing season the farmers go to the bank for a loan. If they are lucky enough to be given a loan, and very few are, the bank charges 15 to 20% interest. The farmers grow a good crop but at harvest they find they cannot sell it. They cannot pay their debts. They owe the bank. The bank won't help them any further. They have produced well but they can't sell. It not because there is no market. There are markets which are short of what the farmer offers but he doesn't know about them. It's important that the farmers know where to go. An information bulletin like ours is necessary so that local farming communities can break out of their isolation.

'During the period of the EDF grant we tried to become self-sufficient by selling the bulletin and trying to get annual subscriptions but we could not get beyond 200 copies. You cannot finance 12 investigators and editing costs on that kind of circulation. Many farmers were unable to afford 100 francs per issue. A large number are illiterate. We ran out of time. A pity. If we had managed to broaden the scope of the bulletin to three districts, a hundred markets, it might have worked. We are going

KABAARU NJEEYGU
bulletin d'information agricole
Edité par SEMIS - village de Pete - département de Podor

N° 25

PRIX : 250 FCFA

ETAT DES MARCHES AU 10/09/91

CEREALES / GAWEJE

JIGGADE / ACHETER à :                    YEEYDE / VENDRE à

SORGHO LOCAL/  SAMME
110  CFA/kg à AERE/NDIOUM          135 CFA/kg à MADINA/AGNAM/OREFONDE

MAIS/ MAKKA
95 CFA/KG à AERE/AGNAM             125 CFA/KG  à OREFONDE
100 CFA/KG à        GALOYA/

PADDY/ MAARO  WUMO
50 CFA/Kg  à DODEL/NDIAYENE        90 CFA/KG à OREFONDE/FANAYE

RIZ BLANC/ MAARO  DUTTAKO
100 à 135 CFA/kg à GALOYA/MADINA   160 CFA/kg  à OREFONDE
               AERE et NDIOUM
140 CFA/KG à THILLE                150 CFA/kg à FANAYE/TAREDJI/DODEL

SUUNA
90 CFA/KG à AERE                   170 CFA/Kg à OREFONDE

POULETS/GERTOODE  beaucoup à MADINA(23)NDIOUM(21)THILLE(20)
    les plus chers :600 à1350 àTHILLE/AGNAM/AERE/MADINA
    les moins chers: 350 à 1000 àOREFONDE/GALOYA/NDIOUM/NDIAYENE

MOUTONS/JAWDI       Pulfuli : beaucoup à THILLE (280) / AGNAM (101)MADINA(110)
            moins chers  : 4000 à 17500 à AGNAM/FANAYE/GALOYA/MADINA
            plus chers   : 5000 à 20000 CFA à THILLE/TAREDJI/NDIAYENE/AERE

CHEVRES/BEY      moins chers :2250 à 8000 F de AGNAM à MADINA et à THILLE/FANAYE
                 plus chers  :5000 à 13000 FCFA à TAREJI/NDIAYENE/GALOYA

BEURRE /    nebam  sirme :
                 1000 CFA  sur tous les marches

to try again.'

'I gather you are once more concerned about water like you were at Nguidjilone, but on a bigger scale.'

'Yes. I'm in that field again. Our research group was blocked and I was asked to manage a village hydraulic programme at Ndioum. It is an EDF programme to supply clean drinking water to villages which are close to the big irrigation schemes that they have laid out along the valley. There's one at Aire of 1,200 hectares.

There's another big one at Diamandou and another at Ndioum. In addition they have built deep wells with solar pumps in all the important villages along the river and they are planning a further series of borewells in the *djeri* for the use of pastoralists and their herds. Those wells will be fitted with diesel motor pumps.

'The job my team and I have is to train the villagers to manage their water supplies efficiently, to show them how to set up a local management committee whose job will be to raise income from each installation and save it to pay for the maintenance and replacement of parts as it becomes necessary.

'There are three different time-tables to bear in mind. The solar panels wear out in fifteen years. The pump itself lasts seven years and the motor five years. Now I think this opens up another whole set of opportunities for the rural community.

'One method is for the village management committee to raise the money from monthly dues from all the users, to bank it safely and collect interest, which can be used to reduce the dues over a period of time. More challenging is the possibility that a growing deposit in safe hands will give the village financial resources to employ in other activities. The management might maintain the monthly dues instead of reducing them and set up a capital fund which can be invested in local enterprises and form the germ of a local bank. It has become almost impossible for small farmers to get agricultural credit since the state, as a condition of structural adjustment, dismantled most of its credit schemes. A well-managed water pump fund could offer the farmers banking terms. The interest would remain in the community.

'Naturally people have to be trained and also have time to weigh up the pros and cons of such an enterprise. I believe the time is ripe. The peasant farmer has had a rough time of it and is much more open to new ideas than in the pre-drought, pre-structural adjustment years. They now know that one gets nothing for nothing. They know that everything must now be bought. They know that they have to organise to survive.'

'Explain "nothing for nothing" for me in Senegalese terms,' I asked.

'Nothing for nothing, because for 20 years they have been working hard without improving their well-being. They know now that in order to develop they must undertake their own development. In the past outsiders brought novel gifts to the village communities without asking their opinion. Say you are a village elder, they tell you to do such and such a thing and you will be given this other thing. This other thing which is brought to you is not seen as being relevant to everyday realities. It's a novelty. Perhaps you can make use of it, perhaps not. It's an object of curiosity for a short time and then abandoned.

'The abandoned machinery and expensive gifts of foreign donors remain a powerful image in my mind from a tour along the north bank from Rosso to Kaedi in 1982,' I told him. 'We saw irrigated *périmêtres* with broken down solar powered pumps, diesel motors without parts, cannibalised vehicles, vandalised mesh fencing. Much of the material sent by donors was destroyed. Nobody had tried to consult the people and train them to use it. There had been no follow up. Now they were in a worse mess than before.'

'It's exactly what I have been saying,' answered Hacchim. 'Outsiders came in and installed sophisticated equipment without prior discussion or taking account of people's daily preoccupations. There was no attempt to show people the benefits of the gear to their own lives or how it could be integrated into their routines. It is not surprising most of it failed. For example where a family is allotted an enclosed irrigated field to cultivate with their own pump, that family must be brought to see that it is to replace the traditional *waalo* fields which depended on the overflow of the river which can no longer be relied upon. It is not something which can be taken or left. It has to become a new habit.'

Hacchim had been critical of foreign aid, so I wondered what his opinion might be of the growth of local non-governmental organisations from his village viewpoint.

'At first European NGOs were straightforward about what they were doing. They had come to help people. But often they did not grasp the immensity of the social factor, the difficulty of building new techniques and ideas smoothly into traditional societies. The result was huge wastage; millions spent with no visible change to show for them. People were not prepared for these kinds of help. Then came the drought of the early Seventies. The NGOs took stock of the real state of affairs. They changed their approach. At the same time many local communities were shocked out of their old beliefs and began to think hard about the pros and cons of change.

'There are now many village associations, associations of development groups, and federations of peasant farmers along the valley who are putting together proposals for projects which answer their problems and their needs. They would like these programmes financed and do not want anything else. The question is whether there are European aid agencies who are open to such demands. There are plenty of NGOs who arrive with their own ideas of what should be done and have no intention of altering their plans. They can still find local people who will cooperate with them to carry out their plans. There are NGOs going about looking for villages in which to set up shop. There are in fact hundreds of NGOs in the district of Podor but one does not see the results or have much evidence of their impact.

'There are other organisations who are putting all their funding into training. Training which leads directly to local action, and is backed by functional literacy work, is really important. Literacy work on its own is very popular at the moment, particularly because there is a widespread movement to preserve and build up the Pulaar language to compete on equal terms with Wolof as a national language. But what will really endure is literacy combined with a practical motive. For example, a market garden or a small business. It is good sense to bring together a number of local people to learn how to manage and run such an enterprise in their own tongue. When the motive is survival, it stands a much better chance of lasting. Literacy in a vacuum may help the individual to escape into the wider world but is unlikely to be passed from one generation to the next. Functional literacy classes, linked say to a communal vegetable garden, in which there are regular records and accounts to be kept and meetings to be minuted by a growing circle of villagers, have a strong chance of lasting. Such a group can even afford to pay a trained agent to teach them. It can then develop other kinds of training.

'In agriculture, take the tomatoes which are grown in large quantities along the valley. The growers often cannot sell them and they go to waste. At Madina we began to experiment with powdered tomatoes and with tomato paste. We didn't make huge amounts but when there is a glut people know the technique and offer the product in the market. It's all due to the training and education people have been given in the women's centre there. For me, that's what it is all about. I always try and put my efforts

**Planting tomatoes in the wet soil as the river recedes**

David MacDonald

into practical activities.

'There is a fresh opportunity to get things moving. There are
changes brought about by the withdrawal of all the state services
on which the farmers relied. There are the practical difficulties of
growing and selling crops in an unprotected market. There are the
effects of drought and of the damming of the river upstream which
is stopping the annual flooding of tens of thousands of hectares of
agricultural land, forcing farmers into new systems of paddy rice
growing in collectively run flooded enclosures. These events have
created shock waves along the valley. People are unprepared.
People are lost. They have got used to receiving everything free.
They didn't know where it came from. They didn't know its price.
Things are really only appreciated when one knows their value
and one has had to sweat tears to raise the money to buy them. It
is only now that the agricultural community has found this out,
and found it out in a brutal fashion.

'From the moment when the state abruptly cut off all the
support it was supposed to be giving to the farming community,
the farmers have begun to re-organise themselves and to try and

remember all the things they had been told in the past and see what might be of use. It may be an unavoidable result of the changes of government demanded by the international donors, but they find it hard to live with.

'The farming community in this part of the country has many practical problems. One is that there is no longer a natural flood. Instead they have expensively levelled fields to be irrigated artificially, which are proving to be too small to be profitable. The result is you cannot feed your family, pay your debts, or recoup your investment in that field. On top of that, seasonal agriculture is always a gamble. You cannot sow and guarantee to harvest at so much per cent profit. You win some, you lose some.

'Another problem is that of selling your crop. You harvest it at the same time as all your neighbours. You put your production on the market at the same time as everyone else. The market is saturated. You are forced to sell at a low price. You get less for your crop than you invested in it. But the price of fertilisers and pesticides never drops. Let's say you have invested 100 francs, you may only get 70 in return and you will then have to sell some of your animals to make up the difference. But that is not all. What is the family going to eat? It depends entirely on that little family field of twelve ares, 16 to 18 at most. It's too small to feed a family. In all the big irrigated systems being prepared it is said that everyone will have at least a hectare instead, but even that is not enough. In short there are the problems of land and yields and there is also the problem of the market. If the state wishes to promote the farming community it should find a way of buying in the crops at a good price.'

'But the IMF and World Bank programme demands a free market economy that makes that impossible,' I interject.

'It would be possible for the farming community to organise itself into large associations and see how they might farm profitably.'

'You have travelled a long way since I first met you and you are still full of schemes. How do you do it?' I commented.

'Well, I'm 45. I am still optimistic about development and I know that there is plenty to do in giving training to my own people, the Toucouleurs, so that they can develop themselves. There's lots to do and I'm not at all discouraged.'

# CHAPTER NINE

# THIERNO BA
# AND BAMTAARE

*To live is first of all to survive, to exist physically, to eat, to protect oneself, and then look for comfort, a practical way of doing things, eventually beauty, amusement, learning, knowledge about the visible world, a journey into the kingdom of divine mystery.*

**A text in the IFAN Museum, Dakar, next to a display of the evolution of the *daba*, commonest farming tool of the Sahel**

Thierno Ba is the director of the PIP, which is based at Ndioum on the hot and drought-prone northern frontier of Senegal. Watching him over a period of time is quite exhausting. He is continually on the move, meeting farmers in their fields, swopping ideas, counselling and encouraging villagers, welcoming visitors, dictating reports. One moment he is speaking in Pulaar, the next in French. One moment he is asking the cook to give food to a trio of ragged *talibes* from the near-by Koranic school; next he is galvanising a room full of young trainers before they go out to their villages. Then he is agonising over a mechanical fault in one of the precious four-wheel drive vehicles without which the team is severely handicapped in the huge, largely roadless region.

Thierno was a man, I thought, tightly stretched between two cultures, as were the people of the river valley. So before I asked him about the way he saw the future development of his people I asked him whether he thought there was a similarity between a central theme of *The Ambiguous Adventure* and the situation the

Christian Aid/Derrick Knight

**Thierno Ba**

present generation faced. This theme simplified was: which way do we go as a people to avoid social catastrophe and, having chosen, what happens if we were wrong?

'I believe,' he replied, 'that since the great drought of 1973 we are in all kinds of ambiguous situations. There is a phrase in Pulaar, *inte annide*, of which the closest translation might be 'ambiguous adventure'. For instance, there is the continuing drought and yet people say that it is God who brings the rain — an ambiguity!

'There are ambiguities in development. It is said that one must do development at the base — the grass roots, a development which creeps along, a development with small projects and programmes. Others say that development must be done very quickly and with big programmes and projects.

'Does development begin in the village development associations, in the local groups for the promotion of women, in the non-governmental organisations with small resources and means which are 'realistic'? Or does it come from the government-to-government approach? Here there is another ambiguity. An ambiguity of approach. Is it to be an approach at the level of the farmers, with all that includes in the way of minimum risk? How they deal with variable rainfall, the kind of crops they choose to grow, how they use fertilisers and so forth? Or is it the government approach which decrees that there must be irrigated agriculture here in the valley to grow rice? Why should we grow rice? The answer seems to be because it has become an eating habit. And it is an important factor in the stability of the urban population.

'Or is it the big business approach to development, the creating of agribusinesses? Some people say that they are not yet a problem here; but agribusinesses don't have to come from outside. Look at the case of the Senegalese Sugar Company (CSS). Their plant at

Richard Toll employs some 8-10,000 people and expert opinion says that the sugar industry is not viable. Yet a former minister once said that it would still be more profitable to Senegal for CSS to go on paying these people and buy in sugar from abroad than to dismiss them and have them adding to the unemployed. [It is one of the government's few remaining enterprises and because it has a monopoly, is able to charge prices at least three times the going price elsewhere in the world. At the same time it is unable to produce enough to satisfy the local market and buys in cheap sugar from abroad to make up its needs. The CSS offers that sugar too at the inflated price and thus is able to subsidise the salaries of its factory workers.]

'We might say that development has to do with transport, roads, and telephone communication. We now have a good road joining the main cities to the communities in the river valley as far as Ouressugui, but no modern road down to Bakel and into neighbouring Mali to boost trade. There are still no good roads into the best farming areas in the whole country, like the island of Morphil, which would enable the harvest to be got to market in good conditions. Now when it rains the whole area is cut off. When you remember that the river valley was once the millet granary for the whole of Senegal and might be once again, one wonders why this essential road system has not yet been developed.

'Let's talk about rain. It has become very irregular, both where it rains and when it rains. Here we are at the end of September, almost the end of the wet season, and there has hardly been any rain at all. If it rained now the growing season would be lost. There would be no point in trying to plant anything. We have not even had 20 mm [average annual rainfall in the Podor region should be between 200 and 400mm]. So you see, there are so many ambiguities from the point of view of development, from the point of view of organisation, from the point of view of traditional or modern ways of life, that we can be said to be, as you have said, at "the high tide of ambiguities".'

'Surely,' I asked, 'many of these ambiguities have always been present in Senegalese society? There were plenty of contradictions in the development policies being followed when I first came here 25 years ago. Kane's novel is set further back in the colonial period. The debate about sending boys to the Koranic or to the

French-speaking school, then called "the school of the enslaved",
seems to be as fresh today as it was then.'

'Yes,' Thierno replied, 'the debate goes on but it is much more
complex and interesting than it was then. In the old days the
ambiguity was — should a boy go to the French school or to the
traditional one? In those days the initiation into manhood was a
real landmark in his status. Now it has much less significance. The
biggest ambiguity in education and training is at the level of the
message being transmitted and whether it is to be in the official
language or not. As you know there are six national languages and
there is one language — French — recognised as the official
language, the language in which we are speaking now. The
question is whether development is going to be conducted in the
official language. Does it mean that everybody has to start learning
French from an early age and neglect or forget his mother tongue?
Or should the child be educated in one of the national languages
for at least two or three years and then learn another language
later?

'There's the tug of war between tradition and modernity. I
believe one should know who one is, what one is, before being
capable of respecting and loving things about which one has had
no experience until then.

'As soon as we became independent we began to have what
we called "development of the communities at the grass roots".'

I reminded him that the phrase was '*les gens doivent se
défendre eux-mêmes*' — the people must take up their own cause
themselves — and I had heard it said back in 1968 by Ben Mady
Cisse, the government's chosen vessel to bring change to the
countryside.

Thierno grinned. 'You are right. We even had powerful radio
sets in the villages so that people could gather to hear the good
word and comment on it — an early attempt at feedback. That
was the afterglow of independence. But there were problems and
it wasn't long before the elders were asking, when is the
independence thing going to end, because they were nostalgic for
what to them was a less troubled past when their authority was
not open to question.

'That was the direction which development was taking then.
We have now reached a point where a whole range of pressures
have come together at the same time. The structural adjustment

programmes and the damaging effects of the drought are two of them, but others must also be taken into account. So if we want to talk about ambiguities, there are so many it is difficult to know where to start or finish.'

Thierno is already a living legend in the Senegal River valley — a guru of a style of development which answers the needs of the farming community; a down-to-earth visionary of change; a strong advocate of the poor; a believer in their ability to emerge vigorously from the present economic crisis. As such he is inevitably the source of controversy.

'At a certain moment in my life, chance took me in a certain direction which I now regard as very good fortune. I come from a family of small farmers. I went to the French-speaking school more or less by accident, since there were only two in my village from my age group who went to school: I had a namesake on the governing committee who wanted me to go. The school was at Matam, some seven kilometres from Ouressugui where I lived. I had to walk there and back every day. I learnt quickly. When I reached the top standard in the primary school I took the exams for secondary education and was offered a place in four schools. I wanted to go to the Ecole Normale William Ponty in Dakar, from which one emerged as a teacher or with qualifications which guaranteed well paid work. But I didn't go there and today I thank God for it. The only school the family could afford was the School of the Agricultural Technicians because it also offered full board and lodging.

'I spent four years there and then immediately started work on the land as a young farm extension worker. I discovered that there was then a kind of training being done which is now called 'encadrement' — a word which has two meanings. It means training, but it also means putting people into a framework. It seemed to be the latter meaning which was stronger. The agricultural technician "knows", and the farmer "knows nothing". So the technician tells him to do this and to do that. The farmer asks why? The technician says: "It is too difficult for you to understand, just do it!" To me it didn't make sense. I didn't understand the thinking behind it. But I was caught in the system because when our district manager wanted something done, I was not able to question him — he "knew" and I "knew nothing", even though it was I who was with the farmers and out in the fields.

'It didn't stop there. The same thing happened to the district manager. When his regional director came visiting, *he* had "all the answers". The district manager knew nothing. When the national director or the Minister came it was the same story. *He* knew exactly what should be done and nobody else knew anything worth knowing. There was a whole hierarchy from top to bottom prepared to carry out instructions from above without questioning. The higher officials had no inkling that the man on the ground was well qualified and had the real experience. Their authority was entirely mythical. They had no idea what went on at the grass roots. They were prepared to ignore field experience, the daily contact with farmers. To them it meant nothing. I was profoundly worried about it. I was sure it was a fundamental mistake.

'I decided to do a further course to enable me to get a better grasp of the problems. I enrolled in the Ecole Nationale de l'Economie Appliqué (ENEA) in Dakar. Before I went there I had been a simple agricultural extension worker. When I came out I had gained a set of new perspectives on the rural economy and its mechanisms. I became the head of a local Centre for Rural Expansion (CER). I had a staff of 10, each of whom had their sphere of work — water and forest, animal husbandry, health, the family livelihood and so on. My job was to lead and coordinate them. Though I worked with each of them to open their minds to the wider issues, I found it slow going to try and overcome the training they had received to give orders to villagers without proper discussion or explanation. It didn't work. It still goes on. It still doesn't work.

'So I went back to school. I took a master's degree in Rural Sociology in Paris. Afterwards I wanted to return to Senegal and work directly with farmers. I had no wish of returning to Senegal to step into the sort of job in a Dakar office to which higher education entitles you. Anyone can become a minister, I thought. Anyone can be the national director of a government service; but not many can work with farmers at the grass roots.

'The more I thought about it, the more I realised that I still lacked some basic understanding. It was how to reach out to adults in a society like ours where opinions and prejudices were already set but needed challenging. So I decided to continue my studies a while longer and I enrolled in the Department of Sciences and Education at the University of Lyon II. There I did a diploma course which enabled me to make an in-depth study of a village development association in the Senegal River valley to examine closely the kind of problems such associations face, how they start, how they run themselves, how they fit into local traditions and customs, what influence they have and so forth.

'What I discovered seemed to me fundamental to an understanding of how village societies are prepared to accept and work with change or not.

'There have been village associations linked to the preservation of traditions, young people's age groups and so forth. I felt it might be worth trying to build up certain members, provide them with some professional skills so that they could give new life to these associations and get them to move forward more quickly.

'The job of the administrative services of the country is make the best use of available skills, to open the country up to new ideas. The task of the village on the other hand is to maintain proper respect for local traditions. If one could mobilise the young to have a broader vision of their role it might be possible for the association to evolve differently and to take them along a development road.

'In the traditional associations the elders have always had the final say. A certain person will be nominated as leader because his father had been the leader. Another will be sent to a meeting or be delegated to represent the village because his father was a reliable defender of village tradition and custom. These customs have to be taken into account when proposing any change or there is likely to be a confrontation between yourself and the elders. "If you are prepared to respect our village association," they say, "we shall be able to agree with you and work with you. When you come among us, wrap yourself in the cloak of the village community and accept its rules."

'In my opinion it is only when a younger, more open leadership replaces those elders that a proper development initiative can begin. Then the door will be opened to fresh thinking and fresh actions. It will allow a modern-style association to come into being because the young generation who have been able to go to school will want to introduce modern ideas. The hold the elders have had over the community will fade away as it becomes clear to more and more people that they are no longer in touch with the times. Even their expertise on the environment is proving worthless as

the climate, the rainfall, the flow of the river, all fail to respond to
their predictions based on known patterns of the past.

'When I had gathered together all this information and
experience, I tried to see if there was a means of achieving "good
development" and a good programme of training.

'It was while I was still doing research in parts of the Senegal
River valley and was visiting Ndioum, that I found the offices of the
PIP. There was a French director and just one field worker at that
time. We had a chat and they told me that they were having local
problems with an agronomist belonging to the state development
agency, the SAED, who was behaving badly towards villagers and
giving them the wrong advice. The PIP's own agronomist was
leaving. Would I be able to join them? I explained that I still had
much to do before completing my research and it wasn't possible.
They said it was a shame and wouldn't I give it more thought? I
said no, I had to complete my master's degree first.

'They wouldn't leave matters alone. They came chasing after
me as I moved from village to village up the valley and repeated
the offer at least four times. Eventually I had a phone call from
Dakar from their president Ahmadou Malick Gaye, asking me to
come and see him. He said to me: "If you really want to help the
region after you finish your studies this is what I propose. I will
enroll you on the staff of the PIP. I will arrange that your flight and
your expenses are paid each time you have to go to France and
back to complete your course. In the meantime you will begin a
programme of action-research." The French university agreed to a
plan of four months in France, eight months in Senegal and I
began work. In 1987 I became a full-time member of the team.'

'Exactly how did you begin to put your ideas to the test?'

'When I first began to look closely at the region in 1984 I
realised how important it was that the local languages be used to
enable the villagers to move forward. I also saw that they would
have to be the ones making the real decisions in their own
development. I realised that it was wholly impractical for a modest
organisation like the PIP to provide technical support, training and
material help for some 300 and more market-garden schemes 50
to 100 kms apart, which is what they were trying to do. The plan
was all wrong. What might be possible was to enable one or two
villages to master the techniques of market-gardening so that
when others came to the PIP for help they could be sent to see

what could be done and learn from the experience of those villagers. We might even be able to train a number of people in those villagers to become instructors themselves to go to other villages and show them how to do it.

'So we began to create these little islands of expertise from which other little islands could take a lead. It wasn't an idea that was worked out from the start. It evolved, and local people developed the idea in their own ways. And at the same time, with the budget we had, we looked for a means of achieving "good development" and a good programme of training. The PIP has become a testbed for development actions which may, unlike those of the organisations in which I worked previously, lead to a good development result.

'We face up to that challenge here every day. What can we achieve here — in the teeth of often adverse political and economic events, and of the state of the environment? What can be done to solve the problems thrown at us by structural adjustment, the withdrawal of the state and the presence of all kinds of non-governmental organisations with their lack of coordination and their different visions of what should be done? Now that there is a growing number of village development associations and inter-village associations, what do all these people, all these civil organisations, hope to achieve?

'So we went and talked with villagers, farmers, herders, local workers to see if we could find one word, phrase or idea which could act as a rallying point, something people felt they owned and which made them feel good. Something about which they all agreed. And the word we found was the Pulaar word *Bamtaare*.

It was a word which had all kinds of depths. I remember a village instructress whom we asked how she understood it. "*Bamtaare*", she said, "is after you have worked with your group of women, after you've done everything you should have done, gone to your room, had a good wash, discussed the day's news and gone to bed." To me it means "well-being", although "well-being" is so widely interpreted that each of us has his or her own idea of its meaning.

'It poses another question. Are the people here looking for a sudden growth of income? Are those with only a bicycle wishing for a car tomorrow? Why not a private plane or a large private house and all the comforts? But we have a sense that the people in some of those countries who have arrived at those levels of income have no well-being. A man or a woman who work hard throughout their lives only to end up in an old people's home, is that *bamtaare*? We ask the question. I suggest that it may not be in that direction at all.

'So at PIP we settled for *bamtaare*. It is very simply when one succeeds in reaching a modest level in one's standard of living which allows one the choice of accepting it or refusing it. When a person is in good health, can eat adequately, can worship freely, has all the basic needs — shelter, food, health — and has earned all the main elements of a modest but decent life. Then that person is able to say, "I accept the limitations or I refuse to be bound by them." It seems to me that this is the key to the kind of training we should be offering. The goal should be how to arrive at that sort of equilibrium. If one swings too far one way it means that one has too little. If someone in the family is sick, one has not got the means to pay for treatment. One cannot feed one's children adequately. If one is too rich, then the danger is that one can do anything at random.

'This is the basis of the training which we are following. Our goal is to enable a person to arrive at that level of equilibrium where he or she can go in the direction they wish. It is a very difficult task but it is what we are doing in a programme we call the Centre d'Entrainement de la Vie Active (CEVA) — the Centre of Training for an Active Life. Those who take part must attain a certain standard of literacy in their mother-tongue and be able to think constructively about what is going on in the world. It implies that when one has reached a standard of literacy in Pulaar one may move to the study of French or another language which will allow one to go elsewhere.

'One must work on the land and discuss problems as they arise with local people. One must always listen to what villagers have to say because they know best what they want. They know their special needs. Even if we are in the training business we should remain modest. I am firmly of the opinion that organisations which support development should not do the development work in place of others on the spot. Development should be done by the local people and we can only support their actions. In this way the people will understand that you haven't come to tell them fairy tales but have come to help them in their community effort.

'....able to think constructively', at the PIP, Ndioum

'Sadly, in the present state of the country's affairs when the government announces that it is withdrawing from many essential services, it is no longer possible to maintain that equilibrium. The government ought to see that there are problems and difficulties and that they have introduced several policies which are unsuccessful. They should try to correct them so that a balance is restored. For me development is a matter of equilibrium.'

Thierno makes himself available to all who wish to ask for help. When he has finished his routine tasks and is not travelling in some part of the huge area which the PIP covers, he daily sits for some hours in the compound of his headquarters and holds an open advice surgery. The setting is the shade of the palaver tree. He habitually wears a simple cotton *boubou* without ornament. Even the least worldly villagers can feel at home. The subjects range from an interpretation of customary law to the interest being charged on a bank loan, from a land dispute to a request for a character reference. Women too come for counselling, no longer afraid to seek help outside the family. The advice is always practical, sound, exactly suited to the listener.

I wondered whether there was a real thirst at the grass roots which opened the way for technical training and health care, or was it only fear of what might happen which was driving people?

'There are several considerations,' Thierno suggested. 'If one sets aside the abandonment of essential services for the people by the government about which much has been said, I believe it is the adult literacy classes which have helped people understand that there are several ways forward open to them.

'First of all they see that the state apparatus is dragging its heels. It is worn out. It is heavily in debt. It gets little done. They see that there have been a number of actions taken to help them which have not worked. On the other hand the literacy classes have shown them that it is possible to learn technical skills in their own language.

'Until then it had always been said that it was only possible to learn about modern techniques in French. Now people see that they can acquire real skills in their own language and even see colleagues who are literate in Pulaar getting jobs as salaried employees. They have many new openings. They run their businesses better. They manage their affairs better. They see that it is possible to argue questions of morality, to develop one's knowledge and to keep business records, all in their own language. In the past they were always told that there was no way of bringing these interests together. In the past when someone was very intelligent the wistful comment was, "Ah yes, if only he had gone to school." The counter-argument is, "Well yes, but if he had gone to school he would soon have lost his powers of memory and of storing information in his head."

'The two were supposed to be irreconcilable. But we have now proved that in learning to read and write one's national language, the two opposing lines of thought can be brought together, because everything is going in the same direction in an equilibrium between tradition and change. Let me give you an example.

'In the past we trained the memory of children by having them repeat verses of the Koran until a clever child could recite the whole of it. Now we can teach a person to read and write so that if he grows forgetful as he gets older he can consult the book and find the text he thought he had forgotten. People are much more confident in themselves than they used to be. They used to leave crucial decisions to others. Now they want to manage as many things as possible on their own. This in my opinion is due entirely to their becoming literate and to their personal discovery. As villagers often tell me, "Before, we were in darkness and now we are moving rapidly towards the light."

I asked him about the connection between the falling standard of living of the rural community and structural adjustment programmes at a national level.

'I think this is a combination of many factors. I will give you a down to earth example. Let us imagine that it had rained this year as it has done in the past. The rain falls generously and at the right time, and the alluvial lands flood, so that people can grow their crops and reap a good harvest, the cows give milk, the fishermen catch enough fish and so on. I am convinced that if that had happened, whatever disasters were taking place elsewhere, whatever international upsets occurred, the peasant farmer would look no further than his own rapidly filling grain store.

'If there are grave problems today, the peasant farmer believes, it is largely because of the effects of the bad drought years and of the villagers being unable to cultivate their crops. As a result they have had to appeal for emergency food aid or for food to carry them through the *soudure* [the lean months before the main harvest]. There have been times when the government should have provided funds and given its fullest support to minimise the effects, but it did too little and too late. It had spent its money elsewhere. If there are any effects as a result of SAPs they are indirect ones. The teacher has left, the health worker charges for prescriptions, agricultural credit has almost disappeared. But it is not because there has been a sudden withdrawal of state services that the rural community is no longer able to make ends meet.

'Another factor is to do with taxes. Because of the 1973 drought people were unable to pay their taxes and their backlog of debt grew into huge sums. The villagers made it a point of honour to pay off those tax debts 100%. Not only that, but they assumed responsibility for the board and lodging of the village teacher who often did not bother to go and draw his salary in Dakar but saved it entirely while he was housed, fed and otherwise cared for in the village community for free. One has known other officials who chose to go and live in a rural community because life was simple for them and they had no expenses.

'Under the impact of the worst years of drought the village people were no longer able to satisfy the needs of those strangers who had come "to spread the good word", to use a village expression, and were having all their daily needs met. That included teachers, health workers, petty officials. Many of them left. It is in that sense, perhaps, that one should look at the impact that decisions made in the capital have on the rural community. When the price of petrol rose or fell it didn't have much impact on rural society because they made very few journeys. Barter was the local currency.

'It was altogether a different matter when the government, in order to meet its debts and other obligations to foreign donors, decreed that the agricultural regime in the Senegal River valley had to change to a systematic irrigated agriculture. It was different, too, when the government abandoned the support it gave to the cultivation of groundnuts because it said, they are now shown to be a cancer risk. In any case, they argue, the world price has fallen because of the competition from soya bean oil, sunflower oil and so on. They see massive irrigation here as an answer.'

The Senegal River valley scheme (which everybody calls '*le barrage*') is a national debt which, officials told me, will have to be paid for largely from levies and other charges upon the rural community along the valley, so I asked Thierno what they had been told.

'It is a massive debt,' Thierno agreed, 'well over 400 billion local francs (334 million US dollars). Senegal has to find 70% of the total, while Mauritania and Mali share 30%. If we are talking about the effects which have already been felt by the farmers, then this is not one. It is in the future. At present the small farmers don't know where and how the water will be metered, how it will be paid for.

'In the Senegal River valley we have had many of the problems since the 1973 drought. What we can say is that *le barrage* is likely to make these problems worse, particularly in relation to the environment. The dams could be used to flood the land up to 25 kilometres on either side of the river, but it seems the authorities have no intention of doing that. It is the holding back of the water that is going to be terrible. The fact is that the people most affected have not been consulted. This is what people should be fighting about. They need to use all the influence and arguments they can muster.

'One local farmer said to me a year ago: "We think the dam is a good thing and we shall have all the water we need." Now he is protesting vigorously. "Why have you changed your mind?" I asked. "Well," he said, "in the past I thought water was the gift of God, God made the water, the water came, flooded the land, the cattle drank it, the crops grew and the water table under the trees rose and the trees flourished. There was an equilibrium. When they built the dam at Manantali we believed that all the water in the Fouta Djallon was going to be saved and held in a reservoir, so that when the rains failed us they would have all that water down there that could be released to make up our shortfall. They would create a flood. So the animals which had been pastured in the *djeri* could come down to the *waalo* when it was wet and green and the annual cycle of crops and the movement of herds would be renewed as it had always been. And the trees would not die any more. It is true that trees have been killed because people cut them, but the main reason is that their roots cannot reach water. Then as the flood water subsides we have a second season of crops, planted stage by stage as the water recedes. And the animals can remain in the valley and provide us with milk for the whole year. We thought the dam would secure the annual cycle we have always practised. As a result we would have everything we had in the good old days. But now they tell us they want to stop all that. Now they are fixing up a giant tap and they will turn it on when they want and close it when they want. That is what frightens us."

'In fact the villagers have been given very little hard information. And of course nobody can see the main dam upstream. It's in neighbouring Mali. There is already an epidemic of bilharzia in the plantations downstream in the delta as a result of the release of water stored upstream which is contaminated. Not only bilharzia but many other water-borne diseases are coming into the valley.

'At Richard Toll they have commissioned a specialist team from France to look at the problems and suggest solutions. Scientists have been searching for ways of combatting these diseases for years and have not found the answers, so the inhabitants of the valley are to be exposed to a whole list of diseases to which they are not accustomed. It is another kind of danger. Yet there is no information given out to warn the villagers. Many officials say you mustn't frighten people, you mustn't tell them about such things. So the official line is to talk about the advantages of the dams and to ignore their bad effects.

'The communities are much more organised than they have ever been, and they are not fooled. In April 1992, the PIP was asked to host a seminar at Ndioum, organised independently by peasant organisations in the valley. It attracted a broad cross-section of peasant associations, inter-village federations, women's and youth groups from Podor to Bakel. They got the idea from a seminar on debt, sponsored by Christian Aid a couple of years earlier, when all who attended it on behalf of popular organisations realised that they had the same problems as those in other parts of the world and wanted to make common cause with them.

'The 1992 meeting marked a big step forward for a rural population which had become aware of what was happening to them and what they had to do. As civil servants abandoned their posts, social services collapsed, agricultural networks were broken up, and government development agencies were stripped of their budgets and assets, rural populations found themselves having to provide alternatives out of their own pockets. For the first time in Senegalese history they felt strong enough to join together to share their concerns and demand some answers.

'At the end of the meeting they agreed the terms of an appeal, addressed both to their neighbours and to the authorities, which made it clear that they had no illusions about the causes of the economic crisis or about the government's plans to exploit the supposed weakness of the rural population. This appeal containing a list of issues which had to be solved, complaints which needed discussion, and needs which demanded to be addressed, was drawn up and endorsed by a long list of community organisations. It was written, not in terms of a political challenge — the signatories have no political agenda or party affiliation — but in terms of an invitation for the beginning of a dialogue with government to discuss matters of some urgency to a majority of its citizens. It went not only to local government officials like the prefect and the regional governor but to the President's Office and all the ministers with responsibility for aspects of regional life. None of them have so far taken up the issues or replied formally to the appeal.'

That position remained true as this book went to the printer. The appeal is included as an appendix to this chapter. The peasant farmer and community organisations have continued to forge strong links between themselves and to press for dialogue with government.

'I believe that the experience gained from making this appeal and its treatment by the country's present leadership will not be lost on the rural population. In practical matters I believe that what is needed is that communities must take complete charge of their lives. They need to belong to local associations which work entirely in their interest. Officially controlled bodies or privately financed groups won't do. They won't do, because too much goes on under the table in such bodies. Communities need their own savings and credit facilities. It doesn't need much to start a new scheme but I think it is a way of getting things going, of getting money to work. Money must stay in the village. Small sums soon add up. These village savings groups can then be the means of attracting outside credit for small projects or even of lending small sums to individuals who are known and trusted. The local savings group will know exactly what resources the borrower has — a donkey, goats, how many hectares of land — and be able to assess his or her credit limit realistically.

'At the present time agricultural credit is very hard to obtain and the feeling is that only those with influence or capable of spinning a good tale or able to offer a bribe succeed. There are always stories circulating about certain high officials or dignitaries who obtain large sums because they were able to offer inducements, to use "*la petite porte*" as it is called.

'It is quite clear that the present agricultural credit system, or lack of it, must be reformed. If not, then community run village savings banks must be encouraged. With the widespread success of literacy and numeracy classes in the valley, it would be a simple matter to organise courses in the management of such activities. Then it should be possible to link them and form a genuine central farmers' bank based on capital provided by the farming communities themselves. It is quite realistic. Once the local savings groups had agreed on a plan, the non-governmental organisations could help with security by providing safes and strong boxes and funds for the training of staff in their own language.'

Thierno reminded me of a comment made to me by an official about the present system of agricultural credit. First, he said, it will kill many farmers, then it will kill agriculture and then the surviving farmers will set out to kill the staff who ran the system.

'In fact it is a good image of ONCAD, the National Office of Cooperation and Assistance for Development, which was set up by the government as a channel for agricultural credit for the cultivation of groundnuts. It got mired in bureaucracy and shadowy dealings. It managed to cripple many farmers and finally it was forced to close down in 1980. It added to the numbers out of work and destroyed many families.

'Now one of its replacements, the CNCAS — the National Agricultural Credit Fund, is going the same way. The CNCAS was supposed to help provide short-term credit for the farmer for his main cereal crop, for essential expenses, fertiliser and tools, for six to nine months with low interest. But the conditions were strict. It only considered legally constituted village groups. It had very little money to lend. So the problem of credit for agriculture remains an acute problem. The government is angry, the big banking interests are angry, the farmers are angry. Everybody is complaining.'

I was summarising the situation in my head as Thierno spoke. The farmers cannot re-imburse their loans because they have not been paid for the rice and tomatoes supplied to the processing factories. The processing factories say they cannot pay the farmers because they have no money until they can sell on the products they hold. The products they hold don't sell because the country has imported similar products more cheaply. The country opened its import trade because it was told to do so by the IMF and the World Bank as part of a structural adjustment programme. A road towards disaster is clearly marked out.

The light was failing, a queue of petitioners had formed to ask Thierno his advice, his help, his comfort. We had to tidy up and bring the dialogue to an end. But he had one last argument to put to me:

'I cannot remember who it was who said that not to engage in political issues was also a form of political action. When it comes down to it, it all depends on the nature of the problem. When people become literate, when they begin to understand what their rights are, one is helping them to live more confidently, more at ease. I tell people time and time again that the power to say yes is only important in relation to how firmly one can say no. I believe that all these things are hastening the time when people will be able to commit themselves politically.

'Development is a form of politics. It is the politics of development. So the way I understand it, there is nobody who is not caught up in politics in some way or other. Of course there are political schemers and professional politicians, but there is also a liberating form of politics. Each of us does politics in his or her own way. There is no doubt that it is a constant struggle.

'What I think is important in an organisation is not the leaders. It is those behind them, those who are motivated, the farmers' organisation who see clearly whether you are doing any good or whether you are doing badly. There comes a time when it is the organisation which decides to back its leaders or not. When that happens I think it becomes a strong and dependable body. Leaders have to realise that they cannot do anything they like, that they have the power neither to build nor to demolish.

'Development at the grass roots is above all building on the kind of actions and courses we are promoting, encouraging the community and farming organisations with whom we are working, and accompanying them at all times and as equals, not as some sort of superior being. That is what I think is important. When we have achieved this, it is certain that some will still be unhappy. It is a tough challenge. It is a perpetual struggle. Its objectives are all-embracing. But I believe that in a democratic country like Senegal the ordinary people have a much greater opportunity to speak up strongly once they know themselves to be within their rights. When they see the state withdrawing from many of its former obligations and when they face so many economic and social problems, one can expect the community organisations to talk about their rights, too, and to choose independent political candidates who will speak up for them because they know now what policies and actions they wish to see implemented. That, too, is development.'

Thierno turned with keen interest to his next petitioner. However tired he might be, he was there to share the pain or the delight of his visitor and to use every opportunity to promote *bamtaare.*

# APPENDIX

**APPEAL BY THE PEASANT ASSOCIATIONS OF THE SENEGAL RIVER VALLEY WHO MET AT NDIOUM ON 22-23 APRIL 1992.**

Within living memory, the inhabitants of the Senegal River valley were able to live by their work.

Crops irrigated by rain, and crops cultivated on land drying out after the annual river flood, guaranteed a subsistence which was completed by animal husbandry and fishing in the river and in the ponds. The trees in the woodlands provided wood with which to build and to cook. They also provided fruit and medicine.

The soil was enriched either by leaving it fallow, if it was rain-fed, or by the annual flood with its deposit of fertile silt on low lying land.

People cared for their environment as they did for each other. Those who went away to find work elsewhere, did it to enable their families back home to have a better life. But they knew that the community they left behind was solidly rooted. The older generation has lived through times when folk had no fear for their well-being. But the very young today only know a time when each is anxious about tomorrow.

The chronic failure of annual rains, the breakdown of the annual flood, has for many years threatened the very existence of those who depend on the river for a livelihood. Those who stay work hard in the fields and harvest very little; sometimes nothing at all. The fish have died. The animals are dying. The trees are dying. The land is becoming exhausted. Those who migrate are compelled to send their loved ones the means to survive.

The Senegal River basin scheme, with its dams designed to raise production, may herald the end of our way of life by taking away all hope. Its criteria are those of the past — edicts issued by the authorities — the need to make immediate profits. We are excluded. Up to now the peasant farmers along the valley have been offered no role in the development of the big scheme.

Faced with these dangers, we the signatories of this appeal affirm that:

> The most important resource of a country like ours is the knowledge and courage of the men and women who live here, our own people.

The real 'private sector', the only possible starting point for a development which respects the declared objectives (ie priority given to the basic need to provide a living for the population of the valley, the creation of local jobs, protection of the environment by harmonised development of all the possibilities of the region), is peasant family agriculture.

This peasant family agriculture can only survive and develop itself with the support of a system of organised community mutual aid which is the action of the peasants themselves.

**1.** We urge all those farmers, herders, fishermen and their families who depend on the river for their living to join such bodies, to put more weight behind them if they are already members, to create new genuine work organisations without partisan or sectarian affiliations, who respect democratic membership rules and have financial management open to all and especially:

- Strong village groups to face up to the tough problems which are beyond the capacity of isolated families. Specifically:
  — management of a communal stock of fertilisers and seeds.
  — the maintenance of an irrigation network.
  — the protection of arable lands.
  — the guarding of growing crops against cattle.
  — the fight against desertification and drought.

- Federations or unions of peasants linking different villages to tackle the problems which can only be solved at the level of several rural communities working together:
  — allocation and withdrawal of land rights.
  — agreed corridors or paths for migrating cattle.
  — management of ponds and wet lands.
  — means of managing and supplying stocks of fertilisers and other field chemicals (other than through the 'Crédit Agricole' scheme).
  — access for women and young people to arable land and the means of production.
  — marketing and processing of crops.
  — mechanisation of tilling and threshing.
  — cereal banks.
  — organising village credit schemes.
  — running rural councils.

— dealings with the local government authorities.

— initiation into the skills of writing and calculations in our own languages etc.

● A close and active liaison between federations and peasant unions in the valley in the hope that, however long it takes, it will be possible one day to form a peasant union in order to be able to face up to the problems which can only be solved at a national level and even for some at an international level:

— the political implications of ownership and leasing of land.

— the management of the dams, in particular an agreed level and duration of an artificially induced flood each year.

— relationships between those on the bank of the river (*waalo*) and the upper levels (*djeri*).

— fair terms for the supply of agricultural chemicals.

— a survey of the potential of local resources, especially of fertilisers.

— fair terms for the marketing of crops.

— conditions to ensure the participation of peasant organisations in decision-making affecting their interests at all levels, from local councils to the National Assembly.

— promotion of the active participation of women and young people.

— promotion of the wider use of written and spoken local languages at all levels.

— relationships with NGOs and aid bodies in general.

**2.** We ask administrative authorities to recognise the peasant organisations of the river valley as valid representative bodies with which to negotiate, instead of trying to work round them as is too often the case at present, and especially:

● To provide the peasant associations, federations and unions with a legally recognised statute to make procedures with officials easier.

● To give properly constituted peasant organisations tax relief on agricultural materials without having to organise as an NGO to obtain it, which only mistakes their role and confuses them with groups intervening in the country from overseas.

● To work out with the peasant organisations a pricing system and regulations for imports which will enable local producers of cereals, onions, tomatoes and other vegetables to be able to compete.

- To work out with peasant organisations a timetable and level of water of the annual artificial flood to be released from the dams which will allow the farmers to make the most of crops sowed as the water level falls and which will enable river fish to breed.

- To work out with the peasant organisations a political solution to the ownership and use of land which gives priority to the present and future inhabitants of the valley and then takes account of the needs of the actual and future inhabitants of the rest of Senegal, and which takes account of the potential of all the land and not only the irrigated land.

- To look for appropriate means of farm management other than through the government 'Crédit Agricole' as at present organised.

- To be responsible for the costs and running of public health measures, especially all those to do with water-borne diseases, malaria and bilharzia.

- To enforce the existing laws governing the work of rural councils, notably those which made provision for the right of public access to meetings, advance notices of meetings, keeping of minutes and procedures for the allocation and change of use of land.

- To recognise the right of all the productive groups of farmers, fisherfolk, and herders in a rural community to elect up to the one-third of rural council members which had originally been allocated to cooperatives.

- To allow independent candidates to stand in local elections.

**3.** We request NGOs who promote or support projects in the Senegal River valley to support peasant organisations directly and especially:

- To give priority as part of this support to all matters which reinforce the independence of peasant organisations; to support production by the setting up of supply lines for agricultural materials and ways through which villagers can become self-financing; to find ways of getting information on what is going on or being planned for the modernisation of the river basin; to provide training facilities.

- To avoid subsidising a privatised commercial sector which, unless it is financially viable, will only make the farming community more dependent.

- To judge peasant organisations by their degree of representativeness, their internal democratic working and the openness of their financial affairs rather than their adherence to western thinking on development.

- To challenge the assumption that women and young people should be automatically supported because it may be just a way of avoiding looking at the real questions of representation and power.

- Not to play the game of European governments who treat "migrants" as a separate population.

**List of peasant associations who are signatories of the appeal of peasants taking part in the development of the Senegal river valley:**

**FEDERATION DES PAYSANS ORGANISES DE BAKEL**
**FEDDE BAMTAARE TOORO**
**FEDERATION DES ASSOCIATIONS DU FOUTA**
**DENTAL GOURE ARRONDISSEMENT DE SALDE**
**FEDERATION DES JEUNES YIRLAABE ALLA YDI UNIS ET
    SOLIDAIRES**
**FEDERATION DES FEMMES PAYSANNES DE LA VALLEE DU
    FLEUVE SENEGAL**
**FEDDE YIWEELE DIAB GOLLADE**
**UNION DES JEUNES AGRICULTEURS DE KOYLI
    WIRNDE**
**ASSOCIATION POUR LE DEVELOPPEMENT DU FERLO**
**ASSOCIATION YANG-YANG DODJI**
**FEDERATION DES PAYSANS DE DEMBANKANE**
**ASSOCIATION DES JEUNES DE LA COMMUNAUTE
    RURALE DE GALOYA**

# POSTSCRIPT

*One straw doesn't sweep the courtyard. One finger by itself cannot pick up a pebble.*
**West African proverb**

The anxieties and disillusion about the future which underlie so many of the remarks and thoughts of the people whom I met in 1992 were not eased away by events in 1993, which saw the continuing downward spiral of the economy and an ever wider gulf between an embattled government and its people.

Presidential elections were held in the spring of 1993 in which several opposition parties were allowed to take part for the first time. They were followed by elections for the National Assembly. The people had dared to hope for change but the government fought with money and lies. Opposition parties were inexperienced, unwary and divided; their challenge drained away. The old incumbent Abdou Diouf, or Ndiol Misere as the press scurrilously call him, won a further term and the Socialist Party (PS), despite a long record of mismanagement and corruption, won a safe majority in the Assembly in May. The murder of Babacar Seye on May 15, an opposition leader and respected judge, widely interpreted as a political killing, did nothing for the reputation of the government and it introduced a new dimension to Senegalese politics which, though often acrimonious, was not known as in some African countries for the routine assassination of key players.

In a gesture meant to defuse some of the increasingly vociferous criticism of the government from inside the country and from its international backers, a number of opposition notables were offered ministerial portfolios and accepted them. Their inclusion in a so-called National Government was largely symbolic and it was interpreted by the sharp-eyed as an attempt to take the sting out of the opposition and to hobble it. The independent press however accused the opposition politicians of seizing an early chance of getting their noses into the trough of available perks and salary privileges.

The new government quickly showed that it had learnt nothing from the recent past. It increased the number of ministries to 29 — an action the ever more critical press noted gave Senegal more than any other African country. Most of them were quite unnecessary. Counting ministers without portfolio and former ministers retained in minor posts but with full privileges and expenses, the real number was 50. They gave themselves salary rises and they opened new embassies which were staffed with political friends.

Within weeks, however, with an economic situation considerably worse, with government funds all spent, the cabinet had no alternative but to present itself once again to the IMF and the World Bank with an emergency plan which might enable them to offer further funds, at least enough to pay the salaries of the indispensable public servants and buy some time.

The outcome was the Plan for the Re-launch of the Economy (PRE). It was a package of measures designed to fill treasury funds. Customs dues were to be levied on all imports. Petrol and diesel oil prices were raised dramatically. VAT was to be levied on a wider range of goods.

The PRE also included cuts in salaries and expenses of ministers, including the President, and civil servants, making it look as if the members of the government were at least willing to shoulder some of the pain of an austerity drive. The President was to have a 50% salary cut, ministers and deputies in the National Assembly 25%, together with reduction in petrol allowances, use of official cars and other personal allowances. An end was ordered to grants for the furnishing of the homes of ministers. Civil servants and all employees of the state received salary cuts of 15% and a loss of many perks. In a call for nationwide solidarity for the government's problems all workers in the private sector were required to donate a payless day a month. Extra taxes were to be levied on private savings.

There was no doubt that Senegal needed a rigorous economic plan to aid its recovery, backed by the whole of the population. But the PRE was accused by the media and by the *patronat* — the local equivalent of the Institute of Directors in Britain — of being a recipe for economic disaster and the further impoverishment of the majority of the population. The tax changes would damage the fragile livelihood of the poor. NGOs, who had customs exemption for goods and equipment imported for development projects, would face large extra costs which donors might not be prepared to meet. Fuel prices were already higher than in any other West African country and bore no relationship to the real cost of imported crude. The rise would be passed on in higher transport costs for goods and people leading to higher food prices, higher electricity and water bills, all of which were already beyond a majority of the population. The salary cuts to public servants would add to the misery of low wages, often paid several months in arrears.

The apparent ingredient of sacrifice by the country's leadership demanded in the PRE was soon unmasked as a fraud by members of the new independent press, notably *Sud Quotidien* which had flourished during the election campaigns and gained a reputation for audacious reporting. *Sud* uncovered a major secret scam over top government salaries. Politicians would lose nothing. For a long time the official salaries of ministers and others those holding office were being at least tripled by an under the table, tax-free cash payment which came out of a 'black' fund. It appeared in no budget nor in any public accounts. Now even the newly elected opposition party leaders and deputies, supposedly elected on a clean politics ticket, had condoned the situation and taken their envelopes of cash. It did not matter that the official part of their salaries might be cut, they did not need it. It was all a sham. Even those Senegalese who had been prepared to give the newly elected government a chance to pull the country together now saw that the whole political milieu was rotten, the appeal to national solidarity a con.

In the meantime the government, any integrity shattered, prepared to implement its new economic measures without

**'Everybody on strike...'**

consulting business, the unions or religious leaders, or testing public opinion. It seemed prepared to brazen it out with tricks and the manipulation of patronage. The international banks, perhaps out of relief that some action was planned to fill the Treasury account even at further cost to the economy, agreed the measures.

The immediate result was the stiffening of opposition and a withdrawal of popular trust. The attempt to push the measure of the PRE led to a full-scale General Strike, the first for 25 years, on September 2nd 1993. An unprecedented grouping of unions, workers, traders, the middle class and political opposition parties brought the whole country to a standstill. 'The country at half-mast,' 'At death's door,' 'Dead cities', were the headlines the next day. It was wholly successful. Other smaller-scale protests were mounted before and after the strike; truckers protesting petrol and diesel rises; traders protesting customs dues. The CONGAD, the council of NGOs, denounced the measures which they said would fatally damage the efforts of all those groups to pull themselves up by all kinds of small projects and self-managed schemes.

The government damaged itself further by ordering the violent breaking up of peaceful protests. On November 9 1993 it used armed police with gas and batons to remove a peaceful sit-in outside the Ministry of Finance. They arrested 170 including women, children, *marabouts* and members of the National Assembly and held them in prison in an open breach of Senegalese constitutional rights. Senegal, once the bright star of African democracy and a champion of human rights, has fallen from grace. Amnesty International too, has sounded the alarm.

Growing unemployment and poverty is fast breaking down the fabric of ethnic, family and religious customs, a worry mentioned by several of my interviewees. People can no longer afford the traditional hospitality to guests and strangers which for generations has been a valued sign of a caring community. At meal times more and more people hide from relatives, neighbours or other visitors to avoid having to feed them. The sacrifice is too great and yet they feel ashamed and guilty. Samba talked about the effect in his own family in Chapter Two, but my more recent conversations show that it has since got worse.

The rural community has seen a fall in its living standards for which it bears no responsibility and which has occurred despite developing its own resources. The problems of getting paid for rice and for tomatoes by the private companies SMT and SOCAS, about which farmers spoke in Chapter Four, remained unresolved by the end of November 1993 — 18 months after the contracts should have been honoured. The economic crisis is causing all kinds of local tensions. For the second year running many farmers, bereft of financial means to pay for the package of inputs necessary for a new crop cycle, have been unable to plant. The interest on the credit they were given by the farm credit scheme for the 1991-92 season is still running. It has eventually to be repaid. The factories remain unwilling or unable to pay their customers. Now there are questions about who is to blame — the factory, the farmer, or the state? The time will come when people refuse to pay because it is not their fault. The withdrawal of the government from many of its former social and technical services continues. The former Senegal Development Agency (SAED), which was supposed to be the advance guard of the irrigated rice era, has shrunk away, withdrawing its remaining services to farmers.

The major overseas donors like the European Development Fund and some European government donors are completing work on present village irrigation schemes along the river valley without renewing their commitments. Private investment remains scarce.

The frontier between Senegal and Mauritania is still tense and the bulk of the refugees from 1989 are still stranded in camps in northern Senegal, with minimal UNHCR supplies. Some have attempted to return home but found that they have been dispossessed. Because many had their identity documents taken in the 1989 conflict, they cannot prove their rights. The Mauritanian officials deny that a problem exists and say that all the refugees are foreigners. Some shooting incidents have taken place on the river. Plans for navigation remain in abeyance; joint schemes for the improvement of the region are frozen. Though fresh water fish, an important part of local diet, have managed to breed in the river and are once again abundant, traditional fisherfolk fear to go fishing in case they are shot at from the far bank.

Fewer irrigated *périmêtres* for rice paddy are being completed. Targets set by the OMVS planners for increases in agricultural production are proving wholly unrealistic. The OMVS managers have still not consulted or advised the riverside population about how or when water released from the upstream dam will be charged.

The engineers controlling the upstream dam at Manantali have not yet given any clear guidance about whether it is their intention to release an artificial flood from the reservoir or not. It seems to depend on rainfall in the southern mountains. If the reservoir is full, they want to bring down the level. It has nothing to do with the interests of the valley farmers. Nothing has been done to remove their fears that the river will remain in the hands of distant engineers who have no knowledge or concern for farming. If the artificial flood is at the wrong time it will drown any growing crops. There is a clash of interests. The engineers warned the villagers last year not to plant on the low-lying land until November when they intended to send down a flood — too late for the farmers who have to plant earlier to harvest a crop before the intense heat of April and May.

Rains fell generously in the wet season of 1993 and the region can expect good crops both on the *djeri* and in the *waalo* as long as no unexpected disaster strikes — a mistimed artificial flood, a plague of locusts or grain eating birds. Grass has grown in abundance where the desert had established itself. It will not revive the woodlands, but has replenished the groundwater needed to support existing live trees.

The government social services have continued their withdrawal. By breaking the links between themselves and villagers, farmers and the unions representing teachers or health employees, the government can now deny responsibility for any social problems in the country.

On the other hand it means that more and more local communities realise that, now and in the future, they have to count on their own efforts and financial resources to improve their standard of living. Peasant associations in the valley are multiplying. They have been meeting in their local areas, working out priorities, forming new alliances with neighbours and NGOs, splitting away from old loyalties and old political patrons.

The people appear to be mobilising steadily. Their voice is becoming stronger. There is a burning hunger for change. The longer the government delays entering into a dialogue over essential practical issues of livelihood and social well-being — real plans, not pipe dreams, for the future of the river valley — the tougher will be its task. The rural population is still almost 90% of the Senegalese people. United, it is a force to reckon with. Its political fidelity in the past has been too easily bought with promises and small gifts. Not for much longer.

# ABBREVIATIONS AND ACRONYMS

| | |
|---|---|
| **CER** | Centre for Rural Expansion |
| **CFA** | Communaute Financière Africaine |
| **CNCA** | National Agricultural Credit Fund of Senegal |
| **CSS** | The Senegalese Sugar Company. |
| **EC** | European Community |
| **ENDA-GRAF** | The Research-Action-Training Group of Environment and Development of the Third World (a Senegalese NGO) |
| **ESAP** | Enhanced structural adjustment programme |
| **IDA** | International Development Association |
| **IMF** | International Monetary Fund |
| **IFAN** | Institute of Fundamental Research for Black Africa in Dakar |
| **OMVS** | Organisation for the Development of the Senegal River Valley |
| **ONCAD** | National Office for Cooperation and Assistance for Development |
| **PIP** | Integrated Project of Podor (a Senegalese NGO) |
| **PSDS** | Programme of Solidarity and Development in the Sahel (of the World Council of Churches) |
| **SAED** | Society for the Exploitation of the Delta and Valley of the River Senegal (a government agency) |
| **SAP** | Structural adjustment programme |
| **UNDP** | United Nations Development Programme |
| **UNICEF** | United Nations Childrens' Fund |
| **USE** | Union for Solidarity and Inter-Aid (a Senegalese NGO) |
| **WB** | World Bank (or International Bank for Reconstruction and Development) |
| **WHO** | World Health Organisation |

# GLOSSARY

**are**  an area of 100 square metres. 100 ares = one hectare. One hectare is a fraction under two and a half acres.

**boubou**  a loose cotton garment worn on social occasions, often elaborately embroidered.

**canari**  a water storage jar which holds up to 20 litres of water and keeps it cool.

**CFA francs**  currency of many West African countries guaranteed by the French Treasury at the rate of 50 CFA francs to one French franc until devaluation in January 1994. Colloquially referred to in text as CFAs or by Senegalese speakers as francs.

**daba**  a traditional short-handled hoe, common throughout the Sahel.

**djeri**  non-floodable farmland in the Senegal River valley, reliant on rainfall.

**Fouta**  the area of the Senegal River valley traditionally occupied by the Halpulaar/ Toucouleur people.

**Halpulaar**  people who live in the middle valley of the river Senegal.

**marabout**  a Muslim holy man and teacher, often gifted with special powers of healing.

**périmêtre**  no English equivalent exists for this technical term for an artificially levelled field for irrigated crops.

**Peulh**  a generic term for a nomadic ethnic group, light-skinned, lean herders and shepherds scattered across the arid drylands south of the Sahara from the Atlantic to the Indian Ocean.

**pirogue**  a wooden canoe (usually dugout) used on the rivers of West Africa.

**Pulaar**  the language of the Peulhs, one of the important national languages in Senegal spoken by all Halpulaar.

**Sahel**  Arab word for fringe. The narrow band of arid but habitable land south of the Sahara desert, stretching from the Atlantic to Ethiopia.

**waalo**    floodable agricultural land along the banks of the River Senegal.

**Wolof**    one of the principal national languages of Senegal and *lingua franca* in the cities.